Archer Milton Huntington

A note-book in northern Spain

Archer Milton Huntington

A note-book in northern Spain

ISBN/EAN: 9783337229078

Printed in Europe, USA, Canada, Australia, Japan

Cover: Foto ©Andreas Hilbeck / pixelio.de

More available books at **www.hansebooks.com**

A NOTE-BOOK IN NORTHERN SPAIN

By

Archer M. Huntington

ILLUSTRATED

New York and London
G. P. Putnam's Sons
1898

This Book
is Dedicated with Sincerest
Love and Respect to
My Mother

PREFACE.

IN the present volume little has been attempted beyond a brief description of certain trips in the North of Spain, and the book, with few exceptions, is made up from notes by the way. Some care has been given to the preparation of the illustrations, many of which are from photographs specially taken, and it is hoped that few inaccuracies have crept into the text. The portion of the Peninsula described has been thought to lack somewhat of that romantic interest which has grown up for the South, but in Santiago,—the early Christian Cordova, —in the small Gallegan city, where, it is claimed, the bones of Saint James still lie ; in Oviedo, Zaragoza, and the little-known towns of the Pyrenees, there is a wealth of tradition and local interest unsurpassed even in the South.

The writer takes pleasure in expressing his great appreciation of the unceasing kindness and consideration received at the hands of Spaniards,—both friends and strangers,—in a series of journeys occupying many months.

A. M. H.

New York, *December, 1897.*

CONTENTS

CHAPTER		PAGE
I.—IN GENERAL		1
II.—GALICIA .		10
III.—CORUÑA TO SANTIAGO .	.	20
IV.—ASTORGA—OVIEDO	.	46
V.—PLASENCIA—YUSTE		59
VI.—MADRID . .		77
VII.—THE BULL-RING		94
VIII.—MADRID—CALATAYUD		123
IX.—THE LOVERS OF TERUEL .		137
X.—ZARAGOZA .	.	145
XI.—HUESCA—JACA .		164
XII.—JACA—PANTICOSA .		184
XIII.—SAN JUAN DE LA PEÑA—THE CAVE OF THE VIRGIN .		198
XIV.—LEYRE—PAMPLONA		221
XV.—ESTELLE.		236
XVI.—RONCESVALLES	. .	248

ILLUSTRATIONS

PAGE

A SPANISH RELIGIOUS PROCESSION (*Photogravure*),
Frontispiece

PALENCIA, THE CRISTO DEL OTERO . . 8

SPANISH STAGE-COACH . . 9

LUGO 11

ARROW HEAD FROM THE LAGUNA ANTELA 12

REMAINS OF A DOLMEN AT NOYA . 12

TOWER OF HERCULES 16

RECONSTRUCTIONS OF THE TOWER OF HERCULES 16

GALLEGAN PEASANT . . 17

A GALLEGAN OX-TEAM . . . 22

THE CATHEDRAL OF SANTIAGO 25

SANTIAGO 31

THEODEMIR DISCOVERING THE TOMBS . . 34

SUGGESTED RESTORATION OF ORIGINAL STRUCTURE . 37

PLANS OF TOMB 39

MOSAIC FROM THE SUBTERRANEAN CHURCH . 41

WHERE THE RELICS WERE FOUND . . 43

CORUÑA . . . 45

MARAGATOS 47

RETABLO BY BECERRA IN ASTORGA . . 49

ASTORGA 50

RELIEFS ON THE CHEST 52

OVIEDO—CLOISTERS OF THE CATHEDRAL . . 55

	PAGE
THE CROSS OF THE ANGELS	57
YUSTE (*Photogravure*)	66
YUSTE	68
THE CROSS	72
RUINS OF YUSTE	73
MOZO DE CORDEL	77
AN ALPARGATA	78
SPANISH SOLDIERS	79
COURT FOR PLAYING PELOTA	81
CABINET IN WHICH THE POEM IS KEPT	83
HOUSE OF THE SEVEN CHIMNEYS, XVIth Century	87
HOUSE OF THE SEVEN CHIMNEYS, XVIIIth "	88
PORTRAIT OF ANTONIO PEREZ	91
HOUSE OF THE SEVEN CHIMNEYS TO-DAY	92
MOÑA	95
A BOX AT "LOS TOROS"	96
CABALLERO DE PLAZA	99
REJON LANCE, USED BY CABALLERO DE PLAZA	101
PARTS OF THE HEAD OF THE PICA	103
THE MULETA	104
PORTRAIT OF FRANCISCO ROMERO	105
BANDERILLAS	106
COSTILLÁRES	108
CACHETE OR PUNTILLA	109
PEPE HILLO	111
BULLFIGHTER'S SWORD	112
PORTRAIT OF ROMERO	114
PORTRAIT OF MÓNTES	115
FIRE BANDERILLA	116
FIRE BANDERILLA STRIPPED, SHOWING ROCKETS	116
PORTRAIT OF ARJONA	119
A NOTICE OF POSTPONEMENT	121
HEAD OF PICA OR LANCE	122

PAGE

CHILDREN MARCHING . 125
SPANISH KNIVES 128
CARDINAL FRANCISCO XIMENEZ DE CISNEROS . 130
TOMB OF CARDINAL XIMENEZ 130
OBJECTS WHICH BELONGED TO CARDINAL XIMENEZ, 131
WOMAN OF THE PROVINCE OF GUADALAJARA . 133
CALATAYUD—PLAZA DE SAN ANTON 135
THE LOVERS OF TERUEL (*Photogravure*) . . . 137
BANNER TAKEN BY ALFONSO VII FROM THE MOORS . 140
THE SEO . . 149
BENEDICT XIII . . 150
THE EBRO AT LOGROÑO . 157
TOWER OF TRUJILLO . . 160
ZARAGOZA (*Photogravure*) 160
PEASANTS OF LERIDA . 164
THE CATHEDRAL OF HUESCA 165
SEAL OF THE TEMPLARS 168
ACOLYTES OF THE CATHEDRAL OF HUESCA 171
THE BELL OF ARAGON . . 176
THE CLOCK TOWER—AYERVE . . 179
PALACE OF THE MARQUIS OF AYERVE 181
THE CATHEDRAL OF JACA 187
PANTICOSA (*Photogravure*) 194
SAN JUAN DE LA PEÑA . 199
THE NEW MONASTERY . . 204
A CHAPEL OF SAN JUAN . 208
EARLY TOMBS 209
ROYAL BURIAL CHAMBER 210
GOTHIC DOORWAY . 212
DOOR OF THE FAITHFUL . . 213
CLOISTERS; SAN JUAN DE LA PEÑA . 215
WASHERWOMEN . 217
A SPANISH GYPSY . 222

	PAGE
Peasants of Navarre	231
Ferry	233
Sanguesa	233
Spanish Soldiers	234
Plaza de la Constitucion, Pamplona	235
Capitals of the Early Cathedral of Pamplona,	237
Estella	242
Olite	249
Roncesvalles	250

A Note-Book in Northern Spain

A NOTE-BOOK IN NORTHERN SPAIN

I

IN GENERAL

"A man has been in Spain. The facts and thoughts which the traveller has found in that country gradually settle themselves into a determinate heap of one size and form and not another. That is what he knows and has to say of Spain. He cannot say it truly until a sufficient time for the arrangement of the particles has elapsed."

EMERSON

IN Spain it is less the " color " and " romance " of which we hear so much, than the strange, sombre setting of it all—the wonderful, melancholy landscape, unvaried, sullen, monotonous to-day, to-morrow ablaze with a fiery life ; impetuous, restrained, indifferent, responsive. Look deep enough into its heart and you may read the heart of the Spaniard.

There is no single meaning in this mysterious expanse of mountain and plain and yellow, crawling river. To call it barren would be as descriptive as to call sky blue. It is far too protean for classification, for the analysis which elsewhere permits a symbolic meaning to single words.

The treeless road, like a strip of gleaming metal beaten out across the distance, and inch-heavy with dust, beneath

a blinding sun, flecked at long intervals by the sullen red
of a Valencian blanket, lies in a wonderful dead silence.
There are no song birds, no trees for the wind to play
through.   Only now and again the long, solemn, mournful wail of a bell comes faintly and awakes us to the fact
that, far off, gray and dull and scarcely different in line
from the vast dead stretches about it, rises doggedly with
line upon line of narrow, round-headed windows, some
square, solitary tower of brick—Roman in shape and tradition.   A sound beyond all description in its meaning, in
its subtle relation to the lives, the destinies, the joys and
sorrows of those we pass.   Their whole existences are
epitomized in its dull reverberations.   " Death " and
" Hope " it keeps repeating, and between there is an ever
unanswered question.

The imagination has wings in this place.   Soon one is
breathing the unreal.   Fanaticism is natural, chivalry a
necessity.   The boom of the outside world dies away and
a new world arises—one of fanciful shapes.   The senses
grow keener and quicker.   The clear, calm air is filled
with a vitality not of the body.   And in the long silences,
when sound is forgotten, we seem to *hear something*.   And
the old priest who sits beside one, in the broad black hat
and gown, would smile, were one to speak to him of it,
and say, perhaps, that the soul speaks, only in the city
you cannot hear.

" *L'Espagne est le pays d'Europe dont nous nous faisons
l'idée la plus inexacte*," says a recent French writer.   And,
in fact, our knowledge, largely had at second hand, colored
with antipathy of race or religion, too often produces an
attitude of contempt, pity, or aversion for the country
which all but blocks the end of the Mediterranean.

Yet she cares less for what you may think of her than

does any other nation in Europe, and you can force her to accept fewer of your ideas than any other. It has been a tradition with her that people beyond the Pyrenees are not friendly people, and she is not prone to look within and discover the cause of their dislike. The United States has taken her the sewing machine and the Life Insurance Company, and she has welcomed the latter at least. She likes gambling games, and will even not refuse to take a hand with Death himself. For have not they been friends of old? But she moves slowly, very slowly, and always considers herself just a little better than you, and will, always politely, tell you so when need be.

Spain gives us pride—which Spain to all the earth
*May largely give, nor fear herself a dearth.**

She is in more than one sense a composite nation, and as such is the more difficult to see and know as a whole. Here the fragmentary middle-age condition of Italy was repeated. Cataluña, Aragon, Castile, Andalucía, are not mere geographical terms. Each presents its distinct national and special character. Tradition, habits, sports, costume, have all their peculiar expression and local difference.

The brawny Aragonese, the harsh-tongued industrious Catalán, the Celtic-souled Gallegan, the dignified gentleman of Castile and Leon, the fiery, knife-loving Andaluz, are united under one name and one religion as Spaniards and Catholics into a loosely knit whole, wherein the seeds of revolution and ism take ready root.

But things have changed since 1819, when Bowring wrote :

" One might surely expect that in a country possessing eight archbishops, more than fifty bishops, and more than a hundred abbacies,

* Churchill.

with a jurisdiction almost episcopal, 'in which,' to use the language of a Spanish writer, 'there are more churches than houses, more altars than hearths, more priests than peasants'; in which every dwelling has its saint, and every individual his scapulary, one might expect to see some benefits, some blessings, resulting from this gigantic mass of

ecclesiastical influence. Let us, then, look upon a picture drawn by the hand of an acknowledged master :

" ' Our universities are the faithful depositaries of the prejudices of the middle age ; our teachers, doctors of the tenth century. Beardless noviciates instruct us in sublime mysteries of our faith ; mendicant friars in the profound secrets of philosophy ; while barbarous monks explain the nice distinctions of metaphysics.

" ' Who goes into our streets without meeting *cofradías*,* processions, or rosaries ; without hearing the shrill voice of eunuchs, the braying of sacristans, the confused sound of sacred music, entertaining and instructing the devout with compositions so exalted, and imagery so romantic, that devotion itself is forced into a smile ? In the corners of our squares, at the doors of our houses, the mysterious truths of our religion are commented on by blind beggars to the discordant accompaniment of an untuned guitar. Our walls are papered with records of "authentic miracles," compared to which the Metamorphoses of Ovid are natural and credible.

" ' In the fictions and falsehoods they have invented to deceive their followers, in their pretended visions and spurious miracles, they have even ventured to compromise the terrible majesty of heaven. They shew us our Saviour lighting one nun to put cake into an oven ; throwing oranges at another from the *sagrario*, tasting different dishes

---

* A religious fraternity composed of persons not necessarily of the church but bound by certain rules. " *Ni fía ni porfía, ni entra en cofradía*," says the proverb.

in the convent-kitchens, and tormenting friars with childish and ridiculous playfulness. They represent a monk gathering together fragments of a broken bottle, and depositing in it the spilt wine, to console a child who had let it fall at the door of the wine-shop. Another repeating the miracle of Cana to satisfy the brotherhood, and a third restoring a still-born chicken to life, that some inmate of the convent might not be disappointed.

" ' They represent to us a man preserving his speech many years after death, in order to confess his sins ; another throwing himself from a high balcony without danger, that he might go to mass. A dreadful fire instantly extinguished by a scapulary of Estamene. They shew us the Virgin feeding a monk from her own bosom ; angels habited like friars chanting the matins of the convent, because the friars were asleep. They paint the meekest and holiest of men torturing and murdering the best and the wisest for professing a different religious creed.' "

How often the question is asked as to the causes which have brought Spain down from her ancient position in the affairs of Europe, and it is a question not impossible to answer, though the great cause is probably to be found in a direction different from that which is generally supposed. Pride, a weak monarch, a dissolute court, religious intolerance, all these are admirable starting points from which to prove a nation's decline. But Spain has been by no means unique in the possession of these requisites. A close examination of the intricate mass of intrigue and counter-intrigue and plot at the capital reveals a condition differing from that of some other countries only in being a little later in occurrence. In fact, all these are mere effects, the cause is the absence of that which has developed the great nations of the earth, the cause on which civilization rests, the great primitive developing agency —the trading spirit. Spain lacks the trading spirit. For seven centuries she was a battlefield. During that time, while she was keeping the Mohammedan wolf from the door of Europe, there was no chance for the development of the trading spirit. What growth came in a measure to some of the coast cities was the result of local commercial relations finding an extension and expansion at sea—not the exchange of commodities between nation and nation. The spirit of getting by the good right arm grew and produced its tradition, while the precarious cultivation of land for food, an occupation ever more and more removed from the leaders, became the work of an ignorant and unrespected class.

With the absence of trade goes the absence of a knowledge of the outside world and, though a certain general knowledge was brought back by the Europe-conquering soldiers of Charles and Philip, it was a knowledge of how easily gain could be made *in the old way*, rather than a stimulus to the merchant.

Without the logical traditions of buying and selling, raised up through generations, Spain could hardly avoid the errors of government which the want of such traditions brings. She could scarcely hope not to become the victim of each and every scheme for a financial millennium, as a nation, which we are all accustomed to smile at when played in the more self-evident form of personal charlatanry. And, most of all, the dignity of work had been lost. The Spanish laborer pitied himself—and was pitied.

Up to the beginning of the present Cuban war, however, a better condition had been developing. Education and a knowledge of the outside world were bringing home to this nation that to be the proudest man in the world, it is well to have a basis for that pride in tangible rather than traditional things, and of so excellent a nature have I found the Spaniard when one knows him, that I cannot help believing in his ultimate development.

But few, I know, cross the threshold of the Spanish house to find how good a man at heart the owner is. He is proud, it is true, and does not much favor the stranger, but it is the pride of a reserved nature, not of a weak one. We must be slow in our judgement of this man. Let us both be charitable ; what he thinks, as what we think, is the growth of a thousand years.

To the east of Cuenca and south of Zaragoza, the mountain district threaded by the ancient Bilbilis road of the Romans is undisturbed by the scream of the locomotive. The valleys of the Guadelope, Gaudalaviar, the Júcar, the Jiloca, and the upper Tagus are yet to be exploited. Only a short time has passed since the long route around by Lérida to Zaragoza was shortened by the new railroad from Tortosa up the Ebro, and it will be long, perhaps, before the coach from Sagunto to Gérica and Teruel finds no passengers.

Some day, when a coast line is completed and the foreigner may run rapidly from Barcelona, by way of Valencia, Alicante, Cartagena, Almería and Málaga to Gibraltar or Cádiz, with the sea always at hand, then the travelling world will begin to have some idea of that wonderful southeastern coast, than which there is nothing more beautiful on the whole Mediterranean.

But to the high central portion of Spain, general travellers will discover the journey, especially if made in the heat of summer, a somewhat disappointing undertaking. Búrgos, Palencia, Valladolid, Zamora, Salamanca, or Ávila are hot enough in summer and cold enough in winter to discourage most sightseers.

The slowness with which Spain, as compared with France, has built her railroads is best evidenced by laying

the official guide-maps side by side.   But the cause also is
to be found on the map.   Fertile fields, reached by low
grades along navigable rivers, present a different tale from
high plains, shallow streams, and mountains whose passage
makes the reputation of engineers.   And so, in many of
the mountain provinces you must still take the stage, and
give thanks that you are so well carried and that you do
not have to go groaning up to town in an ox-cart or astride
a mule's pack saddle.

PALENCIA

THE CRISTO DEL OTERO

It is, in fact, only about one hundred years since the
stage roads began, under the energetic government of the
minister Floridablanca, to have any real existence.   Spain
appears to have been quite as far behind in developing her
road system as, later, with the railroad.

A French minister at that time describes the stage as a
"clumsy, inconvenient carriage drawn by mules, which
have no other spur or rein than the voice of their guides.
On seeing them harnessed together, and to the shafts

merely by cords, and observing them traversing as it were at random, the winding and sometimes unfrequented roads of the Peninsula, the traveller at first conceives himself as deriving all his dependence for safety from the care and kindness of Providence; but on the slightest appearance of danger, a simple and short exclamation from the *mayoral*, restrains and directs these tractable animals." At that time a stage ran between Bayonne and Madrid in from six to eight days!

The great vehicles, especially along in the north of Galicia, where the stage companies in summer do a good business, are packed with travellers. These are piled in helter-skelter, first filling, then overflowing and, though the law is clear that no one shall ride on the front seat with the driver, the *pescante*, that place is usually the first one filled.

SPANISH STAGE-COACH

Smoking and swearing are the chief diversions. In the latter all are artists, carrying invention beyond the pale of credibility. A peculiarly forcible oath is usually the signal for an interchange of good-humored nods.

"That's one on the devil," said a fellow-traveller, leaning over to me, after a lively burst of expletives.

"Why does he swear so?" I inquired.

"Because he is the *mayoral*," said the other with a shrug.

II

GALICIA

"For you must know that Galicia is so poor and mean a Countrey, that there's no place for bragging."
A LADY'S JOURNEY INTO SPAIN, 1692

IN this north-eastern corner of Spain lies the melancholy little land of the Gallegan, a land of rain and mist, where the scenery is exquisite, where hotels are famously bad, man in an early stage of development, and devotion the chief recreation. Galicia consists of four small provinces: Lugo, Orense, Pontevedra and Coruña and is as little Spanish in tongue, manners or habits as is well possible.

In a general, irresponsible way this country may be geographically called square. It is watered by no less than three thousand streams. It possesses one third of the harbors of Spain and has little or no commerce for them, the most hardy race of people and the poorest, the remains of one of the Apostles, and the worst government. It is Celtic to the last degree and its language has been called the mother of Portuguese—the child having become slightly refined and broadened by contact with the world.

As usual with the people of a poor country, its natives are passionately attached to their homes. No people in Europe make such sad exiles. The word *moriña* (home-

sickness), spoken of a Gallegan, draws the mind instinctively to pictures of morbidness and suicide, as the
readers of Señora Bazán are quite aware.

LUGO

With that pride which is the birthright of small peoples,
the Gallegan knows no land so good as his own, no language to compare with his, no literature with such felicities
of expression! For a straggling little literature he has,
and his unknown poets tell with fervor of the scenery, the
age, the dignity and what not of their little, wet half-acre.

But Galicia has, nevertheless, a somewhat considerable
interest for us if it be only in the study of those influences
or lack of influences which bring her to us so unchanged
from the middle-age turmoil. She stood somewhat apart
from the worst of Saracenic invasion, although overrun
more than once. Almanzor reached the very sanctuary of
her patron saint and left it a heap of ruins. Other scarce
less deadly storms have passed over her; but she has been,
on the whole, well away from the modifying and moulding
external influences at work in the Castiles, Leon, Aragon
and Cataluña.

Prehistoric remains have been found to some extent in
Galicia. The caves of Rey Cintoulo near Mondoñedo and
that of *Á Furada d'os cans*, have yielded moderate stores

of fossil bones, and the remains of lake-dwellers, or lagoon-dwellers, are not uncommon at the low mouths of the

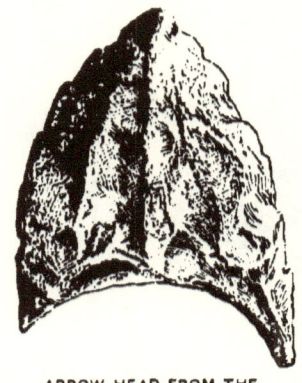

ARROW HEAD FROM THE
LAGUNA ANTELA (ENLARGED)

rivers.   Traces of submerged towns are said to have been found at Santa Cristina, Reiris, Doniños, Carragal, Antela and elsewhere.

The discovery of *Kjockken-moeddings* or shell-heaps somewhat similar to those in Denmark adds another peculiar interest to this coast, although it is to be regretted that more thorough, scientific examinations have not been made of these heaps.   We are told of a writer who, on the discovery of a remarkable deposit, found among the broken bones a human head to which he attached apparently only enough value to take it home and store it carelessly in a closet within reach of his children.   It has disappeared.

Later inhabitants than these have left traces in Galicia. About those shadowy people of the far past we only know however what may be gathered from their broken dwelling-places and the instruments they have left. Later traditions have come to blot them out the more

REMAINS OF A DOLMEN AT NOYA

completely and it is to be regretted that the curious folk-lore of this Celtic northland was not gathered thoroughly long ago. Each one, no doubt, of the prehistoric monuments that are left, has had its legend affixed to it soon or late, and although it is to be supposed that we should have here found in a Gallegan folk-lore many repetitions of older far-removed tales, yet the remaining people would have no doubt had their own as well. Murguía relates the following :

In the mount *d'as croas*, situated in the parish of San Martín Salcedo, Province of Pontevedra, there dwelt long ago an enchanted lady of remarkable beauty. She lived in a palace which existed in the interior of the mount and in which there was so great a treasure that the report of her wealth reached as far as Cádiz.

Many sought to discover her but failed, although the exact directions were set forth in a popular rhyme, yet she was not infrequently seen by the inhabitants who, fearing her, always fled at her approach.

One day a boy who was guarding his father's sheep came upon the lady seated upon a stone. She was combing her hair with a golden comb and when the shepherd endeavored to pass her she called to him and begged that he would give her a sheep.

The boy, greatly alarmed, fled and, arriving home, related to his father what had occurred. The latter, instantly bethinking him that the whole flock might be lost, sent his son back with instructions to give the lady what she wished.

When he arrived, however, at the spot the flock had disappeared and it was only after a prolonged search that he discovered the enchanted lady guarding it.

She then told him to go to his father and bid him come to her at once. The boy obeyed, and soon after the terrified man made his appearance. She reassured him, however, and an interview took place the details of which were kept a profound secret.

It was soon noised about, however, that these two were now charged with supplying the wants of the enchanted lady of the mount, and it was also noticed that their material affairs went well and that they grew more prosperous every day.

But, a long while after this, the man was taken very ill. The doctor gave him up as lost. His wife at this time leaving the house by chance, encountered a lady at the doorway who asked her how her husband was. The woman did not reply, but on re-entering the house was astonished to find the same lady seated beside her husband, and the latter so much restored that he was able to speak and declare himself out of danger.

The curious wife, however, was not long in questioning her husband, and although the latter refused to reply for some time, he at last spoke and disclosed the secret (whatever it may have been) of the Enchanted Lady.

His punishment was not long delayed. During that very night his wife, as she afterward declared, heard strange sounds as of blows, and cries and complainings, and in the morning the man was found dead and covered with bruises as of heavy blows.

The capital of Galicia should be approached from the sea; one might add after a transatlantic voyage. Nor have I in mind any such six days' outing as we grow tolerant of on English or French or German steamers. My own memory reverts to a journey which began in the harbor of Havana, where a shifting, talking, jostling, eager, excited crowd was seeing its friends off on an early spring day; to a steamer whose decks, indiscriminately at

the service of first and second cabin, were made unten-
antable by suffering humanity two hours after leaving
port ; to a cabin where a crowd of thinly clad wretches
huddled and suffered for fifteen days ; to fifteen days of
calm sea and clear sky and smells, and the daily slaughter
of sheep or cattle or fowls, watched eagerly by the passengers from the deck above ; to hatless women in untidy
dressing-gowns ; to men in slippers ; children in bare feet,
a hundred little miseries of food and air, and heat and
noise—and then Coruña. Those fifteen days between
Cuba and the first land will set the fountains of milk and
honey flowing for any imagination. This unromantic,
sombre corner of Spain, too, is a fine preparation for
what is to follow, and if we can find satisfaction here we
shall not fail to be properly impressed in the south, where
costume does not die and the hotel proprietor is learning
his lesson of the value of the picturesque.

Perhaps we may regret, however, after a few days that
the hotel proprietor has not learned a little at least of his
lesson here ; that he had less time on his hands for sitting
by a *brasero* inside the big door, through which, during
the rainy part of each day, the cold, damp air sweeps in
gusts each time an inquisitive guest looks in. A mantle
of fog and mist Galicia wears. Hard and rough old land
though she be, like her native Celt, her tears flow easily.

The Province of Coruña, with a population of over
600,000, has a history filled with achievements on a small
scale. As is the individual Gallegan life, so hers has been
circumscribed. The city dates from very early times,
when the trading-vessels of the eastern Mediterranean
found their way along the coast to make this a convenient halting-place. Her famous Tower of Hercules, com-
manding the harbor and marking a way for her ships,

has had its counterpart from the earliest days. The keels of Phœnician galleys coasting from the ancient

TOWER OF HERCULES
(AT PRESENT)

cities of Tartessus, Gades or Belon, have grated in the pebbly coves at the foot of this tower. The Phœnicians sought Spain, chiefly southern Spain, for her minerals. Their colonies dotted the present Andalucia, and beyond the Pillars of Hercules their galleys began early to steer eagerly to the Scilly Islands of Britain, the "Tin Islands" (Cassiterides).

Tin, from its use as an alloy in copper, became of vast importance to a world whose arms were of that metal. The Phœnicians for a time kept the secret of their discovery. No doubt the last point of land in Spain became of increasing importance to the mariners in frail boats, and the great circular

RECONSTRUCTIONS OF THE TOWER OF HERCULES SUGGESTED BY MURGUÍA

tower of the promontory has perhaps gladdened with its

flaring beacon the hearts of not a few of these forgotten strangers just beginning their return to the distant East.

There were gold mines in Galicia then, we are told, but where is not located, although that they were of any great extent is to be doubted. Even the precious dust of the Tagus could not have been so extensive as would be demanded of a modern mine. With the Gallegan gold, silver was also found as high as three per cent and, in the Peninsula in other places, it is reported, as high as twelve and one half per cent.

Tin of Galicia was plentiful in Roman days as in the time of the Phœnicians and later comers, though it must afterwards have given way in the market before the product of the richer and more profitable mines of Britain.

There have been few world-stirring or epoch-making events in this little out-of-the-world Galicia. Her history like that of other small, self-centred districts is of vast importance only to herself. Her development has been slow and slight, her name little mixed with outside affairs. But she is eternally famous as the resting-place of the Spanish patron saint, Santiago, who lies in the city of his name.

On a recent trip to Coruña, I recall a talk with Juan Diaz, a *mayoral* and a good Gallegan. He had been, he said, a soldier in the war, and had a reputation for hard fighting and the drinking of *aguardiente*.

GALLEGAN PEASANT

I found him in a low room filled with the customary haze of tobacco smoke. Twenty men or more sat about small tables smoking, drinking and talking in monotonous tones. There was some gambling.

2

Their half-eager expression was subdued by that calm
dignity which we are told to expect in Spanish faces ; not
the Latin dignity of Castile but rather the gravity which
among these sturdy people of the misty north country,
where nature has fashioned a new Ireland and a second
Irishman, masks a Celtic explosiveness.

At one table there was heavy playing. Silver *pesetas*
instead of the customary "little dogs" were piling up.
The host leaned indifferently in the doorway, while his
wife poured out a glass of *aguardiente* for a boy of sixteen.
The wind was blowing outside and a swinging door creaked
and groaned unnoticed.

My friend, the *mayoral*, had been drinking and talking
to me for some twenty minutes in a low tone.   He spoke
of the taxes and their increase ; and went on telling me
especially of the pressure of the duties on food, and of the
high imposts on all provisions entering town.

" We are being ground down below what we can earn,"
he said, changing from Spanish to the Gallegan dialect for
the benefit of the others.   The door outside slammed a
period to this preliminary outbreak.

A face or two turned our way ; a chair creaked here
and there.   The greater number were too deeply interested in their game to notice us.   The host in the door
shifted his position and held his pipe in his hand.
Sandé's small, quick eyes recognized the signs and he
began an eager discussion.

Soon he formally laid down his text.   His voice rose
above the wind's roar.   The interest in the play had
steadily waned and all eyes were upon him.   His voice
rang out and I was astonished at the sudden flow of eloquence which followed.   His face, which had been flushed
and excited when he began, became rather pale and his

gestures quick and nervous. Some of his listeners rose, as he came step by step down between the double row of tables, appealing now by questions, now by sarcasm, sneers or direct invective, sending his words in a rapid torrent among them.

Glasses, cigarettes, games, all were forgotten. He held his audience fixed. Soon the excitement was intense. He told them rapidly of his personal service in the war and sketched the crossing of a river, under fire, when he had been a bearer of despatches, establishing his right, like a true orator, to speak to them of their wrongs.

This lasted, perhaps, five minutes, and then Sandé with a fine dramatic flourish of the arm, made his way slowly back and seated himself by me once more, amid a great buzz of tongues and cries and praise. That was all. No one else rose. The bubble had burst. A few moments and play was resumed here and there, then argument died. Fitfully raised voices fell almost at once. The speech was a thing of the past. There was no *result !*

" Do you North-Americans treat your poor as we treat ours ?" the orator said to me, leaning over and lighting the cigarette he had been rolling.

I did not tell him that in the row of tables and the little heaps of stacked-up money, there was perhaps more of an answer and explanation to causes than he dreamed of.

Here in Galicia the blood of the Celt is no mixed stream in the veins of the Gallegan and it would be no far-drawn parallel to find in the eloquence of this stage driver the same original spirit which brought together on a completed scale, thirty years ago, the monster meetings of an O'Connell, or of a Feargus O'Connor, when Ireland was for repeal—without result !

III

CORUÑA TO SANTIAGO

"All within this city is as still and strong as the granite of its own monuments."

MURGUÍA

IT is early morning and there are few words at the door as the *mayoral* springs on the box and takes the reins. Snap, snap, goes the whip. *"Anda! Anda!"* cries Angel Roda, the *zagal*, running along the line of animals slashing right and left.

The *zagal* is the second in command of a Spanish stage-coach. His function is to urge on at every opportunity the lagging or exhausted animals, and his work is much harder than that of his superior. Wherever the coach begins the ascent of a hill this swift little attendant, whose name, of Arabic origin, signifies a brave and courageous young man, is down to earth and swings his long lash which stings and bites the welt-marked sides of the horses or mules. At his onslaught there is a jerk, a sudden lurch and the great coach with its six horses and four mules begins to stagger ahead. Along the streets we roll and sway, over the great slabs of pavement with deep holes worn between, rumbling and heaving on, passing a double line of people all curious to see us swing by; on past the little market-square with its umbrella-covered booths; its lines of brilliant, glazed and unglazed pottery; its piles of melons, figs, oranges, apricots, grapes and nuts; past the fountain where the men and women stop in picturesque groups to stare at us or shout good-bye to Sandé or the *zagal*. We are ever the moving attraction of a double gazing line, till the outskirts of the town are reached and we enter the great *carretera* or stage-road, magnificently kept and dotted in outline, far as the eye can reach, with a double row of upright, conical guard-posts of stone at the sides.

The lines tighten, the *zagal* leaps to the ground from his little seat under the box of the *mayoral* and runs alongside the mules. His whip snaps continuously. The mules and horses leap in the traces; on their flanks where the hair is uncut sullen ridges are raised, and the closely clipped backs are marked as with hot iron.

There are thirteen passengers on board, five on top under the heavy rawhide hood, five in the main body of the coach and two in the little box over the front wheel, shut in with glass like a railway compartment—the *berlina*.

This then is the Pilgrimage to Santiago, the *Romería*. We are going toward the place of the Cid's adventures with the leper. Angel Roda and Sandé, the *mayoral*, seem to feel all our anxiety to reach the pilgrim's goal of the Middle Ages. And not alone of the Middle Ages, for to-day we pass a pair of barefooted pilgrims on their way to this wonderful St. James of Compostella, and later we learn that a number of them go each year, not only Spaniards but French, Italians and others. The cool fresh air blows into our faces as we mount the slopes beyond the valley, and at twenty minutes past one we feel the keen breath of the ocean and a small strip of hazy blue water is in sight. At that moment I chance to sneeze, and Angel Roda leans from his narrow perch to mutter "Jesus-

María!" to keep the devils from jumping down my throat.
Domingo Sandé is dressed in a short velvet coat with a red
faja, or sash, about his waist and a little Basque cap
pulled down over his eyes.   He is small and light and
waspish.   When he is not too busy with his horses, he is re-
lighting his cigarette which continually goes out.   Our companions are a chance acquaintance from Vigo, a Basque of
Bilbao, a silent fellow in green checked trousers from Pontevedra, a strange assortment of parti-colored nondescripts
and two dignified Spanish gentlemen, interested in the min-
ing at Santiago, and whom the Basque hopes to interest
still further, he whispers, in a railroad from Coruña to
Santiago, not only for the mine and its advance, but for a
passenger and freight traffic.   It would cost two million
dollars, he says.   Farm products seem to be all that could
be had for transportation and the passenger traffic must be
light indeed.   The distance is seventy kilometres.

"*Ho-a! Ho-a! ánja! ánja!*" calls the *zagal* as we
reach the road which turns off to Lugo and start up the
grade.   Here we meet a long line of ox-wagons with huge,

almost solid, wheels;
one great s p o k e
across the middle.
They are loaded with
sand and their driv-
ers have taken off
their boots and stuck
them on the uprights
at the corners. Twen-
ty pairs of inverted
feet seem to be thus

A GALLEGAN OX-TEAM

upraised, through which double row we look, as through
a vista, down the side of the hill.

We pass, now and then, women sifting barley and occasionally a load of wood, in short sticks. It is curious to note the devices employed to avoid the use of wood here where it is so scarce. The fences, where stone is not used, are mud walls capped with vine, and a sort of basket-work frame attached to stone uprights is substituted for gates. All houses are of stone, built up of flat pieces on their sides interfilled with mud and overgrown with vine or grasses.

Potatoes, corn, onions and cattle are exported to England. Blackberries, figs and chestnuts grow everywhere along the road. Pine trees are raised for England. The bread I have always been told was good, but it seems to have been my fortune to find it always sour. Their corn-bread or *pan de maís* has usually the consistency of dough and the feeling of damp india-rubber. It contains the vital spark of indigestion.

"*Hola! Apricta! Apricta-a-a! La Bonita-a-a! Brillante! Anda! Anda!*" cries our indefatigable *zagal* as we pass a group of women, beating wheat with heavy flails. The *delantero* or outrider on the foremost near horse drives his spurs home and we start forward for a while at a trot, while boys get on behind as we pass through a little village and cries of "Whip! Whip!" (*látigo! látigo!*) are raised.

One of our passengers is a heavy, thick-lipped man whose underjaw protrudes. He buys and eats raw eggs at each relay station and declares them a most refreshing beverage. The others, especially a monk inside, are satisfied with wine.

At our third halt, on asking for a glass of water at the door of a house, I am cordially invited to enter. By the kitchen fire an old woman sits mechanically turning flat cakes, somnolent chickens roost on perches in two funereal rows along the walls, seemingly under the impression that it is night, or perhaps like good Spaniards taking their *siesta* in the heat of the day. Four rabbits, the not improbable elements of a future pie, skip over each other in a corner, watched longingly by a tall thin cat with numerous kittens ; while quietly asleep across one side of the room, and snoring in peaceful content, lies an enormous hog cheek by jowl with one of the various future heirs of all—a baby of two or three years—sleeping almost at his side. To prevent the escape of any part of the assembled throng a half-door blocked the way, over which only the sleepy chickens may pass, or the cat, when domestic duties permit.

We crossed the Tambre River at 6.30 on a small curious bridge with jutting angles, ornamented by a carved coat-of-arms. Below a grove of tall pines, which rose on a hill to the left, lay a small town.

As we lumber on, the fine, penetrating dust rises in a heavy cloud and the fleas work industriously. We have changed our equipment of men and horses now several times and our last *zagal* is decked in a blazing red coat with black velvet trimmings. One still notices how great is the economy of wood ; even in the frames of the wagons we pass the same sort of basket work used in the gates is employed. Sometimes a network of rope stretched to four uprights is substituted, but this is for carrying cut straw and like material. After six o'clock along these roads when the day's work is ending we pass numbers of peasants—men and women (the man usually walking and the woman riding). One of these latter was tenderly carrying a small, new, brilliantly washed pig—a sight to which one soon grows used in Spain. She was followed,

THE CATHEDRAL OF SANTIAGO

for contrast, by a carriage bearing the flaring arms of a marquis—warning us that we were approaching our destination.

At 7.30 Santiago was in sight and the two spires of the Cathedral rose from the hollow below us between the hills. Scattered houses soon appeared; later the town and its long, broad streets and a little farther on to the right a great gilded Virgin stared at us as we passed, as though saying to herself : " Even here, in my very stronghold, do these find their way !" To the right then, and down a steep hill, and on to the halting place among an expectant crowd, where we were soon in the thick of the fray with the hotel boys.

We fellow-travellers took dinner together and discussed Spain and her great future, and incidentally the olive, its cultivation, and the methods of improvement which the natives were so slow in adopting. A great part of the crop went to the United States, it was said, and the demand was increasing and would increase for there seemed to be little faith in the California olive,—though American petroleum has been sent here crude, and refined in the country, and only recently American butter was tried as an experiment at Vigo and Coruña and Bilbao.

About half-past nine I walked out along the dimly lighted arcaded streets, over broad flag pavements, like those of Coruña, to the Cathedral. With me went the *sereno* or watchman who, wrapped in his cloak, his staff surmounted by a steel axe, was, as he stalked on, a theatre character, majestic in the moonlight. As we stood in the solemn, silent square under the tower with the clear sky and moonlight above and about us, the great bell began to strike. Its heavy hammer of wood sent a strange, mysterious voice across the deserted space. It was a time for still

walking and wondering and half-falling asleep, and so
back into the past, that wonderful past which is not dead
in Spain but sleeps and which at times, and under the
proper spell, seems to revive. Was the sound of passing
feet not that of a great army of departed pilgrims? Was
not the square filled with white, upturned faces in the
moonlight? Were there not thousands upon thousands of
voices mingled together in answer to the great sobbing
beat of that grave singer high above us? Beat! beat!
beat! and again beat! beat! beat! and the moonlight
shivered along the pavement and the ghostly steps were
still and the voices were hushed.

Then, suddenly, at my side, as though the soul of all
had really spoken out with a passionate human cry, there
rose the chanting call of the *sereno*. I started as the long
wail sprang from the hollow stones beside me. It filled
the air; it beat against the black and silver walls of moonlight and shadow; it rose with its wonderful, quavering
invocation and fell to an earthly cry of agony. On the
face of the man who leaned upon his glittering axe-head
I could see an expression of exultation. Into these often-
repeated words he was throwing not only his physical but
his spiritual nature. His very soul, bred up among these
wonderful walls where history had folded her wings while
man went slowly by, had caught up and learned its un-
consciously instilled thread of meaning. This watchman's
call was a prayer for life among such wealth of death.
"*Ave Maria Purissima. Son las diez, y sereno.*"

I asked a boy to point my way and, following his direction as I thought, took the wrong street.

"To the right, Pilgrim, to the right," I heard his shrill
voice call out far behind me, and I waved him a thanks
and went on my corrected way. Beggars asked for the

usual *perro chico*, or little dog, always hoping for a
two-cent piece, however—a *perro grande*, or big dog.
The streets at ten were deserted. Only the *sereno* remained, who here gives his hourly cry after one in the
morning. At Burgos he began at eleven. The *guardia
civil* with his angular hat, bright yellow belt, red-tipped
collars and cuffs and white gloves, so familiar along our
way from Coruña—one meets a pair of them at intervals on every stage-road in Spain—is here little in evidence. I was not much surprised to find Englishmen
sitting at our table in Santiago ; there were, besides, four
Portuguese and two Frenchmen. In what other place in
Europe would there have been no understanding between
these wanderers ? The Portuguese were innocent of
French ; the French ignorant of Spanish and the solemn
Englishmen sat and talked stolidly—in English.

Journeys between Cathedral, University and bookstore
left in my mind a memory of a maze of crooked, branching streets. The little squares lie scattered over the town
like the bodies of strange, deformed creatures blindly
stretching out their convulsed arms in every direction.
Under the low arcades it is cool even at midday and there
is a wonderful calmness—the calmness of a dying city.
Such a sensation one may have in most of the places
along the way in northern Spain. Santiago, no longer
the goal of fanatics from every corner of Europe, no
longer dreamed of and longed for during the weary
months of a desperate personal struggle to reach the door
of its Cathedral, no longer the bestower of eternal life for
those who fall hopelessly by the way, seems to mumble and
gasp and turn cold at the last and the voice of the great
bell, the moonlight gone, the spell broken, sends out a hollow sound that makes us start—a veritable death-rattle.

Before one enters the grand portal of the Cathedral of
Santiago, that grave portal which the feet of countless
thousands of pilgrims have approached in religious awe
and veneration, there must have already come the feeling
of strangeness and isolation which the old town has the
power of rousing. How desolate the city is! How unlike, in the most remote degree, anything we had expected!
These small, narrow, unimposing streets; the poverty;
the stillness! Where is the smell of incense which we
had half-expected to meet at every turn? Why do we
hear no hymns resounding? Where are the throngs that
should be passing along beneath those low arcades? Are
these mean buildings all that the spiritual metropolis of
Spain can boast?

But we may forget the town and all our disappointment
when we look up at the grand *façade* above us. This
mighty pile of stone is the expression of an influence once
felt over all Europe. In the belief that within these walls
lay the body of one of the companions of Christ, the whole
Christian world fixed its attention upon this little Gallegan
town

It must be noted at the first in studying this cathedral
that we are in reality not examining an original building.
The architect did not here strike out along general lines
of his own, but rather closely followed a model already in
existence. This is found to be true of some other cathedrals in Spain, though to a less degree. It was George
Street who first pointed out the resemblance here to the
earlier Church of Saint Sernin at Toulouse, where the chief
difference is in the material used for the work, the one
being of granite, the other of brick and stone. The
French church was begun by Saint Raymond in 1060, and
as Street observes: "*By a strange coincidence, S. Sernin*

SANTIAGO

boasts of having, among the bones of several of the apostles, those of Saint James; though of course this would be strongly denied at Compostella." Street goes on to give the dimensions and details of the building.

The story of the finding of the tomb and remains of Saint James the Greater, at Santiago, is in no way mere tradition in the mind of the Spaniard. The relation is fused and welded into the great mass of Spanish belief. The whole matter rests upon a foundation of custom and age too firm for the assailment of doubt. It is not with history that this may be settled, but with the Church.

At the end of the eighth or beginning of the ninth century, a hermit named Pelagius succeeded in gaining a reputation of the durable nature which only greatness, accident or religion has ever been able to confer on men. In this case the fact to which the celebrity was due was the sight of a sudden shower of stars which fell, it seemed to the observer, upon a spot not far distant. This not altogether unprecedented phenomenon awoke in the breast of the pious anchorite a sensation of the profoundest wonder and awe and, when the same marvellous fact was reported as having manifested itself in a neighboring town, he could no longer refrain from carrying his strange tidings to the Bishop of Iria, Theodemir by name.

Having heard the tale, the good bishop became greatly interested and at once determined to make an examination. Excavations were undertaken on the spot and soon a narrow stairway was unearthed, descending which the searchers came to a door and entered a subterranean church or crypt, where, by the light of torches, Theodemir soon discovered an altar and three tombs. A close examination of these revealed the stupendous fact that the bishop and his companions were in the presence of the

3

sacred remains of Saint James the Apostle and two of his disciples.   On the mosaic floor they could still read the names of the latter, Theodorus and Athanasius, and a picture of a man with a halo bore the name of the saint himself.

THEODEMIR DISCOVERING THE TOMBS

In the manuscript of the *Tumbo A* in the *Archivo* of Compostela, of the year 1129, and in another manuscript—the *Historia Compostelana*, of the thirteenth century—the Bishop of Iria is represented making his discovery.   A description of the first of these miniatures is given by Fita and Guerra :

"An arch, the upper part of which is of gold and the lower of jasper with red and dark-blue veins, sustained by columns of dull jasper with capitals of gold, recalls the primitive vaulting.   From the key-stone of the arch hangs a lamp of that precious metal.   Three

sarcophagi, placed lengthwise and uncovered, fill the space, the one in
the middle standing above the others. The first is of green jasper, the
tomb of the Apostle yellowish, the one in the rear of red marble. Over
the chief tomb, waving a censer with the left hand, and pointing to it
with the index finger of the right, is an angel. A golden halo sur-
rounds his head, the tunic is violet, the mantle green, the wings gold
and violet. At the foot of the sarcophagus stands the prelate of Iria.
His mitre of the ninth century is white with a golden fringe. The in-
fulas fall upon the shoulders and are red. He wears a golden tunic
with sleeves of gold brocade, fitted and forming spirals, and a green
mantle. His right hand grasps a golden crosier with an oaken staff,
and his left also points to the apostolic sepulchre in a questioning attitude. The bishop is graybearded and above his head and running
as far as the lamp is this inscription : TEODEMIR' EPISKOP'
(Teodemirus episcopus). Outside the crypt are seen the constructions
due to the king Alphonso *el casto :* light towers of gold with narrow
windows, houses painted light green with white bands, windows of dark
green, and circular earthen tiles above a golden cornice, and, near the
key of the arch, two small towers or air-vents of reddish color."

Such is a picture of the scene given us by an artist
more than seven hundred years nearer to the reputed
occurrence than are we. Yet even he was three whole
centuries removed from it, and in three centuries much
may be done—with faith.

The explanation of the presence of the body of Saint
James is very simple. At the death of the future Guardian
of the Peninsula, he having previously expressed his wish
to rest in Spain, his seven disciples, largely recruited in
that country, at once begged and obtained his body, and
starting for Joppa, there sought for a ship to take them to
their native land. The ship at once made its appearance
miraculously and *Scyla cum Carybdi atque periculosis syrti-
bus, manu Domini gubernante, devitatis, primum ad Iriensem
portum felici navigio pervenerunt.** Having arrived at Iria

* *Hist. Compost.*, Lib. I., Cap. i.

without one stroke of the oars or the need of a sail,[*] they disembarked, and marching with their burden four leagues to the north, following the ancient Roman road to Brigantium, they arrived at Liberodunum, where they are described by Leo III. as coming upon a monstrous idol, and near it a most opportune collection of stone-cutters' implements. With these they at once fell upon the idol with the right ready rage of holy men and it was soon no more.

Having thus righteously cleared the way, they proceeded to construct, with these same implements, a fit tomb for the holy remains they bore. Soon a small building was completed, and having laid the body in its last resting-place, they consecrated the altar and, after singing hymns, went their way to gather to the fold of the new faith such as they might in the surrounding country.

Two, however, of their number seem to have found it well to stay behind. For the rest of their lives Theodorus and Athanasius remain to guard the tomb and, at the end, their bones find a resting-place to the right and left of those of their master. So for the tradition.

Guerra and Fita, basing their conclusions on the manuscript miniatures, on excavations, and on the construction of like buildings in Italy and Palestine, have made an attempt to give a detailed restoration of the primitive edifice itself. The plan presents a square structure with walls of heavy, cut stone, joined in the Roman fashion, each side or face of the building measuring eight metres. They also give a fragment of Roman mosaic, resembling other pieces encountered in various parts of Spain.

The corner-stone of the religious reputation of the city of Santiago de Compostela—Saint James of the Field of

[*] *Morales: Cr. Gen.*, Tom. 4.

Stars, or of the Field of the Apostle, as Lafuente pre-
fers—was laid with the discovery of the sacred bones.
Throughout the whole
Christian world ran a
thrill of fervent joy at
the announcement.
Perhaps to the court
of the far-off Charle-
magne himself some
worn but eager mes-
senger brought the tale
out of that unknown
Spain of Christian and
infidel, while the court
of that greatest figure

SUGGESTED RESTORATION OF ORIGINAL STRUCTURE

in Europe bowed attentive and awe-struck.

Nearer the scene we find a prompt recognition of the
event in the presence of Alfonso *el casto* who, with his
court, came to pay homage at the miraculous shrine. The
latter was rebuilt by the king's orders. Privilege after
privilege was showered upon the new church, which
promptly arose. All land within three miles of it fell
by royal grant to the monks, and Ordoño I., in 853, doubled
this allotment. In 899 Alfonso III. removed the building
of stone and mud constructed by the pious Alfonso *el casto*
and raised in its place a church of fine marble, brought
block by block on the shoulders of captive infidels from
the shores of the Duero and the Támega.

It is probably in the doubtful battle of Clavijo that
Santiago first appears most prominently as a national
protector. As almost every fact in regard to this event
is questionable, it has not been unnatural that the saint
should have here received a due tribute in the form of ac-

knowledged miracles. A host of infidels are shown on the
point of overwhelming the Christians. The disastrous
struggle of the day has ended and the night has closed in.
The Christians are in despair. The King Ramiro, dis-
couraged and hopeless, has retired to rest, when a wonderful vision comes to him. Saint James, in all the glory
of the blessed, appears. There is a short conversation.
After having assured the despondent, but resourceful
monarch, that all will be well with his arms, the saint
retires !

In the morning the king calls his followers and in
a speech, which Mariana, as usual, gives *verbatim*, informs
them that they are about to be blessed with victory.

The battle begins with fury, and thereupon the saint,
in fulfilment of his promise, appears upon a white horse,
bearing in his hand a white banner with a red cross and
leads the Christians in person. The Moors betake themselves to instant flight and the day is won. Sixty thousand
of the enemy are left upon the field ! *

Almost exactly one hundred years passed away in quiet
after the rebuilding of the church by Alfonso, when one
day the rumor came that, in the Moorish territory to the
south, a danger was threatening. An expedition was
forming under the leadership of that scourge of Christians,
Almanzor. Soon the story was verified by no less authority than the appearance of the unconquered leader himself,
with a strong army.

Whatever may have been the powers of Saint James
at this juncture, he certainly was given every opportunity
to display them, but for all that Almanzor seems to have
had no difficulty in making a clean sweep of the holy town
and of leaving it a mass of ashes. The white charger of

* *Mariana*, Bk. VII. Chap. xiii.

Clavijo nowhere made his appearance. No banner with a blood-red cross was unfurled, and not one of those fine structures which had so long gladdened the eyes of the

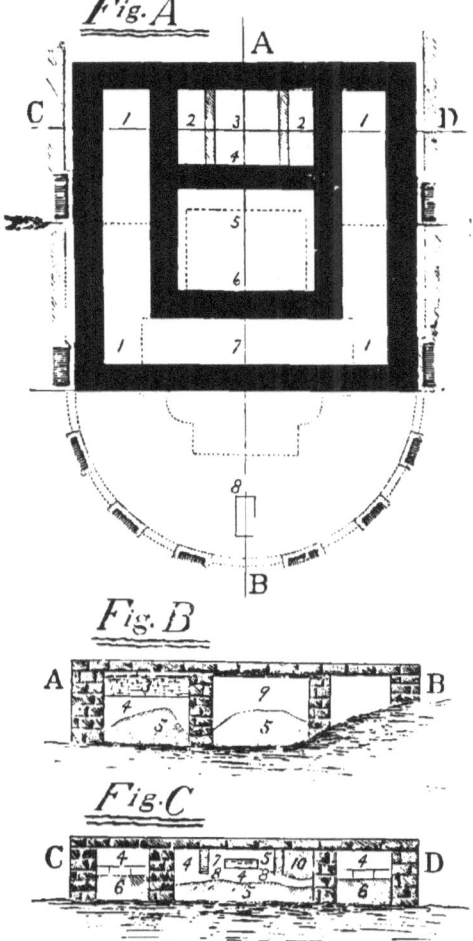

Fig. A—1. Subterranean passage. 2. Tombs of Theodorus and Athanasius, in the floor. 3. Place where sarcophagus of Saint James rested. 4. Where the burial-chamber was entered. 5. Antechamber or subterranean church. 6. Where the subterranean church was entered. 7. Point corresponding to door, facing East on floor above. 8. Where the relics were found.

Fig. B—Longitudinal section AB. 3. Wall of Roman bricks in the tomb of Athanasius, consisting of nine courses of ten bricks each. Above this, an ancient pavement of earthen blocks; beneath, a later one of marble. Over all, a Roman mosaic pavement. 4. Heap of broken granite and marble. 5. Heap of fine, light dust. o. Building rubbish with which this part was filled in the XVIIth century.

Fig. C- Latitudinal section CD. (For 4 and 5 see Fig. B). 6. Earth, rubbish and scattered human bones thrown here in the XVIIth century. 7. Part of an ancient column. 8. Brick walls of the tombs of Athanasius and Theodorus. 10. Earth with which the tomb of Athanasius was filled.

faithful were left to tell the tale. The story of an old man seated among the ruins and questioned by Almanzor, who

spared him when he learned that he was guarding the
remains of one of the associates of Christ, is as reliable as
that the horse of the conqueror burst and died from drinking at the porphyry font in the Cathedral, or that the
divine vengeance fell upon the Moorish host after the destruction of the city.   The rival Christian Mecca was
blotted out by a master-hand at annihilation.   Almanzor
marched away bearing in his train the great bells of the
Cathedral, which he carefully set up in the Mosque of
Cordova, inverted, as lamps, where they burned for the
infidel, we are told, until the good Saint Ferdinand, using,
as had Alfonso and others before him, the backs of Moorish captives as a substitute for beasts of burden, returned
them to their original places.

But it was by no means to be supposed that, because
the saint neither protected himself nor was rescued by his
followers, the profane hand of the Moor had succeeded in
tearing his bones from their place and scattering his dust
to the four winds of heaven.   Nothing was less likely.
When such a rediscovery entailed but a mental effort, it
was not to be imagined that the Patron of Spain would
rest unidentified.

The development of the legend and its far-reaching
influence was soon felt.   Prosperity increased and brought
with it its usual dangers.   The rich gifts which found
their way to the new centre of religious activity were soon
the objects of the cupidity of those through whose terri-
tories they passed ; but above others the gravest annoy-
ance was felt at the depredations of those Moorish pirates
who began to intercept gift-laden vessels and to carry their
arms ashore and into the very churches and towns.   In
these forays Christians were continually carried into cap-
tivity.   Churches were looted and burned, and the whole

population stood at last in constant fear of a sudden raid. In the twelfth century we find some planned resistance to this condition of things. As the Gallegans had no ships, or at best were poor mariners, it was decided to send to Genoa and elsewhere, and skilful artisans were obtained, who, at great expense, after some time constructed two ships, with which the Christians set forth and so ably attacked their enemies that they afterwards dared not show themselves except in force.*

The history of Compostela from this point would fill volumes. It has now assumed a position of European interest. It has grown beyond the condition of a mere town to which a few pilgrims occasionally come. The Christian world has responded to the presence of an Apostle in Galicia. Dante places him in paradise. † " From the twelfth to the sixteenth centuries," says Burke, ‡ " the number of visitors to Compostella was enormous. The roads of Christendom were thronged with its pilgrims. In the single year 1434 no less than

MOSAIC FROM THE SUBTERRANEAN CHURCH

2460 licenses are said to have been granted to pilgrims from England alone."

Passing this long period we come to the year 1589. Spain at that time was still suffering from the crushing humiliation of the destruction of the Invincible Armada,

---

* *Hist. Comp.*, Lib. II., Cap., xxi.   † *Paradise*, xxv., 17.
‡ Following Rymer, X., 11.

and the name of Drake had no uncertain sound in the ears
of the people.   When, therefore, word came that the " *terrible corsair of Isabel of England*" was about to ravage
Galicia, and that his force had already landed and was
creating havoc in the city of Coruña, almost within their
doors, a thrill of horror not equalled since the days of
Almanzor swept over Santiago.

The name of Drake was at that time hated in Spain
as no other.   The career of this "desperate" Englishman,
from the expedition against Porto Bello, through all the
subsequent list of his expeditions, was well known and
greatly magnified by the accounts given.   The indomita-
ble courage and fierceness with which he made his unex-
pected attacks, his reputed eagerness for gold, in which
he was said to far outdo the Spaniard himself, his contempt for the altars of the church, combined to make him
feared and execrated, and it was not for a moment imagined that, having gone thus far, he would resist the temptation which the rich spoil of the most famous shrine in
western Europe afforded him.

A hurried conference was therefore held in Santiago
as to what must be done to protect the holy of holies from
the sacrilegious hands of this freebooter and his lawless
followers.   It was soon decided to transport the relics to
a place of safety.   A certain number were taken to Orense;
but what was to be done in regard to the bodies of the
saint and his disciples.   One account gives us the words of
the Archbishop, Don Juan de San Clemente, who, on attempting to break through the wall, was met by a blast of
air and a strange light, and was forced to desist : "*Let us
leave it to the Santo Apóstol to defend himself and us.*"

The recent discovery of a hurriedly constructed burial-
place and a number of bones in an excavation made in

the Cathedral gives evidence for the belief that the contents of the subterranean church were taken up and re-
buried as a precaution at this time, and that the position,
kept carefully a secret by the few who knew it, was finally
forgotten. It was in 1879 that the discovery of the relics
was made. The search had been undertaken to discover
the remains of Santiago if possible, and at the desire of
the Archbishop of Compostela the final examination was
placed in the hands of a number of scientific men, to whom
the prelate writes, " well assured," he says, " of their *acred-
itada religiosidad.*"

WHERE THE RELICS WERE FOUND

The wish of the Archbishop was to learn how many
skeletons were in this tomb, their age, and whether there
was anything about them to indicate a doubt that theirs
were the bones sought. The commission was conducted
to the spot (in the apse of the Cathedral), where they
found the pavement already removed, disclosing in the

centre of the space a roughly cemented box or tomb of
irregular stones and mortar. The interior of this tomb
was found to measure 99 by 33 centimetres, and to have a
depth of 30 centimetres.

The tomb contained a promiscuous collection of bones,
mingled with loose earth, and the upper stratum seemed
the least affected by the action of time and dampness.
The fragments were so fragile that it was with great difficulty they were sorted and classified. They were afterwards placed in alcohol to give them consistency.

The result of the investigation was the classification of
portions of three skeletons, of uncertain age, but which,
judged by a chemical analysis of fragments of the bone,
and comparison with a Celtic skeleton reported by Gir-
ardin, might well be *centuries old*. Nothing was therefore found to prove that these were *not* the bones of
Santiago and his two disciples.

Half of one Sunday we devoted to returning by carriage to Coruña. The idea that the long stage journey
would be improved upon by this method was, however, a
false one. We started at fifteen minutes past four A.M.,
and drove the first miles through fog, rain and darkness.
Then it cleared and we had all the benefit of the dust in
our low vehicle. Eight hours of this was dispiriting.
Our horse was flogged within an inch of his life by a
merciless driver and kept up by two portions, at intervals
of two hours, of *corn bread dipped in wine*. We watched
this process of partial inebriation with all the interest possible under the circumstances. The horse seemed to be
well inured to the diet, for his pace, though not quickened,
was ever steady !

Peasants in their Sunday best gave us " *buenos dias* "

as we passed by, but there was no spirit left for a reply. We only nodded gloomily. At last, however, we reached the long down-grade to Coruña and could see from far off the English ships at anchor in the bay. At high noon we halted before the hotel.

CORUÑA

IV

ASTORGA—OVIEDO

OF the unbeaten ways of the north there are few of which you will hear less than that which leads, by way of Coruña, Lugo and Astorga, to Leon. Astorga is one of the many places one slips by and never misses. One is in no fear of being stirred to regret later by hearing some casual visitor's stereotyped admiration of a great cathedral or a famous fortress or a marvellous picture, though of a great *retablo* perhaps we might be told with justice, for here is the best work of Jaspar Becerra, thought to have been a pupil of Michael Angelo, the same Becerra whose famous carving of the Virgin was once, after two failures, inspired directly by the Mother of Christ herself, who came at night and set him to work upon a fire-log !

He was a Southerner, this Becerra, from Jaen, born in 1520, and went early to Rome. His career was that of a painter, sculptor and architect. His wife, Doña Paula Velazquez, was from his own land, to which soon after his marriage he returned, and his work may be seen in Zaragoza (a small bas-relief) in Madrid, Granada, Salamanca, Segovia and elsewhere. He died in Madrid (1570) one year after the completion of the *retablo*, his masterpiece, in Astorga. His famous image of the *Virgin of Solitude*,

MARAGATOS

carved from a charred block, has disappeared after work-
ing miracles unnumbered ; perhaps, as has been suggested,
it returned to the flames once more beneath the camp-
kettles of a French general.

Astorga to-d a y
will keep the travel-
ler but a short while.
He may perhaps find
enough of interest
for him to pass some
time in an exploring
tour of the walls and,
if he is English or
American, to Moore's
house. The French
have done their usual
work here and the
ruins are but partly
interesting.

And yet, about
this little time-worn
place a strange thing
has happened. At
the edge of the great
Leonese plain which
here, stretching to
the Guadarramas on

RETABLO BY BECERRA IN ASTORGA

the south, begins to be walled in by the Cantriaban, at the
foot of the smaller mountains of Leon, live the remnants of
a people who seem to have in some way lost themselves
during the successive flux and reflux of Moorish and Christian advance and retreat and to have been cast up out of
that sea upon this shore, here to preserve strange, half-

forgotten and half-modified traditions and a peculiar costume.

Who are they? From what great stock have they been lost? Out of what camp of Taric or Attila have they wandered by night never to return? Speculation has at one time placed them in the ranks of the Arabs, at another found seemingly positive and conclusive proof of their northern descent.

ASTORGA

In costume, if not in physique, however, the Maragatos suggest the East. The great baggy trousers of the men are very Moorish; their love of jewelry, of gold and silver ornaments, the enormous ear-rings of the women, their retirement, their clannishness, their sudden ceasing from their peculiar wedding-dances at the entrance of a stranger, seem more the outgrowth of Semitic, than northern tendencies. The young bride among these people puts off her wedding garment never to resume it until the death of her husband. Their lives are hard ones, in the open air for the greater part, and the women do most of the severe work.

Wailing across their open fields at intervals on the day of a wedding, or other fiesta, come the plaintive notes of the *gaita*, or bagpipe, and their calm, serious faces seem in harmony with its mournful sound.

Leaving our bags at the station we got into a rickety cart covered with a frame-work hood of reeds and dragged by a tired mule, and by careful balancing managed to keep our seats. The first hotel, which is run by the father of the American agent in Coruña (a Spaniard), did not strike

our fancy, so we moved across the street to another and
after a breakfast of *tortilla* and tea, got into our cart again
and were bounced and tossed out to Muria, one of the little
towns of the Maragatos, whom we had come to see.

It was an interesting drive. The country is bare of
trees and after passing out beside the walls and under the
cathedral with its figure of a Maragat standing high up
against the sky, we turned down towards the valley and
plain below. After passing to the left of *Mal de Vieja*
and on crossing a stream before entering Muria, we came
upon a curious little chapel with a flaring blue arch painted
over the door. The town was deserted but we drove up
the main street and found the house of the *cura*, whose
housekeeper (said to be the handsomest woman in town),
after some discussion from a window high up in the wall,
at last agreed to come down and talk at the door.

"Strangers ?" she asked, "and where from ?"

We replied that we were from Lugo ; harmless travellers on a voyage of discovery.

"*Pues*—and what is there for you to see here ?"

Had we not seen her face ? She laughed and we
gained admission to the church. There was nothing
worth seeing inside although our driver and guide were
overwhelmed with its splendor. A statue of San Roque
about ten inches high mounted on its pedestal, stood on
one side having been carried about the town in procession
on the previous day. Everyone was out of the village
down at the threshing-floor in the fields where now and
again we could hear bursts of song and the grinding
wheels of the great ox-carts. The ear-rings of the women
are mostly crescents, again suggesting Moorish influence.
The long, hanging ear-rings of the Gallegans one does not
see here. Wooden shoes—*galochas* or *almadreñas*—are

rare, although they are used, in bad weather. They are common in Lugo.

"Why did n't you bring your wives with you?" asked our driver on the way back to Astorga. "They would like to see Maragatos—there are no other Maragatos in Spain," and he drew himself up proudly. "Have we not here every convenience for travelling about and seeing?" I had been twice jolted off my seat to the floor of the wagon. Before we reached home, he had offered to go with us to the end of the world if we would take him.

On our return to the city a climb to the top of the cathedral tower well repaid us with a view over the wide desolate expanse of country.

In the city of Oviedo there is preserved a chest the fame of which has spread over the whole of Spain and not a little of the catholic world outside. It ranks, among the religious-minded, with the *Pilar of the Virgen* in Zaragoza and the Apostle's tomb at Santiago. It is a holy of holies.

RELIEFS ON THE CHEST

This chest has a history dating from the time of the early Church in Jerusalem. Its contents are intimately connected with Christian tradition. It has a deep mystical meaning for the believer who here finds himself confronted with incontrovertible testimony of the Great Truth. As to this we need say nothing. It will be enough to give a mere outline of the discovery and history of this remarkable chest and of its contents. Its story has been written in whole or in part by various of the well-known Spanish historians and to them the more deeply interested may turn.

The box is about six by three and a half feet in measurement, is of oak and covered with silver plates with bas-reliefs, those on one of the sides representing the birth of Christ, the adoration of the shepherds and the flight into Egypt ; on the other, the revolt of the bad angels, the ascension of Christ and various apostles. The entire top is devoted to the crucifixion.

The thirteenth day of March of each succeeding year witnesses the festival in celebration of the transference of this famous box of relics. This day has been set apart in the church of Oviedo for the due honoring of the largest united collection of great Christian remains in the Peninsula. Let us consider the history of the collection :

According to the Spanish account the chest was constructed in Jerusalem for the purpose of preserving the more precious relics of the Christians there, when, in 614, the Persians entered Syria and Palestine, taking the patriarch Zacarias and many Christians prisoners, together with the true cross, which latter was returned and set up in its old place, only to be (in 637) again taken by the Mohammedans and placed in the Mosque of Saint Sofia in Constantinople ! The Christians then fled, bearing with them their relics and remains, and the sacred chest, it is said, was brought to Cartagena or Sevilla (authorities differ) and was later taken to Toledo where it remained ninety-five years.

From Toledo the revered relics found their way to the Asturias and to the mountain known as Monte Sacro, whence they were brought to the city of Oviedo. In

the church of San Salvador, with the greatest awe and
veneration, the chest was opened.   It is interesting to
note that the opening was attended apparently with some
fatal or diabolic meaning.   Until the time of Alfonso VI.
no one appears to have dared to undertake so dreadful
a thing.

Morales tells how, in his own time, Don Cristoval de
Rojas y Sandoval, being bishop of Oviedo, made up his
mind, in spite of the sacred warning, to open it at all
hazards.   Formal and solemn preparations were made,
but at the moment when he stretched forth his hand to put
the key in the lock, he was suddenly overcome with such a
tremendous feeling of horror and fear that he was unable
to continue.   And Morales reports that, among the various
sensations which he experienced, that of the rising on end
of his hair was not the least fearful.   Examination of the
chest, it appears, took place in the time of Alfonso VI. at
which period it was found to contain many small boxes of
gold, silver, ivory and coral, which boxes on being opened
with the utmost awe, brought to light the following remarkable objects, each relic having attached to it its name :

A large piece of the holy sheet in which Christ was
enveloped in the sepulchre.

The *sudario* stained with His blood, which relic is three
times every year exposed to public view with the utmost
veneration ; on Good Friday, at the festival of the Eleva-
tion of the Cross on the 14th of September, and on the
morning and afternoon of the day of St. Matthew the
Apostle.

A large portion of the True Cross.

Eight thorns from the crown worn by Christ.

A piece of the reed on which the sponge of vinegar
was raised to Christ.

A piece of His tunic.

A fragment of His tomb.

A piece of the swaddling-cloth in which He was wrapped in the manger.

OVIEDO—CLOISTERS OF THE CATHEDRAL

A piece of the bread of the Last Supper.

One of the thirty pieces of silver received by Judas.

A piece of the roast fish which Christ ate with His disciples after His resurrection.

A piece of the honeycomb eaten at that time.

Some of the earth on which His feet rested when He ascended to heaven.

Of the earth on which He stood when He raised Lazarus.

A fragment from the tomb of Lazarus.

A piece of the stone with which Christ's tomb was closed.

A piece of the olive branch which He bore in His hand when He entered Jerusalem on the ass.

One of the three images of Christ crucified which Nicodemus made after His image.

A phial containing the blood and water which had gushed from the side of an image of Christ made by His followers, when the Jews set it up as a mark and struck it in the right side with a spear.

Hair of the Virgin.

Pieces of the garments of the Virgin.

Fragments of linen made moist by the milk of the Mother of God.

The chasuble given by the Queen of Heaven to Saint Ildefonso, Archbishop.

The forehead of Saint John the Baptist.

Hair of the same Saint.

One of his bones.

Relics of the twelve Apostles and the Prophets.

A large piece of the skin of Saint Bartholomew, the Apostle.

The right sandal of Saint Peter.

Part of his chain.*

The pouch of Saint Peter.

---

* The question of which part is at once raised. The subject is a very confused one and the stories are contradictory. Four chains are supposed to be referred to elsewhere in ecclesiastical history as having been used on Saint Peter; two in Rome and two in Jerusalem. It is a well-known story in the Church that two of these united miraculously to form a long one which is now in the church of *St. Peter ad Vincula* in Rome. I have never met with this Spanish fragment elsewhere.

That of his brother, Saint Andrew.

A bone of the hand of Saint Stephen.

Other relics of Saint Stephen.

Relics of Laurence and Vincent, of Saints Cosmas and Damianus and others.

The clothes of Saint Tirso Martyr.

Some of the hair with which Mary Magdalen wiped the feet of Christ.

Four bones of the head of Saint Librada, Virgin and Martyr, with relics of many other holy women.

A blade from the wheel on which the virgin Saint Catalina was martyred.

A part of the rod with which Moses divided the waters of the Red Sea.

A piece of the stone of Mount Sinai on which Moses fasted.

Some of the manna which God rained upon the children of Israel in the desert.

The cloak of the Prophet Elias.

The bones of the three who entered the fiery furnace of Babylon.

At this point the writer halts as though for a long breath and says naïvely : " and besides all the said relics of the Holy Prophets, Martyrs, Confessors and Virgins there are there guarded many more, *whose number God only knows.*"

He is however by no means at an end. There are yet, outside of the sacred chest, other wonders to be told of in detail ; a marvel-lous cross of solid gold, made in that very church by

THE CROSS OF THE ANGELS
(FRONT)   (BACK)

the hands of the angels themselves (which shows that the angels very wisely worked in the peculiar style of the time), and that famous other, called the Cross of Victory, with the aid of which Pelayo defeated the Moors, not to mention one of the six water-jars, the contents of which Christ converted into wine.*

The bodies of the Holy Martyrs Eulogius and Lucrecia.

That of Saint Eulalia of Mérida.

That of Saint Vincent of Zaragoza.

That of Saint Julian, Archbishop of Toledo.

That of San Serrano, bishop.

The shoulder blade of San Pedro Regalado.

Two bones of one of his arms.

The cassock in which the body of Pius V. lay shrouded for three hundred years.

The pillow on which his head rested during that period.

A letter, from Saint Teresa of Jesus, in her own hand-writing.

The completion of this document is of a kind not unfamiliar to a large portion of the world's inhabitants at the present time. It simply promises, with Papal authority, to all such as, moved by God, shall journey to this shrine, the remission of one third the penalty attached to their sins, and a gain of one thousand and four years and six *cuarentenas* (40 days) of indulgence.

---

* It is of little moment perhaps that the good writer here in reading his proof failed to notice that *hidra* had been substituted for *hidria*, the former meaning a hydra, the latter a water-jar. The miracle is rendered somewhat bizarre by the change.

V

PLASENCIA—YUSTE

FROM Madrid to Plasencia is never an inviting expedition, but the prospect of seeing Yuste was quite enough to ease somewhat the roughness of the journey, though it could not drown the incessant rattle of the ancient timbers of our railway compartment. Through a continued hail of cinders we had long vistas of bare, brown fields. Dust, dirt, fleas and fellow-passengers added to the general misery until, at last, we arrived at the station of Plasencia. The station—*only* the station ! To the town we must take stage—six or seven miles.

More dust and fleas and fellow-passengers added to a weary rocking and bumping in the *berlina*, the right side window of which was broken and had been mended with brown paper, just enough to keep out fresh air, and let fine gray dust sift in. But we were resigned. My companion had sunk into silence and we sat staring out at intervals along the heaving, dusty mule-backs. At 4.35, we turned a bend and saw the town lying below us. As we came nearer, the walls could be made out and the whole took form as we passed the Jerte River.

Then, true to the time-honored custom of Spanish stage-drivers, we broke into a gallop, the inevitable method of entering a city after a long, weary journey.

To be sure it deceived no one. No person believed for a moment that we had kept that merry pace through the long period of our martyrdom. No one dreamed that the *mayoral* was smoking any but his first cigar instead of the last of a series ; no one who saw the *zagal* leaping to the ground at each few paces to goad on the mules, pictured him thus nimbly careering from the first. All were perfectly aware that we had lagged and dragged and bumped and choked, and gone far beyond the merest joy of profanity on those miles of seething dust.

We stopped, got slowly down, and Athanasia met us. As soon as we saw her face we deserted our bags, and chanced their following us, that we might be led off at once by her. We loved her from the very first. We knew her to be our guardian angel. Through narrow streets we went under her protection, and into the Plaza Mayor, surrounded by fruit stalls and full of color and odors, some strange, others friends of long standing.

Fruit, fruit everywhere, but we could not stop. Out of the Plaza Mayor at the end by the Café, to the right and along the narrow streets, until hot, thirsty and grateful, we passed at last into the broad, covered court of the hotel of the Romero Brothers, the *Fonda del Oeste*.

The *Fonda del Oeste* is an old house preserved from antiquity, to be devoted to the purposes of an hotel. Up-stairs we wandered through dark, arched passages and at last found our small rooms. Our host we discovered when we went down, seated at a table afar off and we nodded to him but said nothing. We saw that he was old and had taken the place of Spanish age—silence and a corner. By and by his wife, the real host, appeared. Even she had reached an age when it is pleasanter to direct than to do. The real heart and soul of the whole place, we soon saw, was our guide from the station—the ever-present girl of all work—Athanasia. Industrious, excited, wonderful Athanasia. Shall I ever forget her! Her little india-rubber body went bobbing and bounding about unceasingly.

An ornamental daughter of the house, in black and surrounded by an atmosphere of dignity, heightened by a veil and much powder, sat in a central position of the hall and noticed us with some degree of kind condescension. We did not presume to address more than a dozen words to her, which she suffered herself to hear and acknowledge with monosyllables. Later she even smiled.

Outside we had discussions with the fruit women for melons and peanuts. A handful of the latter sold to me opened the sluices of inquiry.

" What do you call them ? " she said. I told her.

" What a silly language," she laughed, turning her fat body half around towards a neighbor and kicking a hog which was rooting among her onions at the same moment.

" The hogs bother you ? "

" Ah, yes. Customers who don't pay ! There ! " This was an accompaniment to a kick sent home. A violent squeal followed and he trotted off, nose and tail up, to his companions. The streets were full of these animals, and they would not move to let one pass. For is not this province the home of the Spanish hog ? Here he is fattened and famous ; from here he is sent out in the various forms by which he is best known after death. But of all is he fairest, best tasting and least like his living self as " *sweet hams* " of Estremadura.

As I write of the hogs of Estremadura I am reminded of the satire of the last few months expressing Spanish feeling against the United States and the amusement de-

rived from the picturing of Uncle Sam and the hog.
Scarcely an illustrated paper or a daily but has had its
fling at so broad a mark. The hog has been represented
as the chief domesticated animal of the North American
people. He is pictured as riding-horse, beast of burden,
household pet, guard, friend and food. It is said that he
has supplanted the eagle on our currency, and that "*the
hog*," valued at one hundred pigs, has become the standard
of values.

At eight we dined with five other guests, and, while still
at table, the muleteers, whom we had previously bespoken,
arrived. They were a good-looking pair with great, gleaming teeth, shuffling feet, broad smiles and the dignity of
good health. Discussion at once arose and every one
joined. Were we to pay four or five dollars to be taken to
Yuste? Two mules for two days, a man and thirty miles.
Five dollars! Everybody shouted in derision. We left
it to our neighbors and it fell to four. There, however, it
stuck. And after awhile, to ease the battle spirit which
appeared on the point of rising, we accepted the twenty
per cent discount and set time and details. As our guides
departed, however, the landlady suddenly sprang to her
feet. Her rasping voice rang out:

"Oh, what a set of fools!" she shouted. "Four dollars! And here was I holding up three fingers all the
time. The thieves!" At intervals after that she would
break out into muttered invectives against the muleteers,
with upbraidings at our childish simplicity.

We were the last at table and received from each de-
parting one a "*que aproveche*" the customary formula by
which one wishes well to one's neighbor and to his diges-
tion. And later, upstairs, as Athanasia handed each his
glass of water, with its white *azucarillo* lying in the saucer

beside it, she called to us to sleep well, her voice echoing
along the turns and passage-ways of the old house.

As all had thought three too early a time for the start,
we had agreed to four, and at that hour we heard the
noise made by the approaching animals. We went down
and found the great doors—a new pair, the pride of the
owner who had discarded the ancient ones as not sufficiently effective—slowly giving back before the energetic
pushes of Athanasia, disclosing dimly outside the splendor
of our two beasts with their muleteers.

We had time to take a cup of smoking tea and, as dawn
broke dimly, scrambled up on the backs of our animals.
Our seats were not, however, of a kind which promised
much comfort for the coming miles. They were the ordinary *albardas*, or pack-saddles, which have the faculty of
straining the legs apart until they ache beyond endurance.
The novice usually clings, I have noticed, with a grim
tenacity to the first position, until clinging is no longer
necessary and the legs have assumed an icy fixedness.

We made our way very slowly along the narrow
streets, the mules' feet slipping now and then over
smooth, worn stones, and the scarcely distinguishable
windows staring at us without expression. Grayness
came in at the end of the streets as the faint dawn grew
brighter, and we left the town and went down the hill and
across the bridge, where low brush fires were sending
up yellow flames to right and left. The rays of the sun
shone faintly from behind the mountain and the valley
was filled with a delicate blue haze. The wind came in
little puffs, cool and refreshing, and brought with it the
early morning sounds.

A woman in a red bodice and yellow skirt seemed to
flare suddenly out of nowhere. On her head she was

balancing a basket of melons. At her throat she wore a crucifix strung on a black velvet ribbon and I could see the little gleaming bit of silver rise and fall at each breath she drew.

"God be with you," she said, as she passed, in soft, serious tones.

Our dog appeared at this moment. He had found an old shoe which he carried in his mouth and worried at intervals. He was short, heavy and muscular, and his bark was like a sharp song of morning triumph echoing in the valley.

Now peasants passed us often, their patient little donkeys buried beneath great heaps of fruit and vegetables. The road was impassable for wheeled vehicles. Our animals picked their way among the rolling stones, now and then thrusting us against the branches of the scrub-oaks which grew irregularly between the great, uneven rocks. Only at long intervals was there a bit of cleared ground, a patch of peppers or corn, with melons trailing along the walls.

After a short halt the mules tossed their heads, rattling the hobbling chains about their necks, and we all mounted again. Our guide sent a long volley of invective in the direction of a dead cow at which a dozen great red-necked vultures were feeding. The profanity was, however, in reality directed at our slow pace. At last, in the far distance, we sighted, between the oaks, the *Puerto* in the mountains by Pasaron, through which we must go to Yuste.

Across a little sandy pool at 8.10. The stream is called the Garganta de Gargüera and there is a bridge which no one takes.

At last we reach Tejeda. The main room of the *posada* has a brick floor and bright, whitewashed walls.

On one side is arranged a good display of blue and white china, sieves of punched rawhide, and household articles hung on nails. All is refreshingly clean and free from evil smells.

As we sit here discussing the preliminaries of food and the possibility of a halt, the mules are led across the room and into the *cuadra*, or stable, a black depth behind, where are dimly visible and clearly audible hogs, chickens, goats and other formless moving masses, too deep in the gloom for recognition. So is the mediæval desire to have all one's worldly goods within one's walls preserved in these little places.

The landlady is a pleasant, toothless old soul, in a very short green-edged dress, and bare feet tucked into slippers. She and a man wearing a purple *faja* and leggings, on whose buttons is a portrait of the Pope, inquire about our trip, the man first carefully removing (one from under each arm) two dried codfish. There is much loud talking. In the *cuadra* the hogs come to the door and grunt ; the chickens crow, until at last the barefooted landlady takes us into her own room, drives out her husband, who has the palsy, and fries us some eggs in oil. We sit down with our muleteer, who first pours red vinegar over his eggs and eats them between huge bites of cheese !

It was about ten when we started on, and we were soon out of sight of the little wayside *posada*. Partridges rose several times before us, doves flew past continually, and once we lost our way, but soon found it again.

" I know the way well enough," said my guide, " though it 's twenty-three years since I went over it. Twenty-three years this coming March. I married from Pasaron and I used to come often enough, then." After this I felt confident of him.

The square tower of the church began to be very near. The little town lies in a break in the hills. We struggled up to it and entered the middle ages. Dark, over-hanging, narrow, filthy streets, filled with vile odors ; half-naked children mingling with hogs, chickens and goats ; women in brilliant colors, with bare feet ; hags peering from grated windows ; and now and then a sinister face at a half-open door. Strange cries, the tinkling of goat-bells, barking of dogs, gruntings, curses, all rising about us in a wild pandemonium.

We had to force our way through it all, now kicking the sullen, angry-eyed, half-savage dogs, now pushing between the great, gray backs of the monstrous hogs. At last we came to a fountain, at the head of the muddy street, over which was written a warning to the people not to defile the water by the washing of utensils therein.

From here we went upward along a street lined with huge wine-jars, the *amphoræ vinariæ* of Rome, and a little farther, we passed the oven where they were baked. Then down through heavy chestnut groves into the open country once more, gaining two splendid views, between the ridges, of the low plain below, with the Sierras in the blue distance.

At a quarter to twelve we passed a cross by the road-side ; an assassination had occurred there, and this had been set up to mark the point where the body had been found. I could not get the details of the story. The spot recalled Byron aptly enough :

> " *And here and there, as up the crag you spring,*
> *Mark many rude-carved crosses near the path ;*
> *Yet deem not these devotion's offering—*
> *These are memorials frail of murderous wrath ;*
> *For wheresoe'er the shrieking victim hath*

Poured forth his blood beneath the assassin's knife,
Some hand erects a cross of mouldering lath ;
And grove and glen with thousand such are rife,
Throughout this purple land, where law secures not life."

Ferns began to cover the rough country, filling the spaces between the gray rocks and coloring the whole landscape curiously. Half an hour later we entered the *robledo* or oak forest of Jaráiz, and in a quarter of an hour had passed through it. At the edge my guide stopped and waited for me to come up. A broad valley opened before us to the left.

" Do you see that patch of trees over there across the valley, under the mountain ?" he said, sweeping his hand out in that direction.

" Yes."

" It is Yuste."

I forced my animal out of the road and upon a knoll, for a better view. The valley lay at my feet, gray, barren, forbidding. No forest was in sight save that from which we were just emerging, and the little clump of trees afar off, at the last home of the Emperor. The usual silence reigned ; only above in the clear air a vulture wheeled suddenly and swept back into the forest from which he had come, curious, perhaps, at our sudden halt in a place where halting had for him but one significance.

The last house of Charles the Emperor. The spot with which the greatest name in the history of Spain is most intimately connected. The one spot on earth where the arbiter of the lives of a wonderful generation came as near as it is possible for such a man to approach the lowest of his subjects. An old, broken man, on whose mind was written the map of Europe and who had lived just long enough to see the danger signals in the north begin to shine.

Low lights which, under his successor, were to flare along
the whole horizon with a blaze which should draw out of

YUSTE

Spain one vast stream of gold
and men, poured in to quench
it, and leave her sapped and
exhausted after a desperate
fight a century long.

"Are you through look-
ing?" asked my guide at last.

We passed around a curve
and into the town of Jaráiz.
The sight of the place seemed
to awaken in the mind of the
muleteer some memories of
the time twenty-three years
past. He peered here and
there curiously through the
dirty streets and at doors and windows, as though he
were living over some familiar scene. At last he stopped
before a door and struck it several heavy blows. For a
time all was silent. Then a window opened overhead and
a woman's face appeared.

"Do you know where the wife of Silo lives?"

She shook her head and stood gazing after us, as we
moved onward. A few steps farther another door seemed
to strike his attention; he delivered a tremendous blow
upon it. A man came out.

"Do you know where the wife of Silo lives?"

"The wife of Silo?"

"Yes."

He turned and raising his voice shouted down the
streets:

"Pépe!" A head was thrust from a window afar off.

"Who is the wife of Silo?" More heads came to windows—lines of them were staring at us. The words were repeated over and over again. At last, far down the street, an old woman called in a high treble:

"It is Bitorina Parejo he wants."

"Ah, yes, Bitorina Parejo!" said a dozen voices.

"Bitorina Parejo?" repeated the man who had called, "she lives there." And he pointed to a house.

"Let us go there," said the muleteer, "she is my sister."

Before I could express any surprise a little woman, past middle age, had let us in, and a family scene ensued. The two had not met in fourteen years!

I remained patiently standing on one side holding the *cabestro* of my mule until the Señora Bitorina deigned to notice me and listen to my plaint of hunger and fatigue. Then she was all attention. The small, nervous creature flew from her newly found brother to me like a highly excited little hen.

"What will the Señor have to eat?" She had said it three times before I could answer.

"What may we have?"

"Oh, anything—there is everything here!"

I told her I would take what she brought me, and gave my mule into the hands of her brother. We went up-stairs to the combined dining and bed-room which was just over the stable.

"It is warmer so," said Bitorina, in answer to my questions. "In winter it is good to have the beasts so close."

The apartment had two small alcoves filling one side. Adjoining it was the *taberna*, a longer and narrower room, the public drinking-place, run by the little woman.

At intervals men kept coming in and going to one of the alcoves. I inquired of the Señora Parejo if some one was ill.

" Ah, yes, he will die, we think," she replied in a cheerful voice. " The doctor said so, and the fever is on him now these eight days."

I went over and looked in. The air was close and heavy, and by the half-light from the candle I could just see the outlines of the emaciated figure of a man. His face was hidden, but a thin hand and arm hung over the bedside. A man, a sympathetic friend, no doubt, was talking to him in a low voice. I wondered how long, between friends and fever, he could last.

The other alcove bed, I saw, was vacant. I was tired, for the *albarda* had worn me nearly out, though I had changed my position continually.

Nothing could have seemed more tempting than the cool white of the bed after the laborious trip, and without a word to the Señora Parejo, I threw myself at full length upon it.

Scarcely had I done so when a shriek arose, and the little woman flew at me like a wild creature. She seized and dragged me off the bed with the strength of two men. I was too dazed to resist, but retreated before her.

" Oh, *Dios mío, Dios mío !* " she shrieked ; " they are ruined—ruined !" She tore back the cover of the bed, and to my amazement disclosed row after row of—biscuits ! Small, round biscuits ! *They had been placed there to rise.* To rise ! Down the centre of the rows my weight had flattened them beyond recognition ; only at the farthest edge had a few escaped.

I apologized as best I could, but the harm was done. Still, the Señora Parejo bore no malice, and five minutes later she presented me with a sumptuous repast consisting

of thirteen small pickled fish, fine white bread, goats'-milk
cheese, wine or water unlimited, and the half of a water-
melon, *sandía*, in the disposing of which my hostess joined
me.   We talked on amiably for some time, and I questioned her about the man who was ill.   He was of the village and unmarried.   The doctor, she said, was a most
wonderful man.   I made no comment, but my expression
may have betrayed a doubt.

   "Oh, but you don't know—you don't know! Why, he
has cured me twice."   I congratulated her.

   "Yes, I was mad—quite mad.   It came from a blow
on the head.   See here, you can feel it."   Sure enough,
when I put my finger on the place she indicated, I felt the
spot yield.   The woman's skull had been fractured!

   "How long ago was it?"

   "Two years."

   "And you have done nothing for it?"

   "Nothing!   Did I not say the doctor had saved me
twice.   What with poultices and hot bandages and the
cutting of the hair, I have had enough done.   But, sometimes, even now, it bothers me a little, and I have had a
headache these three weeks.   Though not when I wear
this."   And she held up a small brass image of the Virgin.

   It is probable that this woman died or, perhaps, became insane.   The operation which was evidently needed
for relieving the pressure on the brain had, doubtless,
never occurred to her doctor, or if it had he was evidently
afraid to risk trephining.   The treatment she had received
told its own tale.

   We left town followed by children and descended into
the valley, where, after a good deal of bad road, we crossed
a stone bridge and began to climb the low central ridge
which divides it.

" You should have turned to the left a good way back," said a boy who was eating figs by the roadside, in answer to our question. " But go on now up through the *barranca*, and then keep to the right by the cross."

THE CROSS

We soon discovered the *barranca* and climbed up through it. The way was difficult, nothing more than the bed of a mountain torrent which had cut deep into the soil between the rocks, leaving great masses of fantastically worn and tottering clay and gravel, ready to fall at the slightest jar.

This passed, we found ourselves on a long slope stretching down to the edge of the woods of Yuste, which we reached and skirted at a stumbling gait, making a long swing to the left. Then we found the cross, and, after it, the entrance.

At the latter, after a refreshing ride through the cool woods, we came upon a group of women washing under the great walnut-tree, where the Emperor used to pass when he came down from the square brick building above, by the inclined pathway on massive arches.

The present owner of Yuste is the Marquis of Mirabel, who keeps an overseer on the grounds. I followed the latter carefully over the place, through desolate halls and bare, dark rooms. By a low door we entered the Chapel —bare and chilling like the rest. A stray beam of sunlight fell on the floor near a line of graves, at the foot of a raised tiled portico where stood the altar. Opposite the low door beneath which the Emperor's head had so often bowed in passing, in a niche to the left and perhaps fifteen feet above the blue-tiled altar base, may still be seen the coffin in which the body lay while at Yuste. There is an inscription below :

Within this box of chestnut
wood was deposited, during
the four years that
it remained in this con-
vent, the body of our Lord
the Emperor and King Charles
the First of Spain and
Fifth of Germany, of un-
dying memory.

The sunbeam faded away while I read, and we left the dreary chapel and continued our walk.

Outside it was little less dreary. Among the grapes and fig trees the hogs were hard at work, and a calf started up from one of the crumbling arches of what had once been the favorite walk of Charles. The path is still clearly marked, but time will finish what it has begun. At its end lies the open forest. I turned back and found the

RUINS OF YUSTE

famous "fish-pond," now almost dry. Ripe oranges hung over the wall and a few of the golden balls had fallen into the green stagnant pool and were floating there, flamingly suggestive of decay. I tried one, but, as was fitting, it was bitter.

The history of Yuste and of its royal tenant has been written and need not be retold. Spain cannot take much

care of her monuments ; a nation so filled with them could
hardly be expected to, perhaps.   They are, for the most
part, slowly creeping back to the elements again, and each
traveller, no doubt, will have less and less to tell.

How the water, down at the entrance, gushes out under the great *nogal* and rushes away with a sound that is a
quick stimulant after dust and hard riding !   The brook is
divided, one stream for the washer-women, the other for
the garden of cactus, fig, eucalyptus and palm.   One last
look I took up through the great branches and wilderness
of leaves, then mounted my mule, and we started once
more for Jaráiz.

Town was reached just as the hogs were coming home
and we all went in together !   The fact seemed to strike
my guide.

"They all know their place," he said ; "they will go
straight to their own doors."

I did not see any when we reached the streets, and
certainly every door was wide open for them, and in the
cuadra of the Señora Parejo was much grunting, as we
entered.

"How do you like Yuste ?" asked a man in the public
room, upstairs, and I told him some of my impressions as
nearly as might be.

"And do you go all over the country like this ?"

"Yes."

"Riding a mule like that—for nothing ?"

"Yes."

"Well, that would n't pay imposts for us," said my
questioner.

"Nor make biscuits," said another, looking over at the
Señora Parejo, who was standing by the door.   Several
laughed out at this but were restrained by a nod towards

the other room from a heavy grave man with a beard. The man with the fever was dying.

They questioned me about the Emperor and about Philip, in a vague way.   I was speaking of Juana when the grave man said suddenly :

"And Doña Carmen !   What a woman she was ! "

" Doña Carmen ? "   My surprise evidently struck all as peculiar.

" Yes, she who changed clothes with her lover, Alfonso, so that he might escape.   You do no know it ? "

I confessed that I had never heard of it before.

" I have the novel of Philip the Second," said the grave man, with dignified contempt.   Then he rose and left us.   I had lost caste, I saw !

A hump-backed boy sat under the greasy lamp.   As he rose to go he came over and said to me :

" I know you were talking about history.   A novel is not history.   We have few books here, but there are *some*."   His eyes flashed.   Was I talking to a youthful Zorilla, a Lope of Jaráiz ? who knows !

I went to bed as quietly as possible—in the bed of my former discomfiture, now ready to do duty in the accepted way.   The dying man next me was breathing hard and I could hear clearly.   The doctor had ordered everything closed and not a breath of air came in.   At first I was attacked by the fleas, but after a while they grew less vicious.   I think a *sereno* gave his long, wailing cry about eleven.   Then I dropped off into a restless, dreamful sleep until four ; the room was stifling by that time and I got up and crept down-stairs.   As I passed the alcove where the dying man lay I could see another man asleep by the bed, in a chair, the candle throwing a yellow light over him.   His hands hung down and his mouth was gaping wide open ; I had a distinct impression that his mouth lacked several teeth.   His head had fallen forward on his chest, and his *faja* had become loosened and trailed on the floor by the bed.   The other's face I could not see, but they had said he would not live through the night.   I thought the life might have been slipping away in the stillness as I crept down the creaking stair and sat on a stone by two ponderous grunting hogs for an hour.

We took a glass of water, put some bread in our pockets, and started at five.   Our return was uneventful.   Only once we lost our way and called to a woman at the door of a house for a glass of water ; she in turn called to her husband inside :

" Juan," she said, " is there any water ? "

" Water ? " came back a distant voice, " who wants water ? "

" Two strangers."

" Two strangers ! " he repeated ; then, after a pause, " No, there is no water."   We rode on.   That night, after a thorough soaking in a sudden rain, we passed again between the newly varnished doors of the hotel in Plasencia, where we were welcomed by the amiable hostess, received a dignified nod and smile from her daughter —still sitting where we had left her—and were overwhelmed by the irrepressible Athanasia.

VI

MADRID*

All about the Puerta del Sol and the
streets adjacent the coffee-toasters take
up their position early in the morning.
One is aroused by the rumble of their ma-
chines, and the odor of the coffee comes
floating in through the open window. On
the sidewalk in front of the *Gran Cafe
Colonial*, seated on a black bent-wood chair
which he has just pushed out before him
through the swinging glass door, sits,
slowly turning the handle of the *tostador*,
a man wearing a dark blue *boina*, gray trousers, and a long, dirty, white apron tied
in at the waist and across the chest with
two strings passing over the shoulders.

From the sack of coffee, lying beside
him on the pavement, he takes now and
then a grain or two and, as his body
swings backward and forward, munches
it with the inexpressive, passionless face
of a ruminating animal. He wears on his

MOZO DE CORDEL

* *The portion of this chapter relating to the Cid Poem was published in* "*The Bookman*" *for September, 1896, and is reprinted with consent of the editors.*

77

feet, great *sabots* or *galochas*; not flat ones with the ordinary heel and upward curving toe, but with two ridges, one at the toe and one at the heel, transversely, which raise the whole above the wet.   They are very dirty, and burned here and there with black marks made by the sparks which have fallen from the charcoal fire beneath the *tostador*.

The *tostador* is a short, thick tube, three feet high, on four iron legs,—the fire inside, at the bottom.   The top, or end of the tube is completely filled with a hollow sphere on an axis, which discloses at each of its revolutions a small trap-door.   Inside the roasting grains toss and scratch and grind against the sides.

A lazy *mozo de cordel*, or porter, wearing a green cap drifts up and lights his cigarette at the fire, saying a dozen words, as he puffs, to the seated man.   His trousers are of coarse, dark cloth, and red stockings show through the

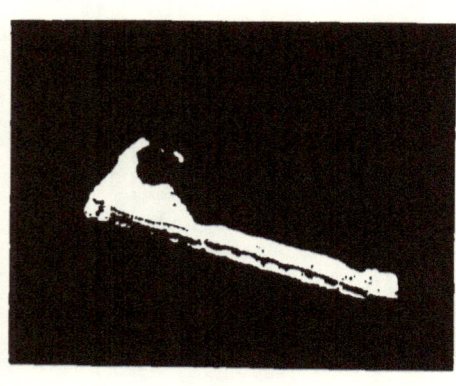

AN ALPARGATA

straps of his *alpargatas*. As he talks he nods gravely to a friend, all in blue, who is seated on the slow-moving hulk of a two-wheeled cart loaded with thin bricks and drawn by a yoke of red oxen. The acquaintance answers, reaching out at the same time to touch one of his plodding team with a long stick.

The coffee-toaster sits, swaying backward and forward, at intervals speaking a word to the small, ragged boy perched on an empty box, marked with three stencilled crosses, who pushes his bare, brown, unwashed toes toward the glow of the fire, which it is his function to stir. A fat old woman, her head bound in a red bandanna, who wears a gray dress and a blue apron, holds her hands folded on her stomach, meditatively, displaying the great silver rings on the middle finger. Between that finger and the thumb is a small bundle of lottery tickets. After an extended conversation with a loiterer on the corner she suddenly swoops down on the patient grinder of coffee and tries to dispose of her wares to him. But he shakes his head. At long intervals, he stops his eternal grinding, to poke back the little trap-door in the ever-revolving gray ball, and there bursts out of the little hole a bluish smoke, bearing rich odor of burning coffee, which rises in a warm, penetrating cloud.

Out in the *Puerta del Sol* the cars are leaving at long intervals, going slowly past,—up the *Calle de Alcalá* or in the opposite direction. The morning sunlight strikes on the net of wires that enters the cupola of the gray building on the south side of the square, and a few men are grouped in earnest conversation at the centre —where a short time ago, as travellers will recall, a fountain stood.

SPANISH SOLDIERS

Soldiers wearing green gloves go by ; street-sweepers

with great brushes and broad, gray hats, each with a brass plate upon it ; *mozos* in black velvet and sandals. Now and then the coffee-toaster shifts the gray ball over, and keeps it turning rapidly in a skeleton frame outside, while he stabs the fire with an iron poker, and brings up an angry, lurid, sparkling flame. Sometimes he glances behind him in through the glass doors of the *Gran Café Colonial.* The front of the building is brown, in imitation of wood, seemingly fastened on by huge spikes, the gilded heads of which only are left conspicuous.

To the right and left of the doors frowns the medallion head of a brown, visored warrior, while its two windows, in each of which is a single marble table, are ornamented by looped-up yellow curtains.

At last he finishes prodding the fire. The red coals are dumped upon the street and are carefully collected in the wooden box marked with the stencilled crosses, while another man, just come from the *café*, gathers up the toasted grains on a great piece of sacking, pours them carefully into a large box, and then, with the air of a con-noisseur, raises on high dipperful after dipperful, letting it run back in a rich, brown stream, still sending out its cloud of steam and delicious odor. Then the *tostador* is left alone on the sidewalk in charge of four small boys, who gesticulate and argue for some minutes, until two men come out and take it in. It is ten minutes past eleven.

Starting at the *Puerta del Sol* and walking up the *Calle de Alcalá*, past hotels, banks, clubs, cafés and museum, you will already have taken, at one swift glance, a consid-erable object-lesson in the manners, language and dress of the modern Spaniard.

If, on coming in sight of the upper end of the *Salon*

del Prado, at the Ministry of War, you turn past the imposing fountain to the left, up the modern, fashionable *Pasco de Recoletos*, and go along the shaded walk until you are almost opposite the new National Library, you will have seen the outside at least of some of the best private houses and public buildings. And if you turn next to the left one block, then to the right, you will pass, somewhat back from the street, the building where the national, or Basque, game of ball (*pelota*) is played in its long, high court. Continue, mount the steps opposite, enter the

COURT FOR PLAYING PELOTA

plaza with the statue in the centre, cross it to the *Calle General Castaños*, and stop before the apartment-house which is number seven, and you will be very near the repository of the most remarkable and famous of Spanish literary relics.

On the third floor of the house before you, the sides of which project, forming a double row of bay-windows, lives Don Alejandro Pidal, former member from Villaviciosa, now Speaker of the Chamber of Deputies, and better known as the possessor of the unique manuscript of *The Poem of the Cid* than by any of his other distinguished titles.

It is indeed a rare thing to seek the most important literary document of a nation in the house of a private citizen, and to the properly enthusiastic there is a slight quiver of fear at the thought of the possibilities of fire or theft, and a vague wish that the little volume had somehow found its way earlier into one of the glass cases of the long library building, of which the green roof may be seen from these upper windows just across the square.

Let us enter the open door, nod to the *portero*, and mount the long stairway to the very top, passing in view of the little circular *ventanillas*, through which, in days not long gone by, we should have had to whisper "peaceful folk" (*gente de paz*) before the unoiled bolts would have been drawn to admit us.

Now, however, we merely ring, are briefly scrutinized, and a few seconds later are admitted to a small study, and Don Alejando is before us.

Señor Alejandro Pidal y Mon, the present owner of the manuscript, is physically above the average Spaniard. He is tall, heavily built, extremely active, and a rapid and most eloquent talker, whether in public or in his own library. He has clear, earnest eyes and a long beard, now turning white, which gives him an almost patriarchal appearance.

He was born in Madrid on August 26, 1846, and his father, first to bear the title of Marquis of Pidal, was Cavalier of the Order of the Golden Fleece, Minister of State, historian, orator, journalist, and one of the founders of the moderate party.

Such was the man who rose to welcome us and whose face lighted up eagerly at first mention of the Cid poem. "It is there," he said, pointing to the side of the small room, where, against the wall, was suspended an elaborately carved and turreted miniature wooden fortress, reminding one somewhat of the gate of Santa María in Burgos. Unlocking the doors of this, Señor Pidal disclosed a metal box through the open top of which could be seen a dark object. Taking out the box and opening it, he handed me a small, black-covered volume.

CABINET IN WHICH THE POEM IS KEPT

The *Poem of the Cid* is, in the eyes of the educated Spaniard, the grandest of epics—the epic of Spain. It is the expression of his patriotic spirit; the embodiment of his memories of the re-conquest; the first child-speech of his nation—of a nation whose earliest memory is of eternal war and of unending struggle toward the south, from which it had been driven. The bearded hero of the poem is the familiar type—the ideal type of a Spaniard *rancio*, warrior and *leader of a faction*.

Much has been written of it. Sketches, extracts, partial translations, rhymed and otherwise, we have already had, and yet the popular idea of the Spanish hero and his poem-history seems to be far from clear.

If we suppose that somewhere about the year 1207 (five years only before the battle of Navas de Tolosa), in the month of May, at a town of Castile, a certain monk, by name Pedro, wrote or copied a manuscript which was in truth a strong, rough song, wherein the especial deeds and

death of this national hero were told, we have (relieved of
scholarly argument and doubt) something of an account
of the document which has brought down to us perhaps
the most vivid picture in Europe of a mediæval warrior.

From that day of 1207, until a more certain one of
1779, or from the moment in which the good Pedro laid
down his pen, as he tells us, in the month of May—and
he could have chosen no better moment in all the Spanish
year to push his writing aside and take a holiday—until a
certain scholar Don Tomás Antonio Sanchez, did the same,
is 572 years, and during that time the world knew very
little about the small manuscript which had been waiting
to be rediscovered at Bivar.

Having read in the History by Prudencio de Sandoval
of certain *versos bárbaros y notables*, which were at Bivar,
and finding in Berganza another account with sixteen of
the verses themselves reproduced, the learned Sanchez
declares that his interest was awakened, and through the
assistance of Don Eugenio de Llaguno y Amirola he was
enabled to get possession of the document long enough to
read and copy it.   The result of this reading and copying
was given to the world in the first printed edition of the
poem.

Probably Sanchez himself no more than half-guessed,
when he first turned the pages of the little parchment volume of seventy-four leaves, how important a find he had
made for the literature of his land.   But his was the joy
of the first discoverer, or, better, explorer ; for those who
preceded him gave but mere hints of the existence of an
ancient manuscript.   It was left for him to find that there
was an account which so closely paralleled history that it
would actually be a point in dispute whether it were not
the very source of that history itself ; for him to regret, as

others have regretted, that the first leaf or leaves were missing and that another leaf had been ruthlessly clipped away at the heart of the text, taking with it fifty lines describing the interesting adventure of the two coward counts of Carrión ; for him to finally wonder and worry as to the author, be he Per Abbat, as the last lines say, or some other of whose work Per Abbat was the mere copyist ; and, last of all, to decide, if possible, whether there had ever been a capital C the more in the blurred date of the blurred last page, making that date read 1345 (era) instead of 1245.

After Sanchez had copied and printed the manuscript (in his *Poetas Castellanos Anteriores al Siglo XV.*), we hear no more of it until after the wars, when it suddenly reappeared in the shop of a bookseller, and was brought to the notice of the government. As the latter at the time, however, could not make the purchase, it was to Don José Pidal, father of the present Don Alejandro, that Spain owes the preservation of her greatest literary treasure.

He, to prevent its going to England, purchased it, and after a careful study published some general notes upon it in his *Estudios Literarios*, under the title of *Poema, Cronica y Romancero del Cid*. Upon the death of Don José the manuscript passed by inheritance to his son, who in turn began a long series of critical examinations of it from various standpoints, resulting in a mass of papers which it is to be hoped will one day see the light, though to a man so busy with political questions this requires more time than is likely to be often at his disposal.

During the period when the manuscript has been in the hands of the Pidals it has been reproduced by various persons. In 1858, M. Damas Hinard printed his famous annotated, critical and sympathetic translation, which would hardly have been superseded were it not for the unfortunate condition of the text (Sanchez) upon which he relied.

"Damas Hinard never saw the original," said Señor Pidal, and he read me a letter from him wherein he earnestly requested to be allowed to study it even for eight days only. This was naturally refused, as it would have necessitated the sending of the volume out of Spain. It was no doubt a serious disappointment for the enthusiastic Frenchman, as he was forced to leave much in his text to speculation, not a little of which was to be afterward corrected by others.

It may be mentioned as interesting to Americans that though the manuscript has not been allowed to cross the Pyrenees, it has made the longer journey to Boston and was there for some time in the possession of George Ticknor. I do not know whether the latter anywhere mentions this fact, but Señor Pidal assures me of its truth.

In 1842, Ochoa reprinted Sanchez in Paris, and Florencio Janer corrected, and, together with Don Pedro José Pidal, again reprinted the first edition at Madrid, preserving faithfully, as is stated in the notes, the orthography of the poem, which was before him. This Janer did in a measure, but not completely, and in 1879, Karl Vollmöller printed at Halle his *Poema del Cid,* "*nach der Einzigen Madrider Handschrift mit Einleitung, Anmerkungen und Glossar neu herausgegeben,*" of which, however, the text only was published. Frere, Ormsby and Southey have made translations pretending to no great faithfulness, though serving the purpose of presenting the story at least.

The manuscript contains seventy-four leaves, forming in all 3735 lines, counting the two restored at the end by Janer.

Sanchez had either failed to notice these at all, or passed them over as an erasure. Each page contains about twenty-five lines, more or less, and measures about 16 x 20 centimetres. The writing is fairly regular, unlined, and, at places, especially on the last page, much blurred and stained. The number of lines or leaves wanting at the beginning it is impossible to tell exactly. The one missing in the body of the text is the forty-eighth, and would correspond to the forty-third, of which it formed one half. The present binding is thought to be of the sixteenth century, and Señor Pidal called my attention to what he believed to be traces of gilding in the depressions of the stamping on the sides, which are boards covered with black *cordovan*. At the edges are still seen the remains of clasps secured by leather.

HOUSE OF THE SEVEN CHIMNEYS,
XVITH CENTURY

Among the old private houses of a city like Madrid, there is no want of interest, although most of them are sadly changed from what they once were. But the traveller must, during some part of his stay at the capital, see that well known old building, the so-called House of the Seven Chimneys.

It is not difficult to imagine how great in Spain, at a certain time, was the expression of luxurious innovation in a house possessing a chimney. *"It is impossible to warm one at the Kitchen-fire, without being choked,"* says Madame Aulnoy, *"for they have no Chimneys . . . there is a hole made in the top of Ceiling and the smoak goes out thence."* When, therefore, the number of these signs of luxury on a particular house had attained to the cabalistic and mystical seven, what power could avert the christening of the building by the first passer : The House of the Seven Chimneys.

The House of the Seven Chimneys has a familiar sound for American readers ; but there is little about the building in Madrid, beyond the name, to suggest the gabled home of the Pynchons. It is simply one of those ancient buildings of which European cities usually possess one or more, and which bring down with them some peculiar history and the suggestion of an age departed.

For the old building, which every *Madrileño* knows, has brought out of the back country of Time strange traditions, half-true, half the outgrowth of idle gossip and superstition. They are no longer told on the corners of the streets neighboring the mysterious building itself by the old women, nor used to subdue unruly children. Only curious persons remember and repeat them now, and they are being put in books so that they may be forgotten with a good grace.

The general outlines of the old landmark have changed somewhat. Windows have pushed their way to the light,

HOUSE OF THE SEVEN CHIMNEYS,
XVIIITH CENTURY

doors been walled up, stucco has overcrept brick, and stone been evolved from stucco, and garden walls have melted before advancing streets. But on the whole, these have been modifications rather than radical changes, and the chimneys—the title to a name distinctive—have remained undisturbed.

Ghosts have been seen to flit over the roof of this ancient pile. Strange lights have moved in its darkened and empty rooms, as the belated tell, and within its walls human bones have been unearthed. Before its doors Don Fernando de Contreras was killed. Esquilache and Godoy have peopled it with memories, and at night not a few citizens of the capital of Spain have, even now, been known to make a *détour* in passing this ghost-ridden precinct.

But of all the tales, one has a more personal interest than the others.

When Philip II. was still blind to the character of his wily secretary, Antonio Perez, and that secretary's word was still the secret means of making and unmaking destinies, in a court where the fortune-seekers were numberless, there came one day into the capital a certain Don Juan Arias Maldonado who, suddenly deprived of a lucrative position, sought his restoration by direct appeal to his majesty the king.

What manner of man, we wonder, was this Don Juan Arias Maldonado. It is not too difficult to discern even through the haze of that confusing period. As a servant of the king in Peru he had, no doubt, amassed considerable of the envy-breeding things of this world, and he possessed—dangerous wealth in the court at that time—a wife of remarkable beauty.

He was a proud, vain man, weak withal, yet with the weakness born of never having done anything with his own hands. He came to a country where men could not shake free from the odor of their class and where the blood of kings had a color peculiar to itself.

A sanguine man, perhaps, and one over-trusting for the possessor of so fair a wife, for when the lady Ana had been but a short time at the court many eyes already turned quickly as she passed, and one pair at least with more eagerness than was fitting.

Perhaps it was in the crowded streets of the old city, perhaps along the shores of the Manzanares which then, we are told, was no sprawling stream, as now, where only washer-women beat their white clothes among the sand, but a beautiful, partly navigable river with oak trees and gardens, and flowers such as now burst out only for a few short weeks in spring and are swallowed up in one common, gray grave of the dust and heat of summer; or perhaps far out in the country, among the groves and gardens where now the Buen Retiro or the Fuente Castellano is lined with tall, and imposing modern buildings; wherever it was the great banker and money lender saw Doña Ana once, and from that moment followed her.

Baltasar Cataño, one of those *flamencos* who had come with Charles to Spain, had been active in the getting of a great fortune. One of the class of money-gatherers of a time when the accretion of money required talents akin to the combined abilities of the politician and the clever criminal, he was perhaps a man of marked ability to which had been added a touch of the qualities of the men from whom he exacted his high rates and clipped his profits, so that even his marriage with Catalina Doria could hardly be expected to deter him from the pursuits of a new vision of loveliness presented to him in Doña Ana, the wife of the petitioner to the king.

Petitioner to the king! They may have been the very words with which he first heard the two strangers described, or perhaps "country fellow," merely, or the more polite words employed to say fool and its synonyms. Certainly not praise would be bestowed on the man of waning fortunes.

And Cataño knew how to deal with such as these. Or better, he knew well enough whose hand held the power—and its price.

It was in the year 1577 that the two arrived at Madrid. Twenty years since the great Charles had breathed his last at Yuste, twenty-two since his resignation of the supreme power into the hands of Philip. New influences were at work, and the chief among them was expressed by the presence of Antonio Perez.

As in Spain at that time there was always not one but a series of dependents, so in the case of the great Antonio there was a second, a secretary's secretary. Don Juan de Ledesma was a man not too far below his master to be incapable of a sufficiently far-seeing treachery and willing policy of deceit, or the opening of negotiations upon almost any basis, provided the signs pointed the way of profit to Ledesma.

To Ledesma, then, Don Arias presented his case. As might have been expected, the wily secretary considered it some time, reconsidered it longer, and then took a still greater period to examine it thoroughly all over again. Months slipped away and daily the resources of the petitioners grew more limited.

ANTONIO PEREZ

In the meantime, however, an unseen agency was at work. The usurer had presented his suit to Doña Ana and had been repulsed. He could not understand it. He had renewed it only to meet the same result. Driven at last to desperation he resolved to gain the aid of the secretary. Ledesma listened. The usual arguments were used and the secretary was won.

The plan was very simple. Ledesma, at the earliest opportunity, was to have a serious talk with his petitioner and to advise him to make a more impressive show at the court, cost what it might. No doubt, the arguments used were not hard to prove to the already desperate Don Arias. He was no longer in a position to deliberate clearly. He could find nothing so fatal to contemplate in the future as the ruin which was already staring him in the face. Whatever doubts he may have had, the good secretary could clear them away by his seeming interest and good-feeling. He would help him. He would advance him money ; he would even sell him a house. Payment was to be considered afterwards. Should the good Don Arias walk to court when others rode ? No, he must ride with the rest.

The good Don Arias rode with the rest. We next see him with the beautiful Doña Ana living gorgeously in the House of the Seven Chimneys—for it was this that the

HOUSE OF THE SEVEN
CHIMNEYS TO-DAY

accommodating secretary had sold them at an exorbitant price. The plan was furthered to its utmost. All manner of extravagance was encouraged and urged by Ledesma, and Don Arias was soon hopelessly involved. His riding was short.

Ruin was upon him. One month was all the time allowed by the eager lover for the destruction of his rival. The creditors appeared. All was taken and the two were upon the street.

At this point the pursuer secretly purchased the House of the Seven Chimneys at half its value, intending to present it as a further temptation to Doña Ana.

But the wily usurer had struck deeper than he knew.

A few weeks more and Don Arias Maldonado was no longer a danger or an obstacle. He died suddenly, leaving Doña Ana penniless.

And so the usurer was successful?

Strange as it may seem, he was not. Doña Ana did not fall into his open arms. She did not fly with him. There was still one retreat left and to it she turned. The Church opened its doors, as it has always done, and she disappeared from sight forever.

VII

THE BULL-RING

" But looked at coldly, so dull is life, that it is better to imitate the Roman Cæsars and quickly spend the fleeting human force than bend to the laws of economy, for misers or spendthrifts we shall end as all that lives by plunging at last into the waves of eternity."

A MODERN SPANISH WRITER ON BULLFIGHTING

WHEN color-photography shall have been developed and we may sit down and study the color of a Spanish street in our own rooms we shall be little better able, I fear, to gain a clear impression from it, than we do now from the ordinary photograph which, we are told, looks so like what we have seen. It is hard to tell why it is that pictures of Spanish scenes are so unsatisfactory. Is it that the rapidity of change is so great, that expression and sound and smells play so large a part in the whole, or that the impressions are so fragmentary and little general that they become confused and lost almost as soon as received ?

It is difficult to describe in words the impression produced by this shifting, impulsive, now sombre, now vivid, street vitality of Madrid, and it seems that on the day of the greatest event of Spanish sport—the bullfight day— this nervous, seething, ill-at-ease mass of life finds a fitting

place to express its peculiar temper in the great open circle
at the end of the fashionable drive, where law and justice
lose meaning, and the impulse to kill is given free play.

Walk up the *Alcalá* on this
day. Down at the *Puerta del
Sol* you will find long lines of carriages and stages and carts, the
mules that draw them decked
with bells and red tassels. A little later the cabs begin to stream
up the broad street, the mounted
guardias in white and yellow and
red stand here and there, peasants from outside the city walls
fill the little curtained cars, shouting boys, sellers of programmes,
and now and then through the
midst of it all dashes an open
carriage in which sit four men
dressed in a blaze of yellow or
green or gold—a fierce flash of
color, passed in an instant.

And so on up the long street
to the great horseshoe-arched
portal of the *Plaza de Toros*, high
above which, on the pointed façade, floats the yellow and red
banner of Spain.

MOÑA

The national sport of Spain
takes undeniably first rank of all others in the matter of
pure cruelty. It has for its object the death, by slow and
deliberate torture, of a fixed number of bulls and horses,
and the performance is of such a nature that it must needs

act directly upon the minds and impulses of the audience for evil. It is impossible that the feeling of mere admiration at the dexterity or boldness of one of the performers should in any great degree raise the beholder beyond the influence of the rest of a tragedy so grim in its details, so unrelenting in its accomplishment, that the whole scheme of human justice appears outraged. I am quite aware in saying this that there are those who are at some pains to defend the sport, and that a great number of Spaniards, while admitting the facts, would regret to think of the loss of the *corrida*. About bullfighting there is nothing to argue. You must accept or let alone.

And yet I believe that nothing in all Spain so thoroughly deserves close attention as this national game. It is the expression of modernized traditions, borrowed from

A BOX AT "LOS TOROS"

Romans and Moors, and has been kept alive in a nation where the freedom and rights of the individual were, in the early days, it seemed, most hard to overthrow.

One's seat at the *corrida* is, more than any other place, the vantage ground from which to view Spanish character. From the under strata of a nation the upper are made. Here one has the under strata stripped for examination. The cloak of custom and convention is flung aside. Actor and

audience are playing to each other.   Both are living out
the tragedy, and if one can forget the bloody side of the
drama played below, one's lesson in Spanish is worth a
thousand times more than the clearest insight into the forms
of the irregular verb or the uses of the subjunctive.   The
education of the bull-ring is an education of daring, of
recklessness, of utter carelessness of life, both in self and
in others.   Such men as the Spaniard Perez, who entered
the cage of an enraged lioness, to save the trainer who
had been struck down, are among its dramatic disciples;
such women as she who, when a tiger escaped in the
streets of Madrid (Dec., 1877), stopped with her child to
watch the creature curiously; such children as those who
followed the same beast pelting it with stones.

The origin of bullfighting is doubtful, but that it is
the natural development and modification of the Roman
circus there can be little question.   It may even be, as has
been suggested, one of those curious inversions of original
custom, so common in history, by which the diversion of
slaughtering human victims by wild beasts has, with the
growth of Christianity, been turned to the pastime of
slaughtering wild beasts by men.   Is there not still hidden
in the spectator's heart the hope of that more exciting
phase of the sport, wherein the modern conditions will
once more be reversed and the wild beast again be master?

If so, in not a few cases has the wish been gratified.
Pepe Hillo, José Rodriguez, Manuel Jimenez (*el Cano*), Cándido, Espartero and countless others have paid with their
lives in the end, and there will no doubt still be added many
names to the list.   Mutilation is an everyday occurrence.
The loss of an eye, as with Dominquez (1857), when the bull
Barabas caught him; of a leg, as with *el Tato* (1869), and a
score of others, are events so common as to be only noted

when occurring to well-known men. Bones are continually broken, but the passion for the sport is incredibly intense and is on the increase rather than diminishing.

It is the custom of Spanish writers to name the Cid Campeador as the first bullfighter, on the most shadowy tradition. There is probably not the slightest reason to suppose any definite form had been given to the sport at that, or at a very subsequent period. That men may have amused themselves in encounters of this description may not be questioned, but if the Cid killed a bull once, it is by no means to be supposed that he ever did so again. Bullfighting would hardly be considered a profitable way of disporting one's self at a time when every faculty was needed to prevent a successful Moorish raid.

Pascual Millán discovered recently in Roncesvalles a record of a *corrida* celebrated in Navarre by Carlos II. in August, 1385. It reads : " The king ordered fifty *libras* to be paid to two men of Aragon, one Christian and the other Moorish, whom we had caused to come from Zaragoza, to kill two bulls in our presence, in our city of Pamplona." Other bullfights took place in 1387 and 1388, proving, as Señor Millán says, the existence of professional *matadors* in Zaragoza in the fourteenth century.

It is said that bulls were fought in Italy about 1300 and after, particularly in 1332, when a special exhibition was given wherein nineteen Roman gentlemen and many others lost their lives.

The Spanish comment upon this event is characteristic : " The poor Italians thought one had but to be a man to do as other men ; they did not take into account that to play with bulls it is necessary to have them born in Spain." Here bullfighting in Italy seems to have come to an abrupt termination. It was promptly prohibited and was not reintroduced until brought back by the Spainards themselves long after.

The development of the sport in the XIIIth and XIVth centuries was slow. It was at this time the diversion of the nobility and was invariably a performance of horsemanship as well as dexterity with the lance. The traditions of this time have been preserved to us to-day in the occasional appearance in the ring of the *caballero de Plaza* who, mounted on an excellent and spirited horse, despatches the bull by the thrust of a broadheaded spear.

An explanation of the cause of the early popularity of the *corrida* is doubtless the facility with which the bulls could be obtained. Along the low lands of the south the animals found an excellent pasturage and were, although

CABALLERO DE PLAZA

not the equals of the bulls of Castile, sufficiently savage by nature. Spain in those days had not at her disposal the resources of Rome. She could not draw a supply of wild beasts from the four quarters of the globe. Lions and tigers were not to be had in her own territory and to send for them would have reduced her sport to a precarious condition. The nation itself was not unified. The want of cohesion represented a corresponding want of inter-course, and the transportation of a single lion from North Africa to Castile would have represented an expenditure of time and money only within the reach of kings. But bulls were at hand and were cheap. They were easily managed; they transported themselves. Afterwards they could be used as food. Economy could go no farther. The sport grew and developed.

It is well known that Isabella the Catholic was most prejudiced against bullfighting from the first and that she even made efforts to suppress it. Her dislike seems na-tural to a Spanish writer on the subject. The ring was in an undeveloped condition. It was crowded with unskil-ful horsemen, and a place of confusion. " If in place of such disorder," says the writer in question, " she had seen a real *corrida de toros*, or at least such as during the past hundred years have been celebrated in Madrid, she would have spoken quite differently."

It is not doubtful that the Catholic queen was some-what tried by the continuance of the spectacle but, as was said, she who could expel the Moors and Jews, could not crush out the national sport, and even the threats of the clergy were unavailing. At last, on the 20th of Novem-ber, 1567, Pius V. issued his famous edict prohibiting it, and placing all princes who should permit its continuance in their dominions under the ban of excommunication, as well as all ecclesiastics who should witness it, together with the bullfighters themselves, depriving the latter of Christian burial, if their lives were lost in the ring.

The thunders of the Church—and it is a commentary on the most Catholic of nations—failed for once. Bullfighting could not be put down. The edict of the Church became a dead letter. And finally the masters of theology in Salamanca appear to have settled the matter, and all was as before. With the difference, however, that opposition, as might have been expected, had added a new impulse, and now all over Spain the talk of the ring grew more and more familiar.

Charles V. killed a bull with a lance in Valladolid at the birth of his son. Fitting tribute to Philip! From that time to the present, with the exception of the short Napoleonic period, bullfighting has never languished.

In 1612 Philip III. granted to Ascanio Manchino special rights controlling bullfighting in Valencia. These rights expired in 1647 (being for three lives) and this is among the first instances where private individuals were granted the privilege, afterward everywhere repeated, from which has developed the present method of leasing the ring.

In the reign of Philip IV. the grandeur and luxury of these entertainments had reached an extraordinary degree. It was the fashion for the nobility to engage in the sport, and the accomplishments of a gentleman included the frequent breaking of lances on the necks of bulls in the open.

REJON LANCE
USED BY
CABALLERO DE
PLAZA

It was at this time that the *espinillera*, or *gregoriana*, (to-day called *mona*) a protection of iron for the legs, came into use.

It is this iron casing which gives the peculiar stiff appearance to the legs of the *picador* when he is mounted. The belly of the horse on which he is astride is the objective point of the bull, and the leg of the horseman hanging before this would scarcely escape laceration were it not protected.   After the charge of the bull and the death or disabling of the horse it is the *mona* which renders the position of the *picador* one of danger for, weighed down by it, he is unable to escape and must rely on the dexterity of those about him to divert the furious creature's attention.   Occasionally his iron protection has been the cause of his death.

When Philip V. came to the throne, the first change in the classes took place in regard to the ring. The king was not in sympathy with this sort of amusement, and it soon fell from universal favor among the nobles.   But it was not to be abandoned.   Seeing their superiors deserting the field, the lower people threw themselves into the sport with passionate enthusiasm.   From that time the change was marked.   As might have been foreseen, what had been the amusement of the court—an amateur's pastime and diversion—became in the hands of its new champions an art reduced to a science, to which successive generations of specialists were to give a code and the necessary traditions.   Bullfighting had really become national.

During this period the Papal strictures had remained an occasional thorn in the side of the conscientious of the Church.   It was at the instance of Ferdinand VI. that these were removed.

It was presented to the Holy See that, in the first place, as the Papal edicts were unheeded they might, with advantage and dignity to the Church, not exist. In the second place it was urged that the agility and dexterity of the bullfighters rendered accident most improbable; and in the third, that the *Hospitals and Houses of Charity would gain greatly from the aid resulting from the fiesta!* In consideration of which the edicts were finally removed, and the acquiescence, if not the approbation, of the Church was made one more active force in the development of the *corrida*.

A new feature at this time was the prolonging of the life of the bull by the use of the long *garrocha*, or *vara* (*pica*). In the days of the gentlemen bull-fighters the *re-joncilla* had taken the place of the lance, and by the sub-stitution of the new instrument for the latter the bull was not killed, but

PARTS OF THE HEAD OF THE PICA, SHOWING WRAPPINGS, IRON SOCKET FOR HANDLE, STEEL POINT THREADED TO SCREW INTO SOCKET AND WOODEN SPOOL OVER WHICH THE WRAPPINGS ARE LASHED

held at bay by the rider—although it was seldom that a fierce animal failed to thrust aside the light shaft or break it short, after which vengeance was at once wreaked upon the unfortunate horse.

The use is mentioned of *banderillas* about the middle of the last century, at the new *Plaza de Toros* in Madrid, given by Ferdinand VI.

A most important adjunct of the *matador's* equipment was now introduced by one of the most famous *toreadors* of his time. This was the *muleta*, a piece of red cloth used to draw the bull's attention aside and to guide his charge so that the proper point of the neck might be exposed to the ready sword. The inventor of this was Francisco Romero. Up to this time the death of a bull had been arrived at after various attempts, and after the neck of the animal had been repeatedly pierced.

THE MULETA

Things had not yet been so changed that those who fought on foot had come to assume the chief glory of the ring. Tradition still accorded great prestige to those who, as the gentlemen had formerly done, met the animals on horseback.

But a number of light, agile men had begun to draw upon themselves considerable notice by their performances on foot. They developed the art of planting the keen little darts, the *banderillas*, on the neck of the bull, darting upon their prey like swift, gleaming flies, fixing their little stings and vanishing before retaliation could reach them.

Romero developed the office of the *matador*. Awaiting the approach of the animal he guided its charges dexterously past his own body until the favorable moment arrived when by a single swift thrust the sword was planted, and a moment later, the great beast sank dead. The stroke was as brilliant as it was merciful.

Romero was born probably about 1700 and was by profession a shoemaker ; but his passion for bullfighting was early excited and he found means to be present, in one capacity or another, at the *corridas* of the nobles until at last, these taking an interest in him, he was given an opportunity of learning the art. And to such purpose did he work that he became famous as the great master of the time. He was in fact, in some measure, the father of the present bull-

FRANCISCO ROMERO

ring and his career in it covered some thirty years. His son Juan followed the profession of his father, as did his grandson Pedro.

A striking figure now appears upon the scene. A man of enormous physical force, of black, melancholy eyes, dark-skinned, and of an expression so strange and unaccountably compelling as to be remembered as his most peculiar trait. This man was Manuel Bellón (*el Africano*).

His history is romantic. When a mere child he became enamoured of a young girl and, on the appearance of a rival, dealt with him to such purpose that he was obliged to fly to Africa to escape the punishment for homicide. It was by this flight, perhaps, and his naturally dark skin that he gained his title of *Africano*.

He seems to have made a long stay on the other side of the strait, devoting himself to a wild, savage life as a hunter, and when, pardon for his former crime having been obtained, he returned to Spain he brought back a physique quite as strong as when he left and a skill not diminished by want of practice.   For a time he was without an equal.

Martin Barcáiztegui (called Martincho) a shepherd from Oyarzun near San Sebastian, was famous at this time for his daring and astonishing feats.   His most notable performance was the receiving and killing of a bull while seated in a chair, his feet bound and holding no other *muleta* than a broad hat in the left hand.   This feat, which was per-

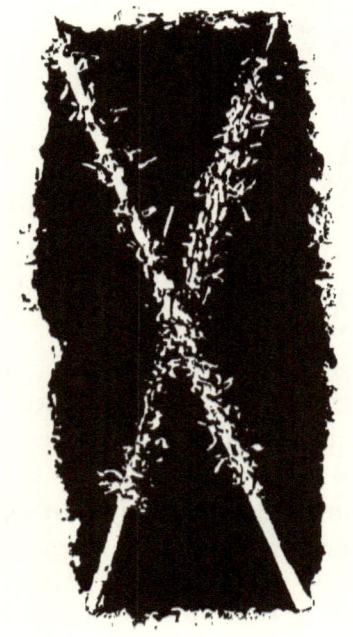

BANDERILLAS

formed repeatedly, is of such a remarkable nature that it has been doubted. But Francisco Goya, whose savage and cynical temperament fitted him not a little to tell the tale of the ring on canvas, was the friend of Martincho and has painted him in the performance of it, and all contemporary authorities verify the fact. Martincho retired finally. He died at Deva, on the 13th of February, 1800.

A more skilful and not less daring man of the same period was the famous José Cándido. His early life is not known beyond the fact that he was born in Chiclana.

Cándido appears to have been a man no less anxious to achieve the impossible than was Martincho, and his first feats bade fair to give him the distinction.   With only a broad hat in his left hand he managed to despatch the animal with a single blow of a dagger instead of the usual sword. But this was only the beginning. The ring was to owe him one of its own most brilliant feats,—the *salto de testuz.*

Facing the bull in the centre of the ring, at a considerable distance (20 or 30 *varas*), he would make a straight dash at the animal. The latter instantly lowering its head to catch the advancing enemy presented the sought-for attitude, and the next moment the *matador* had sprung upon the forehead, stepped to the broad back and dropped to the earth in a graceful attitude over the tail of the bull.

On the 23d of June, 1771, Cándido met his death in Puerto de Santa María. Slipping in the blood of a fallen horse, the bull caught him, transfixed him through the kidneys and, after tossing him about, finally hurled him to a considerable distance.

The audience at once left the plaza and a doctor was sought unavailingly. When one finally reached the scene from Cadiz the victim was beyond recovery. He left his clothes and the money gained that day to the poor; 3300 reals to each of his sisters ; to his wife and daughter, his "houses, vineyards, possessions, cattle, sheep, over 5000 doubloons in money," etc.

Carlos III. once more made the attempt to stop bull-fighting. He failed, as the Church had done. During the 28 years of his reign to 1778, there took place in the plaza of Madrid 440 *corridas* and about 4500 bulls were killed. Several *toreadors* were injured but no lives were lost during the entire period.

There now appeared a man considered more remarkable than his predecessors by all writers on the ring.

This is Joaquin Rodriguez, known as Costilláres. He is the inventor of the *volapié*. In the mind of the *aficionado* this bullfighter still has a place of honor from which no subsequent comer can displace him.

Costilláres was a native of Seville, and was born in the *barrio* of San Bernardo before the middle of the XVIIIth

COSTILLÁRES

century. His father was employed in the slaughter-house of the city and as soon as Joaquin was old enough he was taken as assistant. But the instinct of the bullfighter is, it has been said, akin to the poetic instinct in its assertiveness! The son of a mere killer of cattle in the common way became the most artistic chief in the trade of his time. It needed two generations to arrive at so phenomenal a result!

Meeting the then famous *matador*, Pedro Palomo, the young man attracted his attention, gained his friendship and support, was given lessons by him, and, at the age of sixteen appeared in his *cuadrilla*, for the first time before the public.

As was natural, his first work of importance was that of *banderillero* and so well did he do this that, with the advice of the best *toreros* of his time, he took the sword of *matador* at the age of twenty and was presented to the world in that capacity in his native city by no less a man than Manuel Bellón, *el Africano*.

Costilláres is famous for his careful study of the circumstances of each various act made in the ring. He made it a point to *know* the animals with which he played his game of death, and varied his method of attack in each instance. He seemed to have possessed the true insight into the character of each particular bull and dealt with him accordingly.

Up to this time in the ring there had been a grave difficulty in the use of the long and more piercing *garrochas*, or lances, by which the bull was much more exhausted through pain and loss of blood than at present. It frequently happened that when the *matador* arrived for the finishing stroke, the animal could not be induced to charge. He would retire to the encircling wall of the *barera*, where, too weak to jump over and escape, he would refuse for the moment, to notice his antagonist and stand panting and exhausted. This had always been a trying and annoying moment for the *matador*. Forced to abandon the chance of a brilliant stroke he was obliged either to advance and kill the animal by repeated thrusts or have it done for him by a treacherous stroke from above such as that by which the *puntillero* ends an expiring bull to-day. Costilláres discovered a remedy. He invented the *volapié*. The date of the introduction of this *suerte* is 1770–80.

The *volapié* consists in completely reversing the usual order of attack. Instead of awaiting the bull the *matador* advances slowly toward him, the sword poised, and then, dropping the *muleta* before his eyes and past his muzzle, induces the animal to thus lower the head exposing the vulnerable point behind. Instantly the sword is driven home and the bull falls dead. The one great danger of this is the pos-

CACHETE
OR
PUNTILLA

sibility that the bull may at the instant of the taunt
have still sufficient strength in him to rise with a last
supreme effort and charge.   In this event, called *en un
tiempo* (together), the bullfighter is in extreme peril as
there is no time or space to change his position.   He
must now succeed.   His life may depend on the steadiness
with which the long, keen blade is sent home.   And here
it is that the mettle of these men is shown.   With a clear
realization of the meaning of their position they will stand,
with rare exceptions, unflinchingly, and calmly go through
their part.   Few bullfighters lack this sort of cool bravery
although, naturally, the better ones possess more of it.
They combine agility with what seems a reckless boldness, which is usually made successful by the actual calmness of the actor.

Costilláres appears to have been a man of authoritative
disposition.   He was the first to form a united *cuadrilla*,
of which he remained the acknowledged chief.   Among
his disciples was the famous *Pepe Hillo* about whose name
a host of traditions and tales has gathered.   He died one
year before the latter at Madrid, on the 27th of January,
1800.   Costilláres is also famous as having in his day received, for a single performance, no less than 3000 *reals*, a
sum unheard of before that time, but which would be little
enough to-day.

Two *torcadors* now occupied the ring : Pedro Romero
and Jose Delgado.   The former presented a careful, dignified, exact performance to the public ; the latter : one of
incredible dash and spirit.   Both were of incomparable
ability in their special lines.   But to *Pepe Hillo* (Delgado)
has been given the popular affection so that there is no
aficionado in all Spain who is not ready to go into ecstasies
at the mere mention of his name.

If the portraits of *Hillo* which have reached us are life-like, his character is not far out of keeping with his appearance.   Shrewd, jovial, honest, and with keen appreciations, he was the man of all others to take the public fancy and hold it.   No doubt he possessed personal as well as public attractiveness.   He is described as full of fun and wit, gorgeous in his dress, lavish of money, kind to the unfortunate of his own profession as of others

PEPE HILLO

and combining with it all a most remarkable dexterity and skill.   He was a spoiled child of his time.   Women of the highest rank lost their hearts to him and not a few were the scandals which linked his name with that of some illustrious dame of court or society.

He was born at Villalvilla in the Province of Sevilla, on the 19th of September, 1768.   His father was later a shoemaker, a trade which the son also followed.   Abandoning this the young man entered the slaughter-house of Sevilla, and later, under the instruction of Costilláres, he entered upon his future career, and was soon far ahead of his fellows.   His dash and abandon were what most told with his audience, coupled as they were with the rapidly acquired, but not the less accurate, knowledge of his part, and he soon began to divide honors with his more severe and classical competitor, Pedro Romero.

Led on to the most reckless acts by the recognition he received, he was repeatedly wounded and in more than two dozen instances received serious thrusts from the horns of angry bulls. At the bottom of this was the ever present desire to surpass all others, especially Romero ; and the public, recognizing the supreme efforts he was making, soon joined him and ranked him, though possibly unjustly, above his rival.

It is strange that the death of *Pepe Hillo* was by a cause he had himself feared.   Both he and Costilláres had

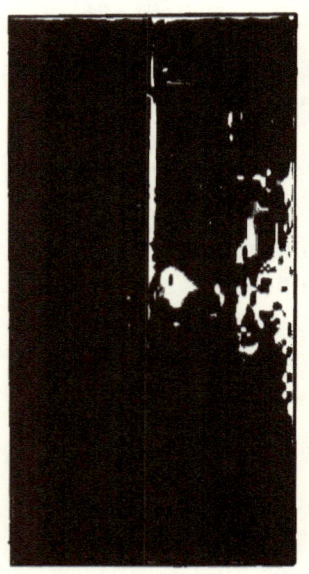

requested, in the year 1789, that Castillian bulls be eliminated from the programme, the reason for this being the known savage and uncertain temper of these animals. Twelve years later he was to be killed by one of these very Castillian bulls.

His end (in his thirty-third year) is one of the most dramatic and at the same time ghastly scenes of this theatre of death.

The seventh bull was in the ring and had already received three or four lance thrusts, although it had repeatedly fled from the horses, of which it showed fear.

BULLFIGHTER'S SWORD   Antonio de los Santos succeeded in placing a pair of *banderillas* with great skill, and he was followed by two other *banderilleros* who added three more pairs.

After this the *matador*, *Pepe Hillo*, took the sword. Making three passes of the *muleta*, two in the ordinary way and one after the manner known as *al pecho*, he finally advanced to give the fatal stroke.   It failed.   The sword inflicted only a long flesh-wound and the next instant the tossing horn had caught in the clothing of the *matador* and he was hurled with great force to the earth, striking upon his shoulder-blade. Whether he was stunned or not by this blow is doubtful, but a moment later the furious animal was upon him and its horn had plunged deep into the stomach. Tossed aloft on the creature's horns it is said that he was seen to make a desperate effort to free himself, but the raging animal, having at last something upon which to wreak its fury, kept possession of the body for more than a minute, by which time the contents of the abdomen and chest cavity had been hopelessly mutilated. Ten ribs of the unfortunate man were broken, and he was practically dead when a final toss set him free from his frightful position. Fifteen minutes later he breathed his last.

Such, briefly told, though without the close phraseology of the ring, is the famous death of a most famous bull-fighter. It happened in the presence of a vast assemblage of people, and it is one only of many which the same audience has witnessed. It is not to be wondered at that the tiger in the streets of the capital aroused no more serious fears in the breasts of women and children accustomed to this spectacle. It was, in fact, the tiger which should have felt ill at ease.

Pepe Hillo was an ignorant man, if a bullfighter can be called so. He could not write beyond the signing of his own name, which he wrote : Joseph Hillo. He was pre-eminently an actor, and though he played tragedy in the end, his whole life was one continued comedy part. He has become by his death a hero, and remains a sort of Byron of bullfighting to this day.

The great competitor of Delgado, Pedro Romero, who is said to have killed no less than 5600 bulls in his life, has been called the Cæsar of the ring. His fame rests upon an invincible calmness, an absence of display, the refusing always to employ a brilliant artifice or *suerte*  when the rule of the ring did not warrant it, and on a dispassionate self-assertiveness of manner. He was unquestionably the greatest bullfighter of the three (Costilláres and *Hillo*, the others) but could never win the hearts of his audience as *Hillo* could with his wonderful brilliancy and recklessness.

ROMERO

His chief skill was in the dexterous use of the *muleta* and in the fact that he *received* the bulls in the greater number of cases. He was born at Ronda, Nov. 19, 1754, and died there at the age of eighty-five, Feb. 10, 1839. He had retired from the ring in 1799, in his forty-fifth year. His career as a bullfighter, though ended before the public, was extended later, however, for he was appointed with Cándido to a professor's chair in the Bullfighters' College, founded in Seville in 1830.

With the death and retirement of so many of the best bullfighters, and with the complications with France, ending in the Napoleonic time, there closes one phase of the Spanish bull-ring. Up to this time its development had been steady. Romero, Martincho, Cándido, Rodriguez, Hillo and the second Romero, had one by one brought their special aptitudes to bear on its growth and permanent form. It was now approaching its present conditions although many new methods were yet to be introduced. In the lull that followed there is little of importance to add and it was not until long after the re-establishment of the monarchy under Ferdinand VII. that the gossip of the bull-ring was again found interesting.

In 1830, however, the suggestion that a bullfighter's college be established showed a return to more normal conditions and the sport once more revived. It was in 1833 that we have its first example of renewed vitality.

In that year there appeared in the Plaza of Madrid a young man who had been the disciple of the new school. Shortly after the school itself was a thing of the past, but its scholar was rising to higher and higher place in the profession dear to the people. The young man was Francisco Móntes, and he was probably, taken in all respects, the greatest *matador* that ever lived. He was born in Chiclana, on the 13th of January, 1805, and received from his father, Juan Felix, a good education.

MÓNTES

The latter, losing the position he had held, was reduced to work for a living, and the young Móntes took up the trade of a bricklayer, at which he worked until the death of his father.

Attracted to the ring, however, he was one day seen practising, either at the slaughter-house or in the open, by Cándido, who gained him admittance to the "School of Bullfighting" of Seville, with a daily pension of six reals. The young man's fortune was made.

Owing to the exceptional advantage of having been the pupil of Pedro Romero himself, Móntes at once developed the extraordinary aptitude of which he had shown signs at the very first and, as Romero had foretold, he was soon a marked man.   In 1831 he became *espada* without passing through any of the lower grades of the ring, and in

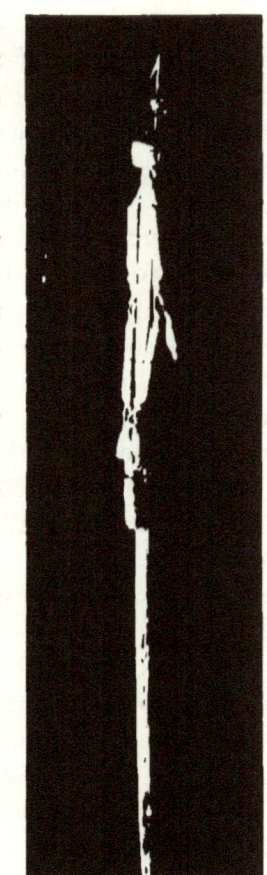

1833, as said, made his appearance at the court, *alternating* with the brothers Ruiz.

The applause which he met with was phenomenal. He at once rose to the first rank, and his astonishing activity, firmness, agility and calmness were discussed from one end of Spain to the other. He was, it seemed, the first to successfully combine the two schools of bullfighting—the calm, determined and assured style of the Rondeñan and the light-moving, subtle method of the *Arte Sevillano* of which the unfortunate Hillo had been so brilliant an example.

FIRE BANDERILLA

FIRE BANDERILLA STRIPPED, SHOWING ROCKETS

The history of any one of a class of men furnishes its special light on the whole, and the history of Móntes is a clear guide to what

manner of man the Spanish bullfighter really is. This
man is the one great perfect exception to his whole class
in the chief requisite for its success: self-control. Móntes
was one of those who early controlled himself and later
controlled his environment. When his father had lost
his means of support the son did a thing most remarkable
in a Spaniard, but more so in one who had already a leaning to the ring. He was educated and he became a
bricklayer. He took the work nearest, and when the
time came he was ready for the next work.

Much of his success was doubtless due to his arbitrary
control over his associates. None disputed him or his
authority; in his *cuadrilla* everyone had his place and
was found there. When his favorite pupil José Redondo
failed to plant the *banderillas* through what Móntes considered carelessness, he called to him:

"You are a fine *banderillero!* Keep out of the ring for
the rest of this day and learn how the others fasten the
sticks." And the other, the one man who in the ring, it
has been said, in some degree equalled or even surpassed
Móntes in *receiving* a bull, obeyed him without a word.

After 1845 his ability began to show signs of weaken-
ing and in 1846 this was more marked, although he then
appeared in the Royal Corridas with great credit. In
1850 he returned to Madrid for the last time, and in that
same year he was wounded in the ring (June 21). The
whole city was in commotion at the news. The house
where he lay in a critical condition was besieged, and when
he finally rallied and returned home to Chiclana in September, it was with the prayers of all Madrid. He died
in 1851 of a fever, hastened, it was said, by excesses into
which he had plunged from some secret trouble.

His peculiar quality was physical strength especially in

the legs and waist. This gave him an advantage in the ring in most of the *suertes*, and his complete training, nerve and dexterity did the rest. He was the pupil of the best bullfighter of the past, and surpassed his master. His appearance was always that of a man older than he was, but in the last four or five years of his life he seemed to break completely.

The time of and following Móntes is called the Renaissance of the ring. The sport again revived all over Spain, and this period lasted for something near twenty-five years.

During that time new men appear who, though adding but little to the list of traditional feats, have gained recognition as masters.

Let me say here that while there is a natural tendency to express righteous indignation at the whole scheme of the Spanish national sport, it must be borne in mind that probably, of all sports indulged in by men, it is the most difficult of successful accomplishment, and demands more of the qualities which go to make up physical bravery than any other. I therefore speak and think of the bullfighter as a man with a distinct career, and rather as a supremely skilful athlete, than a highly developed species of butcher. Self-denial and self-control are quite as much the chief attributes of his ultimate success as they are in other departments of the sporting and athletic world, and the element of danger is quite as great.

During this golden age two names are especially marked. Those of Francisco Arjona Herrera, popularly called *Curro Cúchares* and José Redondo (*el Chiclanero*). The first of these was born May 19, 1818, in Madrid; the second in Chiclana, birthplace of Móntes, in 1819.

Arjona appears to have been born a bullfighter. His

early childhood was given up to teasing cattle after the manner of his elders of the ring, and at twelve he was a member of the School of Bullfighting of Seville, where he was promptly recognized as promising material and taken under the patronage of Juan Leon. At the age of fifteen he killed a young bull in public!

At seventeen he was already a promising *banderillero* in Leon's *cuadrilla* and in the following year killed bulls in earnest. From this time his remarkable agility became famous. In 1838 Leon caused him to join the *cuadrilla* of the then well-known Yuste and soon the provinces began to send up to the capital remarkable accounts of the twenty-year-old bull-fighter who had appeared. Two years later he made his first appearance in Madrid in the ring of the

ARJONA

Puerta de Alcalá, *alternating* with Juan Pastor, (*el barbero*).

His improvement was steady and in 1845 he appeared with Leon and José Redondo in Madrid. At this time Móntes was passing from view and the two (Redondo and Arjona) were the coming men. *El Chiclanero* soon took the lead, however, in public opinion. In 1868 he went with his *cuadrilla* to Cuba and died in Havana of yellow fever the day before that set for his first appearance there.

He was uneducated, but of a generous disposition. When Mendizabal, the statesman, was stricken with the illness which later ended his life he was in reduced circumstances. Arjona came to see him, like many others, and said in his frank way: "Señor Don Juan, here, you shall suffer for nothing! Let a hundred doctors come; I'll pay. I bring no more now, *caramba!* but I leave this and I will come back," and he slipped eight thousand reals under the pillow, and went away. At another time (in 1860), when the troops were leaving for Africa, he was present and gave his money, cigars, and handkerchief to the soldiers. He then went to a certain general and said: "I have nothing more on me, but all I have at home is for the army. Dispose of it for its maintenance—seven hundred goats, seventy hogs and some cows—all I possess."

He was a man of impulse, unable to control his envy of the success of others, and never had the respect of his subordinates. He would take no advice in the ring and had a peculiar style of bullfighting of his own which was as often condemned as praised.

José Redondo, *el Chiclanero*, was left by the death of his father, in 1836, without resources. Turning to the bull-ring he soon gained some success and from that advanced so rapidly that two years later, in 1838, Móntes, chancing to see him perform, said to him:

"In you there is the material for much; if you will work you will go where few go."

The words of the master of the ring confirmed the young man in his determination. He rose rapidly. In 1839 he was without rival as a *banderillero*. In 1842 Móntes gave him *alternative* in Bilbao, although he was unfortunate at first, being wounded seriously there, and barely escaping with his life. A year later his reputation was assured.

There was still to be added to the art of bullfighting one other *suerte*, and this one of the most graceful and difficult. The *volapié* of Costilláres, the *salto de testuz* of

Candido, the receiving of the bull by Móntes, were each a step in the growth of the ring to its modern conditions. It remained for Antonio Carmona (*el gordito*) to invent the *quiebro*.

Antonio Carmona y Sisque was born in Seville on the 19th of April, 1838, and he is said to have killed a bull, with the utmost skill and grace, in 1854, being then sixteen years old. He rose rapidly and in 1857 was already famous for his skill with the *banderillas*. One year later he introduced the *quiebro* and at once took his place at the front among the best men of his time.

It is unnecessary to describe this performance further than as a swift bending of the body to right or left, as the case may be, without moving the feet from their position,

PLAZA DE TOROS

La corrida ____ de abono anunciada para hoy, se ha suspendido por __ ____ __ ____

y se verificará __ __ __ __ __

Los que hayan comprado billetes para esta corrida, y no quieran conservarlos en su poder, pueden devolverlos al Despacho de la calle de Sevilla, hasta las de la tarde de hoy.

Lo que se avisa al público para su conocimiento.

Madrid __ de __ de 189

LA EMPRESA

A NOTICE OF POSTPONEMENT

avoiding thus the onslaught of the bull. It is sometimes performed with great effect *kneeling*. It is done close upon the animal and not uncommonly results in the wounding of the *torero*.

We have now come to a point where the methods and tendencies of the modern ring have been practically developed. The art of bullfighting is upon the basis of trained skill. The path of the *torero* is marked out and his individual desire for reputation can no longer be gratified as it was in the days of the founders of the ring. The audience has learned what to expect from its favorite and is intolerant of minor innovation. New *suertes* are not likely to be introduced. The consideration of the modern ring is, therefore, little more than a repetition of the older sport shorn of the interest attendant upon its growth and development.

HEAD OF PICA OR LANCE

VIII

MADRID—CALATAYUD

WE are leaving Madrid and have clattered down from the *Puerta del Sol* through wet streets, in the small uncomfortable hotel carriage. The train stands waiting by the gloomy platform. Each *Guardia Civil* is buried in his cloak ; a faint line of cigarette smoke arises here and there about the half-hidden faces of the waiting passengers. The woman who sells papers, matches, novels, and the " Lives " of great Spaniards, at the little stand, is shut in despondently and rolled up in shawls. She peers inquiringly up and down at every passer poking her fat neck out like a turtle from its shell and drawing it in again with a slight, audible grunt of disgust when no purchases are made. Of all those volumes with flaring and attractive titles she sells not one and even the newspapers are going off slowly. A bedraggled woman with a big-eyed baby is saying good-bye at the door of a third-class compartment and the "*Señores viajeros al tren*" begins to be slowly chanted by the guard with all the solemnity of a lineal descendant of the most religious of nations. A narrow line of gray light shows above the roofs of the cars, gleaming under the steady downpour that spatters upon them, and out over the platform floor in a fine descending mist ; everywhere a sombre gloom.

123

Two men get into my compartment dragging and lifting a boy, a little fellow of three, wrapped in a *capa* after the fashion of his parents. The miniature garment is lined with red and purple velvet and falls in folds below his small, white, sharp features and wide-open eyes. "*La capa todo lo tapa*," I think, guessing the gaunt little form below, and, glancing over him, wonder how many listless, work-wanting generations it has taken for some stern, straight-backed, Moor-spiking progenitor to dwindle across posterity and end in this.

I settle back in my seat followed by the piercing black eyes that watch me curiously, pondering me deeply, doubtless, and arriving perhaps at profound conclusions as to my nationality and value.

And then with bell and chant and slam of doors and a little jerk and rumble we start out into the gray, solemn landscape. Madrid, like Rome, has a desolate environment. Far away the naked mountains raise their sombre, repellent outline against the sky, and the bare, broken plain is as cheerless at times as the Campagna itself, though it may claim as an advantage the absence of the lurking malaria of the older city. A dreary place, indeed, is central Spain, save for those few wonderful weeks of early spring, when the choked or scorched vitality of the whole year seems to wake and set the blood of all things leaping. Then a carpet of green, sprinkled with millions of flowers, stretches on every side, and the fresh, cool air from the hills steeps itself with perfume and comes to temper the sun's heat like the soul of the wonderful revival. And two months later—but let no one think of it! It is the hundred years of Xerxes; and how greater an army!

A change is being made in some of these outlying portions of the city. Arbor Day (March 30,) has come to be a public festival in Madrid. Early in the morning one sees the preparations in the city, and, long before noon, a ceaseless stream of pedestrians is moving up the *Calle de Alcalá* and out into the parched, half-built-up districts and then, on beyond, to where the ground has been prepared for the planting of the trees.

Later come the carriages—long lines of them—handsome coaches, French and English traps, English coachmen, not a few, excellent horses, and no small number of well-dressed men and women.

There are few places where so many specimens of Spanish humanity may be found assembled as at this new festival. The promised presence of the Queen Regent or the young King hurries an enthusiastic crowd beyond the city, and the long road is for hours tramped by a ceaseless throng of spectators.

CHILDREN MARCHING

Then come the children. They are marshalled in lines and numbered, and in small squads they march or ride in

cars to the scene of the ceremony. Little fellows they are
with olive skins, inquisitive faces, and more restless, eager
eyes than their elders ; eyes soon to become less eager,
less restless !   And there each one plants the tree which
is supposed to be the symbol, in a measure, of his life,
and with the action is chanted a song which is almost a
hymn in the solemn simplicity of its wording, its mingled
sadness and hope ; the hope that though the hand that
planted it may be taken away, yet one good deed done
may be left to thrive upon earth for others, which in
Spanish is sentiment and in English is apt to become
sentimentality.

Two thousand four hundred children form for this
day's celebration, and their restless lines stream onward
from the earliest hour.   The starting point is, naturally,
the *Puerta del Sol*, where the cars are jammed with load
after load.   Forty thousand persons turn out to witness
the spectacle.

During the first experiments of this festival some difficulty was found in the management of the great number
of little boys, but no mishaps occur usually and the day is
one that deserves to be made as much of as it is.   Perhaps no spirit of reconstruction could have found a happier
expression than the reclaim of this waste with trees,
and the day may not be far distant when the summer
months will be less fierce for the poor of a city partly
surrounded by a forest.

The old familiar station cries rise fitfully outside, in
spite of the wet, and at each new stop the fat, dripping
guard stands with outspread fingers, striving not to look
less and less important as his cheerless, soaked figure
grows more wet and bedraggled.   At the smaller places
where the bustle is not enough to drown the voices we

can hear, "*Aguardiente—Aguardiente*," or "*Agua fresca*," rising sharp and harsh through fragments of dismal, dispirited conversations, between whose long pauses the water drips and gurgles. The woman behind the little stand where the white liquor is sold does a good business this cold day. I say at the smaller places, although it would be hard to recall clear impressions of any large places along our route. How the faces stand out afterward in one's memory! Knowing, serious faces whose eyes meet yours with a strange inquiry, as though asking your name and country. Not like French eyes these, or Italian or German. There is pride and grave dignity in them, and underneath them are deep rings. The shoulders are too often apt to droop, and the quick fingers, forever rolling cigarettes, are too nervously deft.

There is a man of perhaps twenty-five by the picket fence of the station, leaning under the eaves of a low shed. He is wrapped in his great *capa*, and the smoke from his cigarette puffs out and is flicked away in the chilly gusts of wind that now and then dash the fine, misty rain in his face. He scarcely stirs, only the eyes move restlessly from point to point. Not a face at the train window escapes him. He has made profoundly original inward notes on all that he has seen. He has studied the English woman who is standing by an open window with her husband and his intuitive glance has fallen before her stare of curiosity; and, as he drops his eyes, he half smiles and mutters a word behind him, and some one there bursts into a fit of laughter.

The country is almost treeless, the towns at too long intervals, and they themselves as treeless and desolate as their descendants of South America or of Mexico and Arizona to-day. Low, *adobe*, tile-roofed structures, with

crooked streets beaten by time and weather since the sub-
siding flood taught men how good a thing was mud for
building.   Here and there splash a few disconsolate, hope-
less-looking creatures, man and beast—one's awakened
sensibility can almost feel the sucking of their feet in the
mud.   Mosquitoes come in at the half-open window with
gentle buzz, and bite vigorously.

Many of those we pass still carry the great Spanish
clasp-knife—the *navaja* of which one hears so much.   But
in the north
these murder-
ous weapons
seldom serve
a more dan-
gerous pur-
pose than the
cutting of
food or the
ordinary uses
of the pocket
knife. It is in
the south that
the flashing
blade is ever
ready to leap
out and it is
there that the

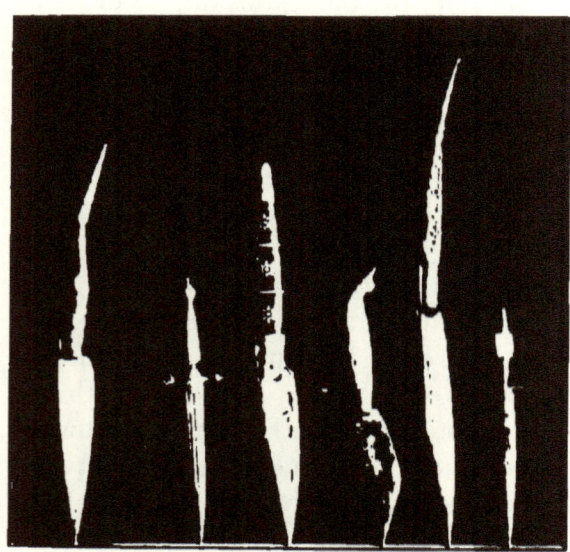

SPANISH KNIVES

click of the ratchet is as deadly a sound as the warning
of the rattlesnake.

Rain has been rare this season.   Only a few days ago
the whole earth was parched and cracking, pools dried,
the streams mere threads, muddied by the thirsty cattle.
Now the water has come with a rush, as it always does in

this treeless land, and all along up the Henares past
Alcalá, is one continuous mud-brown, or light new green.
In the valley of the Jarama, bulls are feeding along the
marshy banks, each with heavy buttons on his horns, not
to be removed, perhaps, until the distant day when he
shall be ready to enter the ring at Madrid and furnish
amusement to a shouting audience, and a little more reputation to Mazzantini, or Bombita or Guerrita, if that last
successor of Lagartijo may have by that time become
reconciled to the Madrid ring.   The streams are swollen
and angry.

The boy opposite me grows restless.   His little white
hands appear from beneath the folds of the *capa*, and I
see them twitch, and clasp and unclasp.   What will become of him, you wonder?   He is quite typical enough
in these days—not alone in Spain!   But the Spanish
phase is peculiar.   Lean over and speak to him, ask him
some simple question,—or some question not simple.
Will he stare at you with the shy healthiness of an Anglo-
Saxon or a German?   Not at all; he will treat you most
seriously, he will consider what you say, he will answer
you after thought.   He will waive his meagre little hands
with expressive gestures.   He will explain or argue, or
politely doubt; he will be a little grown-up person, in fact.
One of those wonderful small creations whom women like
to pet and dress and make much of, and who, thank God,
do not live out half their days.   As you talk with him and
see the little hollow rings about his brilliant eyes and notice how unsteadily the heavy head seems set upon the
frail shoulders, you somehow feel that his very talk is
sapping some hidden source and he is already but the too-
slight covering of an over-intense flame.

"*Alcalá de Henares!*"   Why does the guard not continue : ancient Complutum, birthplace of Cervantes and Solis, site of the great University, burial-place of Ximenez. One might almost add, burial-place of that famous Complutensian Polyglot Bible, afterwards made inaccessible by papal limitation. The place is to-day but a shade of past glory. There is the true sense of desolation about it ; the arid plain creeps up and envelops it. The noise and stir, which we like to think once livened the city filled with its student vitality, has died to a memory.

CARDINAL FRANCISCO XIMENEZ
DE CISNEROS

The great buildings and long streets have a still greater mournfulness, in that they recall so different a past. The inhabitants are poor. The limp of pure idleness has become chronic.

TOMB OF CARDINAL XIMENEZ

It is hard indeed to conceive of this place as much of a respite after Toledo, for that gay though mediocre schemer, the Duke of Uzeda, son of the once great and all-powerful Lerma, who, banished by Philip IV. for eight years to the latter place, was able only

with the greatest difficulty to gain permission to come to
Alcalá. He seems to have been utterly miserable during
his exile and died here in the spring of 1624, a year before his persecuted father had fretted his life out in Valladolid. His sufferings are not hard to understand after a
walk through the streets of his place of exile.

The old gate of the *Mártires de Guadalajara* no longer
stands. The spot may be found, however, if you look.
Through this portal, in 1568, with great pomp and ceremony, the remains of the
patron saints of the city,
Justo and Pastor, were
brought. Their story is interesting.

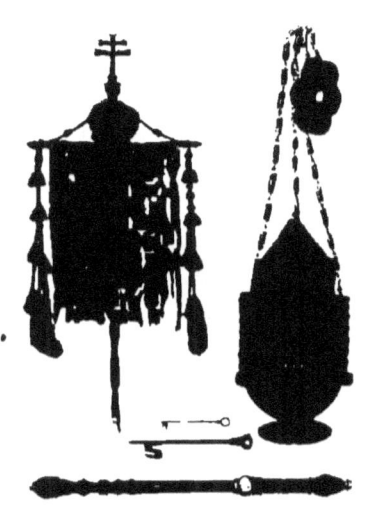

In the days of Diocle-
tian and Maximian, * Da-
cian, hater of Christians, was
sent to Spain. From Ge-
rona, his path was marked
by the blood of martyrs.
San Felix, Santa Eulalia,
and a host of others fell before him, and he at last arrived at Complutum. Here,
however, he encountered a
somewhat remarkable case.
Two little boys, by name

OBJECTS WHICH BELONGED TO CARDINAL
XIMENEZ. STANDARD, CENSER, KEYS
OF ORAN AND STAFF

Justo and Pastor, † of seven and nine years respectively, suddenly abandoned their customary occupation
of learning their letters, and announced themselves
Christians and sons of Christian parents. Word was
brought to Dacian, and the two infantile fanatics were

* Aug. 6, 304, *Esp. Sag.*, 175.   † *Ibid.*, 172.

apprehended.   The fierce Roman may or may not have smiled slightly at the appearance of these heroic upholders of the early Church.   We can hardly imagine him taking the affair with all the seriousness portrayed by his historian.   However, impervious to the joke or not, he took what seemed to him the natural method in dealing with such a case,—he ordered the young saints spanked.

But this punishment seems to have had no fear-inspiring effect, and the two are next seen on the fatal stone where their lives are to be sacrificed.   The moment of the ordeal approaches.   Justo with heroic fortitude supports his brother with the firm words of a man of eighty, and we are at some difficulty to prevent picturing to ourselves an involuntary stroke of the beard.   "Sons of martyrs are we and, that we fall not from the firm faith of our fathers, we come to offer our lives in defense of the faith," etc.*

The fatal ceremony proceeds and, as was to have been expected, a miracle is worked.   The two sage young lives are closed ; but at the place where their knees pressed the stone—"softer than their persecutors' hearts"—hollows form themselves, which signs remain to this day and of which the devout historian remarks : " And this about the stone   .   .   . we read it not in books but we saw it with our eyes, it having pleased our Lord that, for the greater glory of these saints and spiritual delight of their followers, this blessed stone should be preserved until now with such manner of hollowings in the two marks, that no one could deem them fashioned by the hands of men." †

Along the route we are following black grapes grow plentiful in the gravelly soil.   Above Jadraque stands the castle, and over behind the hills, out of sight, one may

* J. de Morales: *Hist. Ecles. y Seg. de Guadal.*, 92.
† A. de Morales : *Cr. Gen.*, Tom. v., 57.

follow in imagination the line of the Cid Campeador to Atienza, or Miedes, or Gormaz, for, on his exile, as says the Poem, he here broke through the hills and entered Moorish territory to carry on the Christian advance and finally take Valencia, premature though it proved. Later I am to cross this same country on mule-back and make a more thorough examination of the castle on the hill. Now it is but a glimpse and on, passing through interesting scenery on the ridge of the Sierra Ministra, and so down the Jalon past Medinaceli and Monreal de Ariza where Antonio Perez was born.

At Ariza one must again think of the Cid. This place has its castle as well. "Between Ariza and Cetina my Cid encamped," sings the old poet, be he Per Abbat or other. Here comes the Cid, if you like, with his *faja* loosely bound about his loins. "The ruffian under the dripping hat?" Why not? Notice the gigantic beard, the broad back, the dignity. He is a beggar? What of it? He needs but "*moros en el campo*," and his good sword Tizon and horse Babieca, and we may stand aside and see good fighting.

"We Spaniards," said a friend of mine in Madrid, "are all brave, that's not the trouble! I will toss a *perro chico*

WOMAN OF THE PROVINCE OF GUADALAJARA

into any regiment you like and it will hit a hero. But the trouble is the fellow knows he is a hero and wants hero pay, *i. e.*, he wants a general's commission next month and if he does not get it—there's food for a revolution !"

The chief engineer of a railroad chances to be in the same compartment and gives me some insight into the construction of this Spanish line, destined, as he says, one day when the way by Canfranc and Huesca should be open, to be the shortest route to Paris. He gives detailed accounts of the financial wreck, consequent on inflated first values, of road after road in various provinces. A sturdy, white-haired old man, angular and erect, who takes his snuff well, and with delicate flirt of the fingers afterwards, he lacks but a few last-century details to set him quite out of a modern environment. Among other things I recall his detailed list of disasters of which he had been a personal witness during his engineering career. He sat and told them off on his fingers dogmatically, and explained their cause at length. Since that time Spain has been stirred up by a new series of unprecedented mishaps of which the floods, the disaster at Mallorca, and the dynamite explosion in Santander are examples. The collapse of the roof of the Cathedral of Sevilla, broken *pontanos* in the east, the sinking of a battle-ship, and floods again have made up the list.

Supper at Calatayud. The place lies beneath a barren ridge, surmounted by a desolate castle, which has almost become re-absorbed into earth, watching, through long years of decomposition, the mouldering, minaretted city at its foot. The Towers of Calatayud with their graceful, tapering steeples, so exquisitely harmonized, are fair preparation for the Ebro city.

Those who travel in Spain will, little by little, come to link certain hours of the day with certain odors. One of

my friends claims that he can tell by one sniff abroad what
hour should be striking. But as there are phases of this
fact which are unpleasant, we may refrain from detailed
descriptions.
There is, how-
ever, one odor
which is pecu-
liar and I am
just reminded
of it. Look
out of the car
window. A
man, a woman
and a girl are
seated on a
bench and be-
tween them is a
small, reddish,
earthen bowl
from which ris-
es steam. The
wind wafts this
gently away
and across in-
to your nostrils
and you sniff
vigorously.

CALATAYUD—PLAZA DE SAN ANTON

You like it? You like it very much. You wish you knew
what it was; you wish, at the hotel, you could get it; you
never will. They will give you what seems to be it,—but
no. You must ride your six leagues before you deserve
to taste of this dish of large, beautiful *garbanzos* and red
sausages and meat and other pleasant things.

After supper the engineer gives rapid little sketches of his life in the hills.   He has shot bears and wolves in his youth and has a long scar on his right arm as a memento of one of his encounters.   He is filled with the natural enthusiasm of the strong, healthy, solitary, out-of-door man.   He turns with the impetuosity of a boy from swift, nervous descriptions of the snow-covered mountains of Sobrarbe, above La Ainsa, to a torrent of invectives against the present political order of things.   His love for the Church might have been touching, had the inquisitor not peeped out for a moment at the mention of the Protestants at the capital.   For the established religion, or rather its priests, he had no criticism beyond : " *Buena gente, buena gente.*"

IX

THE LOVERS OF TERUEL *

WHEN French critics found Boccacio guilty of plagiarism from their own early tale-tellers, I am not aware that any like plea was put forward from Spain in behalf of the little town of Teruel and of a story whose scenes laid there have become familiar as a popular drama to the entire Spanish-speaking world.

The fact is, however, that in the instance which we are about to consider, we have only to read the Italian and then his reputed Spanish original to find that they are one and the same, and that the merest variation of minor details is all that differentiates the tale of Girolamo and Salvestra of Florence from that of Marcilla and Segura of Teruel.

It was in the middle of the fourteenth century that Boccacio wrote the former. The latter is reported as taking place between the years 1212 and 1217. The one has remained a classic from the first ; the other has been passed from hand to hand in the form of poems, history, novels and dramas—now well, now badly used—until at last, on the night of the 19th of January, 1837, Don Juan Eugenio Hartzenbusch became suddenly famous throughout Spain by the production of his drama, *The Lovers of Teruel*, wherein the whole story was related and given its final shape.

* Reprinted from *The Bookman*, August, 1897.

The name of Hartzenbusch as well as the phase in Spanish literature expressed by him, is not as well known as it should be. A mere outline of his life will, however, here be enough. His father, a cabinet-maker, was a German, his mother a Spanish woman, and the young man for some time pursued the trade which was offered to him in the employment of his father. During this period he devoted himself to translation chiefly, and should have gained, it seems now, more reputation than he did. Later, he was to figure as a leader in Spanish literature of his time, as prose writer, critic, bibliophile and scholar, head of the National Library, Academician, and popular favorite. He died on the 2d of August, 1880, at seventy-four years of age.

In the town of Teruel, in the twelfth century, was enacted the popular story which has come down to us to serve as material for plays, romances and poems, and which has brought with it much of the middle-age spirit, recalling a greater story by a greater pen. The history of the Montagues and the Capulets finds a peculiarly similar parallel in the story of the Aragonese families of Segura and Marcilla.

When Alfonso II. reconquered the ancient Roman city of Teruel from the Moors in 1171, there were in the Aragonese army no braver men than Blasco Garcés de Marcilla and his brothers, descendants of the King of Navarre, Garcia I., through Fortún Garcés, his grandson. These were among the settlers who here took up their abode for the advance of the Christian cause and the holding of the newly acquired city.

The son of Don Martín Garcés, brother of Blasco, also named Martín, married Doña Constanza Pérez Tizón. Their son is one of the chief figures in the story which

has made all famous.   Juan Diego Marcilla was born in
the year 1190.

Of the Marcillas and the family of Muñoces there have
come down details of bloody encounters in the streets, of
factions and night attacks, of sudden murders and of quick
revenge.   The name also of Segura is a marked one, and
it was from the house of Segura that the other chief character was descended.   The two family mansions were
found in the present street of " The Lovers," at that time,
however, known as Ricos-hombres and San Bernardo.
The new name records the tradition.

At the end of the twelfth century these houses were
occupied by Don Pedro de Segura and Don Martín Garcés
de Marcilla respectively, both of noble descent, and the
daughter of the former, Doña Isabel de Segura, born in
1197, appears to have been early the object of the passionate attentions of the son of the other house.   It was not,
however, until 1212, when the young lady had reached the
advanced age of fifteen, that her hand was formally asked
by Diego.

Don Pedro de Segura figures in the traditional attitude of the conservative and prudent father.   He refuses
the advances of the young man on the ground of the latter's want of fortune compared with that of Doña Isabel,
who, as the sole heiress of her father, possessed thirty
thousand *sueldos*, without taking the house and its contents into consideration.

Whether it was actual poverty, or whether the fact of
Diego's being a second son acted as the cause of his re-
fusal, is not clear, but it is certain that the lover insisted
manfully upon his claim, and undertook to furnish the
wanting fortune, to which end he asked that a space of
time be given him, that he might seek wealth in arms, the

only means at hand.   Diego left Teruel at once and enlisted in the combined army of Pedro II. of Aragon, Alfonso VIII. of Castile, and Sancho II. of Navarre, which was at the moment formed into a coalition, afterwards to be famous in Spanish history, for the meeting and destruction of the Moors.

It was in fact that moment in the history of the Reconquest when the most serious effort so far undertaken against Spanish-Arabian influence was to be successfully carried to an end in the bloody battle of Navas de Tolosa. Here it was that the Christians, united and determined, met in desperate conflict a great Moorish army, and in the crushing defeat of the latter laid the axe at the root of Mohammadanism in Spain.

BANNER TAKEN BY ALFONSO VIII FROM THE MOORS AT NAVAS DE TOLOSA AND NOW AT LAS HUELGAS, BURGOS. IT MEASURES 3.30 METRES BY 2.20 METRES

It was a short time after he had left his native city, that Diego is said to have taken part in the struggle, he being one of those who, with the king of Navarre, attacked the tent of the Mohammadan leader, breaking through the chain which surrounded that tent, by which the right was gained to wear a chain around the margin of the shield in memory of the deed.   In various parts of Spain broken fragments or single links, said to be part of that chain, are still to be seen.

He continued his struggle against the Moors, gaining

great reputation and money; but as he seems to have been somewhat forgetful, and spent more than five years —the allotted period—in the undertaking, he arrived at Teruel to find that Isabel had become the wife of Don Pedro Fernández de Azagra, natural son of Fernández Ruíz, second lord of Albaracín, having surrendered at last to the insistence of her father.

The story goes that it was on the same day on which the lover returned that the marriage was celebrated. But, when he learned of it from his parents, in desperation, he secretly obtained entrance to her room, where a somewhat unnatural, but altogether dramatic scene, we are assured, took place.

After the husband has fallen asleep, Marcilla addresses Isabel and implores her to give him one last kiss. (Boccacio varies the story here by making him beg to lie by her side, which being granted, he most inconsiderately dies by holding his breath.) But the resolute lady resists his advance; and at repeating the same request, he suddenly adds : " Farewell, Segura," and falls dead.

We are, unfortunately, here deprived of those precise details with which Shakespeare might have presented us. All happens in the most dramatic and perfect manner, however; conscience and the heart work out the grand total without recourse to the meaner agencies of sword and dagger.

Isabel, terrified, perceiving that Diego is dead, awakes her husband, but fearing to relate to him at once what has taken place, she begs him to tell her some diverting story. Having during its recital recovered her presence of mind, she informs him of what has taken place, pretending, however, that it has happened to a friend. Azagra promptly brands the lady of the story as most unkind and selfish in

not having kissed her lover and for having thus let him
die.   Whereupon Isabel discovers the truth to him, and
points out the body of Diego.

The astounded Azagra rises and, after considering for
some time, and not knowing what else to do, secretly carries the body of Marcilla to the door of his father's house
where, in the morning, it is discovered.   A great cry is
raised, but to no purpose.   The body is without any sign
of violence, and the corpse is finally prepared for burial
with great pomp and splendor corresponding to so noble
a family and to the riches which Diego had brought with
him from the war.

More tragedy now follows.   With great accompaniment of clergy and troops the body is taken to the church
of San Pedro ; whereupon Isabel, overcome with the pain
of having been the cause of the death of her betrothed,
resolves to go and give Marcilla the kiss which she had
denied him in life.   In a rough disguise she mingles with
the women going to the funeral, and, arrived at the church,
approaches the body, removes the cover from the face of
Diego and kisses him upon the lips.   At the same moment
she expires upon the coffin.

The climax has now been reached ; the dramatic impression produced.   All stand in horrified silence.   Then
follows the discovery that Doña Isabel Segura is the person disguised.   Whereupon Azagra relates in detail all the
circumstances of the preceding night, and it is determined
that the two bodies shall rest in the same sepulchre !

Such is the popular story.   But the curtain has not gone
down finally ; there is an epilogue to be said.   An epilogue
dealing in grave-yard trophies half-recalled to the flesh.   In
the Church of San Pedro in Teruel, to-day, are the veritable
human documents for the proving of the tale to sceptics.

The two bodies remained interred, it appears, from the thirteenth to the sixteenth century, and in the latter (as certified to by notaries), in the year 1555, Miguel Pérez Arnal being judge of Teruel, during renovations of the ancient chapel of the Church of San Pedro, with the object of constructing that which to-day is dedicated to the medical saints, Cosme and Damián, two remarkably preserved bodies were discovered; and when it was sought to learn whose remains these were, it came to light through the records of the church that they were those of Juan Diego de Marcilla and Isabel de Segura, and that no one had been buried either before or after them in that chapel.

Having been replaced in their former position, when the reconstruction of the chapel terminated, they were again exhumed on the 13th of April, 1619, and from that date until 1708 rested as peacefully as possible in a cupboard, whence they were removed to the cloister and again set up in a cupboard with a marble inscription above them:

Here repose the celebrated
Lovers of Teruel, Don Juan
Diego Martinez de Marcilla
and Doña Ysabel de Segura.
They died in the year 1217,
and in 1708 were transfer-
red to this church.

Finally, in 1854, the people of Teruel, realizing at last the importance of their mummified lovers, had them placed upon a walnut stand, supported mechanically in a standing position, and clothed in light gauze skirts! It is impossible to conceive of anything more grotesque or amusingly horrible. The romantic and passionate story ends in a show-case. The dusty, bony corpses raised to a horrible similitude of life, are even so adjusted as to suggest an affectionate gaze toward each other,—a gaze emanating from profound sockets above which are two bald and glassy heads. Marcilla is the best preserved, the lady having been injured and having lost an eye in the exhumation in 1555.

X

ZARAGOZA

King Charles, our mighty Emperor, did remain
For seven years complete in lands of Spain—
From mount to sea laid low that high domain.
No castle that resisted could withstand,
Nor town nor wall still rose within the land,
Save Zaragoza, which aloft doth stand,
Held by the king Marsile, who loves not God.

CHANSON DE ROLAND

NOTHING so clearly impresses upon the traveller the marked divergence in character of Spanish cities as a trip from Madrid to one of the provincial capitals. In Zaragoza this is especially emphasized. The capital of Aragon might surely be expected to represent a type of peninsula city not greatly unlike others of the same population. It has been subjected to somewhat the same conditions as others. Sufficiently removed, in early times, from the inaccessible central portion to be in no great danger of isolation, a Roman, Christian, Moorish and Aragonese city in turn, it came at last, like the others, to be a part of a single nation. Through all these modifying conditions, however, an individual type was formed and maintained.

Active and intelligent, the Aragonese of to-day has a love of letters and the arts, though in a more sober and restrained manner than his brother of Cordova or Sevilla. He possesses a certain good-natured dignity. He is strong, a fighter, a drinker of pure wine and *aguardiente*, a tall, lusty fellow of the mountains and the glaring, bare, broken foot-hills of his native province.

Typical Spaniard, in the Castillian sense, he is not. His language is less pure, his manners harder, his jests more coarse and direct. He is less subtle, less wrapped in the mantle of courtliness. But he is a good, healthy, whole-souled, earnest man, and you can trust him. He has learned a little more than the Castillian, and a good deal less than the Catalan, about commerce ; he has managed to keep within his walls a fading essence of Arabic tradition ; from the Basques he has received some influences, from the French others, and he might tell you that the Castillian and he were once brothers—who had changed however not a little since that good old time when both had nothing else to do but hunt Moors from year's end to year's end.

And, as in the man, so in the works of his hands. Who, on approaching an Aragonese town, will fail to note the peculiarity of its architecture ; these delicate towers which rise, and which seem to have lost the sharp outlines of Roman structures while retaining somehow, the suggestion of Roman forms. We may well stop before this so-called *mudejar* architecture, this subtle fusion of the severity of the older style with the delicacy of moorish brick-tracery and tiles. What fine results these architects obtained by a few changes in the surface of a brick wall ; what lightness and grace in the peculiar half-finished outline !

The Church has set her seal upon Zaragoza. Instinctively, as we drive along her streets we look for the

approach of processions. An odor of incense seems to
lurk in dark corners ; the deep swelling of voices singing
comes from the doors of the churches we pass. A funeral
procession stops us, the great torches flaring in the wind.
There are a thousand suggestions of the presence of the
Church. A church living and active, not surrounded
by depths of silence in deserted streets and squares, as at
Santiago. Although the city does not lack for history not
of a religious nature, certain memories are forever linked
to her name which mark her as a sort of storm-centre of
spiritual happenings. Very early in the Christian life of
the peninsula we find this Roman place named as a field
for the preaching of the new belief, and it was here, probably, that Prudentius " The Horace and Virgil of the
Christains" was born, whose hymns were to mark an
epoch in christian poetry of the fourth and fifth centuries,
and whose denunciation of a vestal at a gladiatorial con-
test might be well read in some *palco en los toros* these
days. " I will struggle against heresy, defend the Catholic
faith, annihilate the sacrifices of the pagans, destroy thy
gods, O Rome !" says that unhesitating Spaniard. His is
but a single name in a long list—martyrs among them,
whose bones, we are assured, are preserved in this city to
this day.

But all attractions considered, the traveller will, I
suspect, not spend very much time in Zaragoza, not more,
probably, at best, than sufficient to see the monuments,
the river and the people who pass continually along her
streets. It is not here as it is in Madrid. The *Coso* offers
no such stream of different types as does the *Calle de Alcalá*.
There we have the whole Spanish world at a glance ; here
but one individual—the Aragonese. Variations of the
type are interesting, but they are only variations after all.

The architect or the historian will alone stop long, for one finds in this place of the foot-hills, far from the softer and more refined influences of Castile, and just removed from the life of the bustling and cosmopolitan Catalan, a certain harshness. Do we not begin to feel it when rumbling along in the hotel omnibus from the station, and has it not grown to a fixed conviction before we cross the stone bridge over the Ebro to take our train for the north? Is there great regret as we look down into the dull, muddy current below us for the last time? It is in the air this feeling, in the color of the sky, in the motion of the river; the strange, florid tiles of the Pillar and elsewhere, reflect it. Even the lame, savage beasts of burden seem to be imbued with the spirit of the place and anxious to set their white, gleaming teeth in passing shoulders. In the very streets it is, in the women's sharp voices at early dawn, wailing their long dispiriting, half-arabic cries to let you know that they are selling little hot, sugar-coated cakes on the street corners.

Perhaps the enthusiastic travellers watching every detail, as they first enter, may be saved this shiver at the threshold. There is quite enough in the mere street names of a Spanish city to impress its peculiar individuality and excite one's curiosity. No modern rectangular lanes, sawed out and numbered. What various impressions one gets from these names. Shall we go indifferently by the street of *Alfonso the Battle Wager*, of *Argensola*, of the *Swan*, of the *Chain*, of *Jaime the Conqueror*, of the *Dances*, of the *Maidens*, of the *Flowers*, of *Heroism*, of *Independence*, of *Jesus*, of *Justice*, of the *Wolf*, of *Mercy*, of the *Martyrs*, of the *Moors*, of the *Eleven Corners*, of the *Fish*, the *Pen*, the *Dog*, the *Turk*, the *Cows*, the *Virgin* and the *Violin*?

On the morning after my own first arrival I can recall
with what eagerness I was out at six, bound for the Cathedral of the Seo. The city
possesses two cathedral
churches but neither one
takes rank as a first-class
building of its kind in any
way. The one is not
beautiful, in spite of its
tapering tower and delicate
brick-work, nor is the other
less frightful for all that it
possesses the wonderful column of the Virgin. " The
one is an ancient severe
church, raised to the Saviour ; the other a modern
theatrical temple dedicated

THE SEO

to the Great Diana, for now we are in the Ephesus of
Spanish Mariolatry."

The ecclesiologist will discover much, no doubt, to
condemn in the Cathedral of the Seo. He will find no
difficulty in criticising the irregularities of its architectural
treatment, of its lighting or vaulting or its great breadth,
of its pagan details, its capitals, its gaudily gilded bosses.
Street has already pointed the way for this criticism.

But if we can forget all this, and by a no great effort of
imagination bring up the past of the old building and its
associations, we shall be repaid for our visit nevertheless.
Let us recall for a moment Luna, the antipope who built
the *Cimborio* and from whose hand the Church received, in
the first years of the fifteenth century, the famous Gothic
busts of Saints Valero, Vicente and Lorenzo, which were

formerly carried in processions, but are now only placed on the high altar on great feasts.*

History offers nothing so calculated to attract in a broad sense as the story of those characters which we can fairly say made a good fight. It does not so much matter what the fight was about, with whom or what; that it be a hard and unconditional struggle is the chief requisite, and

BENEDICT XIII

the interest of the reader is not the less enlisted when the struggle is as unavailing as it is protracted, and to which only death comes as a reward. In the case of Pedro de Luna, known as Pope Benedict XIII, we have a tragedy of fruitless endeavor and unrelaxed determination which was to go unrewarded. It is the story of a striking character: of a man who rose justly to a place of marked eminence in the affairs of his time, and who yet saw that time gradually turn its back upon him. The Church rejected him; the world cast him off;

---

* Around the base of the bust of Saint Valero, within the sculptured head of which the authentic skull now rests, is written on a silver plate:

"Dominus Benedictus Papa XIII, prius Vocatus Petrus de Luna, Sanctæ Mariæ in cosmedin Diáconus Cardinalis dedit hoc Relicarium Beati Valorii huic Ecclesiæ Cæsar-augustanæ anno Domini MCCC nonagesimo Septimo Pontificatus, sui anno tertio: inhibendo sub pœnna excomunicationis quam contra facientes ipso facto incurrant ne quovis modo alienetur cui sententiæ absolutionem Sedi Apostolicæ reservavit." On the bust itself is:

"Hic est caput Beati Valerii confessoris A Episcopi huyus Eclesiæ Cæsar-augustanæ."

only within himself was found the confidence and determination to maintain his position as spiritual ruler of
Christendom.

Pedro de Luna was a native of Illueca in Aragon, and
in his youth followed arms as a profession, but, soon tir-
ing of this, turned his attention to more congenial labors
in the University of Montpellier, where he filled a chair of
canonical and civil law.   After this he entered the
Church.   In 1307 Pope Gregory XI. created him cardinal at Avignon.   When Robert of Geneva died there,
after a pontificate, during which was presented to Europe
the farce of two popes hurling anathemas at one another,
one in Avignon and another at Rome,—as Wyclif said,
" like two dogs snarling over a bone,"—Cardinal Luna was
unanimously elected to fill his place.   He was recognized
by France, Aragon, Castile, Savoy, Lorraine and Scotland.
The satisfaction of the Aragonese knew no bounds.

The story of the bitter struggle which followed and
how Benedict was soon abandoned by most of his friends
and returned finally to Aragon, is well known, as is his
obstinate resistance to six successive popes from Boniface
IX., to Martin V., never for one moment yielding his claim
to the tiara.   Here we find the chief quality in the nature
of this man ; it has been called by one of his historians
"his lamentable tenacity." The dramatic end of the scene
is placed on a little rock of the province of Castellon, in
the Mediterranean—the miniature Gibraltar, Peñiscola.

"It is not in Constanza," said Luna in reply to the
embassy sent to him by the council then gathered there,
"but in Peñiscola, where is found united the Catholic
Church, as at one time humanity was shut up in the Arc
of Noah." In the end he was left to himself in his fast-
ness on the Mediterranean across whose waters he might

anathematize in imagination his rivals at Rome through the long, tedious years of his unyielding prison life. It was on the 23d of May, 1424, in his ninetieth year, that the sturdy old warrior died and it has been positively asserted that he was poisoned. It was even said that a certain monk Tomas had performed the deed and that he was afterwards punished.

It is probable that no character in command in the religious life of his time, possessed such force, as is evidenced in the unswerving determination of Pedro de Luna and it is possible that, had he been able to maintain his position as head of a united Catholic Church, some of the chaotic condition and degeneration of that Church might have been averted, at least for the time being.

There is a tale, well known in Zaragoza, which we must recall when we first stand inside the door of the Seo. It is the story of that Pedro de Arbués,* called Master of Epila, Inquisitor of Aragon, who in the year 1485, while praying before the altar, met his death at the hand of assassins.

At that time there lived in the city many converted Jews and descendants of others who had professed that religion, and who, from their power and wealth, held some of the highest official positions, and even had strong influence at the Court of Ferdinand, not the least among them being Gabriel Sanchez, the treasurer of that monarch.

It is said that Sanchez, replying to certain relatives who sought his protection from Zaragoza, indicated to them the advisability of causing " to disappear from the

* See Gascón de Gotor ; Zurita, etc.

world" a certain functionary of the so-called holy office. The insinuation coming from such a quarter, produced its effect. The Zaragozan converts, or *Judaïzantes*, held secretly several conferences and decided upon the murder of Pedro de Arbués, the functionary in question, communicating this resolve to like converts in Calatayud, Barbastro and other Aragonese towns. Although the replies of these are unknown, it is certain that a meeting took place in the house of a certain Louis Sanchez Santangel who then lived in the parish of San Felippe y Santiago. There were present, beside the last mentioned, the lawyer Jaime Montesa, Gerónimo Sanchez, Gaspar de Santa Cruz, Juan Sanchez, García de Moros and various others. Certain of them stated that processes had been begun against them by the Inquisition, they had reported it to their friends at the Court, and that the only method by which they might free themselves from the consequences, according to high counsel, was by the death of the Inquisitor of Aragon, in the certainty that the act would intimidate the functionary who should succeed him.

The proposition seems to have met with instant approval. Secrecy was solemnly sworn, and for the realization of the plan it was decided that Sanchez, Montesa and Gaspar de Santa Cruz should collect money for the payment of those who should be found to do the deed. It was later asserted that part of the sum secured went into the pockets of the collectors !

One by one Montesa brought to his house such as he thought would be willing to contribute, and the sum needed was soon gathered. The whole body of conspirators then again met. A heated discussion took place during which García de Moros inflamed his audience to the

point of action and it was unanimously decided that the
moment for the selection of the instruments of the deed
had arrived.   For this work Montesa and Pedro Sanchez
were delegated.

Repeated conferences were now held between this
committee and a certain tanner, Juan Sperandeu, and a
man named Matthew Ram, ready to undertake anything
for a price. With these were associated for the crime
Juan de Abadía, urged on by Luis Sanchez Santangel,
who promised him money and protection, Vidal Durango,*
a French servant of Sperandeu, Tristán, a follower of
Matthew Ram, and three others whose names are not
known.

Four days before that of the accomplishment of the
deed, all those who had originally met at the house of
Luis Sanchez Santangel and some others were cited to
meet after vespers in the sanctuary of the Portillo. Several of them again met on the following day.   In both of
these conferences certain details were settled and assistance was assured to the perpetrators of the deed.

It now remained but to fix the day for the execution
of the plan.   In a conference held between Sanchez,
Santa Cruz and García de Moros, on the thirteenth of
September, in the house of Micer Montesa, the following
night was settled upon, and between eleven and twelve of
the fourteenth, Juan de Sperandeu set out for the house
of Juan Abadía who had gone to bed.   He made him get
up, dress and arm himself, and together they went to the
house of Sperandeu, where they found assembled Matthew
Ram, Vidal Durango, Tristán and three others, their
faces covered with masks.   Together they now repaired
to the *Coso* and entered by the *Trenque*, crossing the

* Or Duranso.

Boticas Hondas in order to pass before the house of the governor and finally through the *Plaza* of *La Seo*, they passed into the cathedral of the same name, by the door leading from the street of the Pabostría, that being open, owing to the beginning of matins sharply at twelve o'clock.

Matthew Ram, Sperandeu, Vidal Durango and Tristán entered the church ; Abadía remained at the door on watch. After some time the latter, finding that they were long in reappearing, also entered and beheld the Inquisitor of Aragon in the priestly garb, kneeling in fervent prayer near the column, by which was the pulpit wherein it was his custom to preach ; a short distance behind him he saw the assassins. At this moment the voices of the choir rang solemnly through the church. Abadía approached Vidal Durango and in a low, earnest voice said : " Strike him, traitor, that 's he." Thus urged, the other did so, inflicting a severe wound with his sword, piercing the throat. The victim rose staggeringly to his feet, whereupon Sperandeu threw himself upon him and stabbed him and he fell to the pavement. The murderers fled.

At the noise and hurrying the clergy left the choir and came upon the Master of Epila, bathed in his own blood. He was taken to his home where two famous surgeons at first sight declared his wounds necessarily fatal. Between one and two, on the morning of the day of the 17th, he died.

The crime perpetrated, Micer Montesa, Luis Sanchez Santangel, Gaspar de Santa Cruz, Pedro Sanchez and others secretly gave themselves up to the greatest rejoicing, relying upon the promises of impunity which had been made to them from high quarters.

Punishment, however, soon followed. Arbués was

succeeded by Pedro de Monte Rubio, and the perpetraters of the crime were soon sought out. Pedro Sanchez was burned in effigy; Montesa, García de Moros and Alonso Sanchez were burned. Santangel was condemned to be decapitated and his body burned. Francisco de Santa Fe committed suicide in the Castle of Aljafería where he was confined. Sperandeu, Ram and Durango were drawn and quartered and burned; Tristán was burned in effigy, having escaped from Aragonese territory. Juan Abadía suffocated himself in the castle with the aid of a glass lamp.

One must not leave the Seo with its traditions until he has walked slowly around it and studied, step by step, the details of its carving and altars.   I recall now how I hurried through this church in my eagerness to reach the *Pilar* which I had seen rising in its grandeur not far away —and how I came back here again after I had been chilled by the grave barrenness of that monster.

The girls by the fountain were drawing water as I passed.   I could hear the click and rattle of the long tin tubes which they reached up to the falling stream to direct it into their jars.   A pretty sight, which one may see all over Northern Spain, most gracefully picturesque, perhaps, in Lugo, where the ancient walls seem to have housed and kept from contamination more of the old spirit than elsewhere.

Attention has been called to the fact that Zaragoza until 1845 possessed no regular public fountain.*   It was on the 14th of October, 1833, that the corner-stone of the one then known by the name of Isabel II was laid in the present Paseo de Santa Engracia where it still stands, though it is now called the Fountain of Neptune.   An in-

* Madoz.

scription marks the place as stained with the blood of martyrs.

The Ebro is muddy and yellow and has more the look of a river than streams usual-ly seen be-tween Spanish banks. It is always a fine river a f t e r rain, and from Tortosa all along up its sprawling yel-low course until beyond Logroño, the traveller will

THE EBRO AT LOGROÑO

get many a fine view. Well off the line of travel is the valley of this stream below Zaragoza, and many a hard day's ride may one have down its course from Caspe to the sea.

The heavy boats, with which the soldiers practise, are drawn high up out of harm's way, opposite the gaudy dome of the *Pilar* Cathedral. Before the door of this last I soon found myself standing, having passed the women selling long strips of pastry by the Lonja, which is one of the sights of the city with its carved heads and over-hanging roof.

Here, then, is the wonderful " Pilar," which has made the present and past religious reputation of Zaragoza ; one of the most important relics of the Church of Spain. Not only is it intimately connected with that great Spanish peripatetic, Saint James himself, who was its discoverer, and by the actual existence of whose remains at Santiago it is so easy to prove the truth of the whole story, but the Virgin herself saw fit to render this stone a thing of supreme holiness by the touch of her divine feet!

Saint James, it appears, first sought the Virgin and kissing her hand, prayed that he be allowed to preach the faith of her Son. She responded by pointing out the profitable field for conversion in Spain and promised to indicate to him later where he might build a church in her memory.

Forthwith Saint James, setting out from Jerusalem, arrived in Spain and, after he had been to the North, in the Asturias (Isturias), to the city of Oviedo (where he made a convert), to Galicia and to Castile, he finally reached that part of Spain known as Aragon and its capital city of Zaragoza. (*Cæsar-augustana civitas ad Iberi fluvii ripam.*) All of which is told in detail in the *Historia Apparitionis Deiparæ supra columnam, beato Jacobo apud Cæsar-augustam prædicante.*

It was here that the Virgin made good her promise of direction as to the church which should be erected in her honor. In the middle of the night the Saint—he had passed a very fatiguing day with his converts—had the ineffable pleasure of hearing the voices of angels singing *Ave Maria Gratia Plena*, and soon after beheld the Virgin herself seated in mid-air upon the famous marble column, as is fully described by historians and pictured in prints of the scene.* At each hand stood a choir of a thousand angels. Saint James fell upon his knees while the mission of his divine mistress was made clear to him, and he was in-

---

*Ecce, inquit, Jacobe fili, locus signatus, meoque honori deputatus, in quo in mei memoriam tua industria mea ecclesia construator : conspice quinimo pilare hoc, in quo sedeo : nam Filius meus, Magister tuus, per manus angelorum illud transmisit ex alto, circa cujus situm capellæ altare locabis. (Esp. Sag., 30, 428.)

structed as to the building of the church in her honor and
for the preservation of the sacred column which had been
sent direct from heaven.

And so, it is related and believed, the Saint constructed
his church and received and guarded the sacred relic
within it and, after all was done, he went out of Spain
and returned to Judea, whence his body was afterwards
brought back by his faithful followers and taken to its
last resting-place in Galicia.

But the sanctified seat of the Virgin remains to this day
and is one of the chief sources of income to the marble-
workers and silversmiths of the old town. You may go
behind the altar and kiss it through an opening if you are
a good Catholic. Thousands have made the pilgrimage,
which is each year celebrated with great pomp on the
twelfth day of October.

The church is gigantic and ugly. A heavy structure,
whose roof exteriorly is decorated with flaring tiles; the
cold, classically-grand interior is redeemed only by the
wonderful Gothic altar, the work of Damian Forment,
whose great carving in alabaster may be seen in Huesca.

There was one thing especially well worth visiting in
Zaragoza on my first visit; the beautiful, leaning New
Tower, *La Torre Nueva*, recalling Pisa. They were
taking it down at the time and I made the ascent of half
a dozen buildings to get a farewell impression of it from
every side. Later I distinctly remember the sense of
regret when, forgetting the fact of its demolition, I came
to the silent plaza where it had stood and found the pavement laid over what had been its foundations. The
vanishing of a monument like this has something so
humanly sad in it that it makes an impression never to be
lost. No doubt the little square of San Filipe where it

stood so nearly four hundred years will soon establish a new individuality of its own, in which the image of the grand old land-mark will be but a ghostly memory.

How much might be written of the tower in the Spanish landscape! Turn where we will, it is ever present. Are we trudging across some field with which the name of Trajan or Hannibal is linked, let us but raise our eyes and there, just ahead, it stands against the blue cloudless sky. From Trujillo to Tarragona we meet Roman towers ; one bears the name of some great general or emperor in every province. Ruins often, mere fragments of suggestive out-

TOWER OF TRUJILLO

line, to be sure, but how clearly have they given a form to those severe and grave buildings which have followed them !

The landscape of the Middle Ages has as little escaped. See the towers of these crenelated fortresses, these churches of fair Gothic, these cathedrals of Castile and over all Spain, these palace forts of La Mota or Segovia. Everywhere the tower is a marked outline against the horizon.

The grass is growing over a thousand that have vanished and left no trace, as this Torre Nueva has vanished. Some have met the fate of this—Calatayud once possessed a leaning tower—others have sunk slowly down and become convenient quarries for later builders, and not a few were re-created and served to shelter some French

garrison of Napoleon from the too eager enemy whom they could never quite conquer.

The Torre Nueva was built in answer to a desire on the part of the people of Zaragoza to have a lofty clock-tower from which the hour might be read or sounded in every part of the city. The decision to build it was reached in 1504, and the question was then laid before the King, who gave his consent to the plan and added his aid. It was decided to put the Master, Gabriel Gombao, in charge of the work, and with him were associated Juan de Sariñena, a Jew named Ince de Gali, and the Moors Ezmel Ballabar and Master Monferriz.

What a light is thrown upon the peculiarities of the strange architecture of these Aragonese buildings when we read the names of the men who worked upon them! What influences but those of Moor and Jew and Christian could have produced such results as these? This tall, tapering frost-work pile had in it the strength of the iron-armed men of the North combined with the subtile art and delicacy of the Arab.

In fifteen months the great tower arose in the little plaza, and in 1512 the two great bells, which had been cast by Jaime Ferrer of Lerida sounded the hours of day or night to the city below them. The building was 300 feet in height and 45 in diameter; it was octagonal in plan at the base, which form was modified, however, as the structure rose and a star-shaped plan broke the monotony. Again and again the form changed as the work went on, in the effort to give lightness and grace, and well did the fanciful brick-work answer the aims of the architects laboring upon it.

How many people are kept employed here at religious

11

art ! Shops on every hand are devoted solely to the manu-
facture of miniature representations of the Holy Virgin on
her Pillar, and the windows are filled with long lines of
them in marble, alabaster and silver.   Demetrius and the
silversmiths who "made silver shrines for Diana," and
" brought no small gain unto the craftsmen," find worthy
descendants in the city of Cæsarea Augusta.

The best view of Zaragoza is from the bridge.   Standing on the great stone-arched, square and octagon-towered
line of masonry, with the muddy, shallow, hissing Ebro
rushing below, the city panorama is spread out in front
with the cathedrals on either hand, the towers of La Magdalena of San Pablo, of San Gil and the rest, rising in the
background.   It is most striking.   Along the river, high
walls of masonry stretch away to the bend, where they are
sunk and disappear in the tree-bordered banks.   There are
traces of Roman walls by the river too, if you care to
search ; walls erected twenty-three years B.C.   The gray,
desolate country rises in rolling bareness beyond, and
reaches out to the great barrier wall of the North.   From
this vantage-ground, the picture is, perhaps, most impressive
on one of those luminous, star-lit Spanish nights, when the
deep intensity of the unclouded sky forms the silent, mysterious back-ground familiar in the East.   The lap of the
water comes weirdly from below, and its steady sobbing
rush past and into the dark has a strange whisper.   Far
away, it catches a faint, lustrous gleam and shimmers
across the shallows between the little pebbly island facing
the end of the city river-wall, which is there broken and
has fallen in great heaped-up fragments from the roadway
edge.   The Seo tower rises then with all the impressive-
ness of its tapering symmetry, and even the great " Pilar,"
etched out in bolder masses, loses its tinsel cheapness in

the outlined grandeur of its high, uplifted domes and pin-
nacles, silent in strength of vastness against the blue.

Nothing disturbs. The distant cry of the *sereno* floats
faintly, or from far off comes the echo of the quick blows
of his staff on the stone pavement. At long intervals one
hears the tread of an approaching person, beginning dis-
tantly, drawing nearer, passing and dying away. The
individual casts at one a side-glance, half-inquiring, half-
suspicious, though, in these days of the *Guardia Civil*, his
hand may have lost somewhat of its old instinctive grasp
for pistol or knife.

XI

HUESCA—JACA

IT was seven of a clear morning when we started up the valley of the low, sandy and muddy Gallego. The fact that we were rapidly leaving the influence of the

PEASANTS OF LERIDA

capital, as far as dress at least was concerned, was soon evident. Peasants on the train passing us from Lerida now wore a different costume from those of Aragon, and we were soon to see the peculiar dress of the Pyrenees. Leaving the river at Zuera, by 9.30 the foot ranges came in sight and fifteen minutes later we stopped at Huesca.

The Province of Huesca offers a somewhat new phase of Spanish life to the traveller. It has had the happy fate of escaping the tourist, and, although less rich than other provinces in the rare and wonderful of art,

THE CATHEDRAL OF HUESCA

is yet famous for its hardy, law-making people and for a few solid and severe monuments. This barren mountain country preserves a primitive people, in primitive towns, and much of costume and native peculiarity remains, which is going, or has already gone, from more travelled districts. In Barbastro, Banabarre, Boltaña, Fraga, Jaca, Sariñena and a dozen other places there is a wealth of types and traditions.

Spain, divided into Departments in 1809, was cut up into Provinces in 1833. Under the Department system, Huesca was capital of that of Ebro y Cinca. She now has 363 *Ayuntamientos*, an area of 424 square leagues, and a population of 263,230. The wines are excellent. Oil, fruit and vegetables are abundant, and the sportsman may have partridges and rabbits to his heart's content or, if he choose to work hard and long, may find an occasional bear in the mountains, or, I am told, even wolves, foxes, mountain-cats, wild-boars, hedge-hogs or deer.

The king of these mountains is the great eagle, but you must go high up among his fastnesses to have a shot at him. Like all wild creatures in Spain, he is wary and will not wait your coming. His brothers, the vulture and the hawk, are seen less in this district than elsewhere, more to the south.

The country continues barren. Trees are marked rarities except away from the larger places. Near the towns the demand for wood cuts everything down for miles around. Where wood is so expensive, it is strange that it is not more grown as an article of trade, and stranger still that the fact of its diminution is not more clearly realized by the natives. One recalls those vast forests in Luxemburg which might well be reproduced in Spain. Oak, hemlock, box, bitter-sweet and juniper are common, and not a few medicinal herbs, but all are fast thinning before the increased demand, and on every high-road one meets the heavily laden *burros* driven up to town with the precious spoil of the hills.

Huesca is an ancient city of over ten thousand inhabit-ants. The Templars took up their abode here after 1143 through the donation of Count Berenger of Barcelona. The seal of the order, found impressed in wax at the end of the past century, was affixed to a document dated 1204. Pedro II. appears to have been the first king to employ seals in Aragon, the sign only having been used previous to his time. The abbreviated legend on this of the Tem-plars is intended to express : *Sigillum Domus Templi de Osca.*

But the end of the Templars arrived in 1312–1317, when they were blotted out by papal bull, and an edict in relation to this was discovered in the archives at Ager by Villanueva and pub-lished by him in his *Literary Expedition.*

It is but a short walk to the height on which stands the church of St. George, whence one has a splendid view of the town lying on its little point of rising ground in the valley. The houses are not covered with the cheerful red tiles of other places, but have a yellowish, muddy look, and the white-washed window-frames are suggestive of eyes. In the midst stands the cathedral, sharp-cut against the abrupt hills of the *Sierra de Guara.* Beyond, the ruined castle of Monte Aragon, and still beyond, the hazy outlines of other broken ranges. To the north is seen a giant cleft through the rocky wall, called the *Salto de Rol-dan*—tradition stretching its hand far back to the days of Roland.

Above the narrow break, steel-blue clouds hover ominously and promise rain. In splendid contrast is this threatening north of mountain and dark, to that soft south lying behind us, where great masses of white, fleecy cloud roll over a clear, blue sky, and the country dies off into uneventful mysterious haze. Bees are swarming from a tiny hole in the wall of the brick church behind me. Their faint, warm, summery buzz mingles with the distant barking of a dog, the tinkle of a goat bell,—there are no other sounds for the lazy air to bear up the hillside to me. On the other hand, toward the northwest, rises a bold peak, the light catching upon it fantastically.

Slowly the clouds close in about the sun. At last only one broad ray of light is left, plunging boldly down through the heavy masses, just wide enough to strike broadly over the town and cover it with an intense light, while all beyond it is in semi-obscurity. For a few moments it forms an exquisite picture. Then slowly the shadow falls more and more over the edge of the mass of buildings, blotting them into dun-colored unobtrusiveness, and inch by inch creeps up towards the centre and the cathedral. There it stops lingeringly, and gradually every other portion in the town becomes dark. Then the great building too, fades, and a swift sparkling and flashing on the spire is the last of it.

The buzzing of the bees grows intense behind me. The windows stare wide open. They are empty sockets now, glaring from what almost seems a vast heap of skulls piled one above another in hopeless confusion. Butterflies and great black flies are flitting and darting in the weird, uncertain light.

The rain is coming soon. A·black, rolling heap of cloud, formed like a human head, with a great white tongue lolled out, has pushed itself out from the mountain behind and stretches its open mouth down towards the town where, as though in alarm, the bell of the church begins tolling tremulously.

An old man, who seems to be in charge of the place, looms weirdly from nowhere, and invites me into the church with a hollow, wheezy voice. An old woman, one more creature of the night, with straggling hair and broom at present arms, suddenly stands eyeing me from a shadowed doorway, while a strange, dissipated cat, with a red nose, suggesting chronic influenza or the gin-bottle, follows the limping master with plaintive mews and climbs the wall at languid bounds before him. Two minutes satisfy my curiosity as to the interior to which I am invited, and a very hospitable offer of food and shelter from the old man I am forced to decline, which, however, is not taken in bad part. I manage to get back to the hotel just as it begins to pour straight down and hiss on the stones.

Opposite is a printer's shop from which a weekly newspaper is issued, and an annual, *half-peseta* guide of the town. The printing-press of this establishment is to a degree simple. It is run after the ancient method—man power—and the old fellow who keeps industriously turning the wheel talks on willingly enough in answer to questions, while his boy, who removes the sheets here and folds others there, stares at us in wonder. There are two compositors, to judge by the litter, but only one is mechanically bending towards the light, which to-day is feeble and at brightest moments cannot be more than tolerable. There is much dirt on the floor, much waste paper about, and the place is redolent of tobacco, local tradition and the proud memory of days when once *four* dailies flourished. True, that was in war times. One may well imagine that only war news could wring excitement from these dull hills.

At three, it clears, and in front of the church I pick up a small boy of religious mind, as guide, all but losing him, however, at the very first, by refusing holy water on entering the church. It takes a *peseta* to destroy his religious convictions, a high local price.

The cloisters are interesting and behind the high altar there is a piece of Gothic work recently discovered and long covered by a picture. The picture itself is shown in the sacristy where four or five priests are gathered about a long table.

To the cathedral—a short, splashy walk through misty rain. I remember now nothing but the little boy tramping along with down-turned hat-brim in sturdy disregard of the wet—truly unlike his prototypes of Valencia and Granada. Legitimate descendant he might be of Sertorius, in this once chief city of that enemy of Rome.

ACOLYTES OF THE CATHEDRAL OF HUESCA

The present Cathedral of Huesca stands on the site of a more ancient Gothic church converted into a mosque by the Arabs and made Christian again by Pedro

I. who conquered the city in 1096.ᐧ The solemn purification of the church took place on the 12th of December of that year, after which, until 1300, it saw no changes. The bishop Adamaro then finding the edifice in a condition of partial ruin determined to undertake the construction of a new one. His resources for the work were meagre and it was not until 1515 that the present structure was completed, through the aid of Don Juan of Aragon and Navarre, natural son of Carlos of Viana, who donated 1500 golden florins to the work. Its architect was a *Vizcaino*, Juan de Olótzaga. The church has been much described. On the right rises the not uncommon octagon clock-tower of Aragon. The building taken as a whole is dignified, strong and severe.

The great work of art of this cathedral is the *retablo*, carved in alabaster, by Damian Forment, a work possessing a peculiar personal interest in the two medallions representing the sculptor and his wife. It was begun on the 10th of September, 1520, as is stated in the contract made by the bishop, Don Juan of Aragon and Navarre, with Damian Forment, " Excellent Sculptor, by birth a Valencian." The famous artist was also the maker of the remarkable *retablo* of the Church of our Lady of the *Pilar* at Zaragoza. Thirteen years—and the time seems little enough—were employed in this work, and the patience with which the delicate details have been wrought out, has produced one of the finest pieces of altar-carving in Spain. 110,000 *sueldos* was the price received by the sculptor, a sum considered rather high at the time.

At the entrance of the *Musco* of pictures I almost overran a little deformed wretch with twisted hands and feet, who promptly offered himself as guide. " I will show you, I will show you," he kept repeating, stumbling along on his distorted ankles, his feet flopping over horribly at each

step and his great nervous, flapping arms hanging list-
lessly, or cast out abruptly to steady himself.

At the *Museo* he hunted up an old man as wretched, if
not as deformed, as himself, and the two struggled upstairs
together, where they were joined by an ancient dame, the
wife of the antique keeper, and all three miserables together, by dint of much united manipulating, key turning,
twisting, groans and sighs, managed to open the mysterious lock of a mysterious door, whereupon with much ceremony I was invited to enter the " Great Gallery."

I entered the Great Gallery and found myself in Egyptian darkness. Here and there, through the long closed
shutters, a ray of light, more intrepidly daring than the
rest, pushed its way in, making a faint sparkle on the
faded gilt of the picture-frames, or piercing down, struck
in little round or zig-zag splashes on the dark, brown,
streaked floor. The old woman went about opening the
creaking windows.

" You don't have many visitors ? " I remarked to her
husband.

" Very few, very few." He shook his head sadly,
watching me curiously from the corners of his eyes as I
wandered about, and stopped finally before several early
panels.

" Those," he said pointing to the row, "go to the Col-
umbian Exposition in Madrid. Twenty-five of them,—
if they will pay the freight there and back," he added in
a parenthesis. The old woman re-appeared.

" Here, take the keys and open the other room," said
her husband without moving. I stopped her and asked
how long she had been there.

" Thirty-five years—and a good many more in my
own place."

" You remember the French then ? "

She was going out but now halted suddenly, and came
tottering back, the great keys hanging jingling from her
hands.   A little flush of excitement had risen to her cheek.

"*I* remember the French !" she said.   " They were in
our town—in my father's house too.   There were a lot of
them—but I can just remember it—when I was a girl.
Yes, they ate up the sheep.   They killed twenty at one
time and ate them—and they burned the house—I can
just remember it—when I was a girl."   She shook the keys
in her excitement.   "And then they were always trying
to make me talk their language—but I never could—only
a few words—I remember the word for cow was *vache*—
I can just remember it—when I was a girl."

A thoughtful, far-off look came dimly into the face of
the old creature.   What had come back to her mind ?
Was it the memory of the one who had taught her that
unpoetic word ?   Some gay young Frenchman—when she
was a girl ?   I tried to look into her past, to see her
younger face through the wrinkles, and picture her as a
girl.   It was like looking through prison-bars into a dim
room.

" Do you ever have any English here ? " I asked.

" No—not many," said the old man, "and when they
come they only talk their own language.   What a language
of dogs it is !   You are French are you not ? "

" American."

" But you do not speak Spanish in your country ? "

In answer to my inquiries he told me how to get out
to Monte Aragon, and fell to talking about the old place
as it was long ago.

" There were as many windows as there are days in
the year," he said.

"And the singing," added the woman, "that used to be fine!"

"Yes, every day the monks and the procession and the singing! There was one young fellow there then— what a voice he had! He went to Madrid afterwards and all the world went crazy over him. Such a face! You would have thought an angel from Heaven was singing. He went away and made money—a great deal of money. He sent it home for a while. But then there was a woman and he stopped. There is always a woman!" And the old fellow tried to throw some intensity into his leer up at me.

And so these two old creatures talked on, never telling me anything I wanted to know, but giving a picture of long lives of small deprivations and continued patience in failure, which were perhaps after all as important as the Cathedral of Huesca itself.

I followed my crippled guide. "I can't earn anything" he said, holding up his misshapen hands, "so in the summer I guide strangers." We went to the palace of the Kings of Aragon—the Institute—and saw the room where Ramiro made the famous bell which was to be heard all over Aragon.

The story is told that the King when hard-pressed by his nobles, sent a messenger to the abbot Frotardo of San Ponc de Tomeras with a letter in which he begged his advice as to the treatment of his rebellious subjects. The reply of the abbot was laconic; leading the messenger through his garden, where a number of cabbages were growing, he selected in silence the tallest heads and cut them down with a stick. He then told the messenger to return to the King and tell him what he had seen. The pupil of the monk had no difficulty in reading between the lines, and a few days later his edict went forth for the assembling of the nobles and the people for the purpose of casting a bell which should be heard all over Aragon. All who could respond to the summons flocked to the city, not certain whether to laugh or to marvel at this new ca-

THE BELL OF ARAGON

price of the King. Five of the chief men of the kingdom, of the house of Luna, were taken apart into a small sub-terranean room and executed. Their bodies were then shown to the populace, and tradition affirms that by a rope suspended from the keystone of the arch of the room the head of the chief traitor was hung in imitation of the clapper of the bell. It is somewhat dis-appointing that the story of the Bell of Aragon cannot quite stand alone. In substantiation of it, the discovery of decapitated bodies is asserted to have been made in the ruins of the church of San Juan of Jerusalem, when the latter was taken down to make room for the present Bull Ring. But decapitated bodies merely, do not prove the story.

After a night on an improvised bed of chairs, enlivened by an unsuccessful attempt to escape vermin, I am up at dawn and striving to hurry the arrival of the *tartana* or-dered the previous evening.

At 6.40, in the little canvas-covered, two-wheeled, one-horse affair, we start for Monte Aragon. As we drive along the *carretera* the morning air is cool and fresh. We meet donkeys loaded with brush and faggots from the hills, though we stare in vain across the treeless miles for the source of supply. At seven, we leave the highway and turn into a small, rocky road which soon brings us into *Quicena*, where our first sight is a Madonna-faced little girl, leaning on a pile of striped blankets hung from an upper window.

"Who has the keys to Monte Aragon?" calls my driver to an old woman in black, about whose swollen left cheek a black handkerchief is bound—national sign of a raging tooth.

"The Alcalde," she mumbles with difficulty, and he goes to get them. In a few moments he returns loaded down. They are four in number, the ordinary huge iron implements, which he throws with a crash on the seat. A little further on we reach a mill whose exterior walls are decorated with a drawing of a remarkable railroad train, the artistic efforts, no doubt, of one of those small, flour-covered, large-eyed boys who stand staring at us. The climb to the castle is somewhat steep, but, up at last, we discover a fine ruin, though everything that could be taken, and was worth the taking, has been carted off to Zaragoza. The place where the famous *retablo* of Damian Forment stood is only a hole in the plaster and I return rather disappointed to the mill, where the people down-stairs, sitting up to their knees in corn-husks, ask me how I liked the castle, and give me a glass of clear cold water.

Finding no comfortable seat, and seeing the cart unharnessed before the door, I walk up innocently and scramble in over the back, whereupon, as might have been

12

expected, it turns over on me with malignant agility. Covered with dust and mud I emerge in silent humility.

" We don't get in that way," says the driver, gravely.

We start on our way a few minutes later, a black-eyed girl's shouts of laughter sounding longest in my ears.

At twelve the coach starts for Jaca. In the compartment in front with me is a man from the mountains and a *cura*. Spain and its condition become the subject of discussion, and the man from the mountain is loud-tongued in denunciations of the Government, after which the bad grape crop has its turn and the same speaker tells, finally, how twenty years before, he had driven goats from France to Huesca by this route.

The stage slows suddenly before a house painted yellow. Only a little girl of six or seven is in sight.

" Here *niña*," says our *mayoral* holding out a letter, "take that to Juan and say that José forgot to leave it as he went through last night, on account of the rain." The child takes it, the whip snaps, and we are off again. Further explanation of this delay of the mails is not thought necessary.

The land has its usual dry and barren look; only the trees by the roadside, with holes dug about their roots for water, suggest aided vegetation. The *carretera* winds steadily on between them, always in good condition, with conical stone guards at the elevated places, and now and then small heaps of broken rock, ready to instantly repair the first wear in its surface. The roads of Spain are excellent, especially in the North. Lizards and tumble-bugs are the only living things. Suddenly the man from the mountain bends over.

" There !" he says, divesting himself of his shoes and stockings and stretching his toes apart with seeming great

comfort—" Now they won't hurt me." By and by he rests
his head upon my shoulder and falls into a peaceful sleep.

There are no fences. Now and then we pass the lines
of *mojoneras* or division posts, a direct inheritance from
Rome and the memory of the great god Terminus. At
a quarter past one the first road guards appear. They
stand, immovable, one on each side of the way. Fifteen
minutes later, at Plasencia, we meet the other stage.

At two, our six horses and two mules begin to pull
more slowly up the ascent, and the blue haze on the distant edge of the valley is deeper. There are shadows of clouds on the mountains. Up through a
water-washed *arroyo* and over the rise along the
straight bit of road, then on and down to Ayerve,
lying on the floor of a valley and
under the side of a mountain, up
which it partly creeps.
Above, on s e p a r a t e
peaks, stand a monas-
tery and some ruins.
To the right rise the
walls of the cliff, and
straight ahead, through
the pass, more rugged
peaks. The s q u a r e
t o w e r o f the church
overtops the town, and
we drive in and through
the *plaza*, curving with
the street line to the
right and stopping un-
der the clock-tower,

THE CLOCK TOWER—AYERVE

with the dilapidated palace of the Marquises of Ayerve

opposite. A little girl of about fifteen, with a green handkerchief tied over her head, wants to get down from the top of the stage here, but refuses to be taken in the arms of the *mayoral*.

They bring the ladder and she comes down slowly, tucking her dress about her. "Come—come," says the *Zagal*, steadying it, "I'm blind. Don't be afraid," and everybody laughs, even the hatless, white-haired beggar with the crooked crutch.

By highroad from Huesca to Ayerve* is some 23 kilometres, and the town is as gray and treeless and uninviting as is most of Aragon. Its history, however, as is the history of the greater number of these little northern cities is one of continual strife and slow development. It was from these desolate places that Spain drew her best forces in the eternal struggle toward the south.

"Ca!" answers a man, with a Basque hat pulled down over his face, to my question about the palace and its owner, "sold everything. Once the family had fine estates here, but they are all gone now." At this moment, a mangy, half-clipped mule and his driver come slowly out from beneath the arched portals of the palace of the ancient Marquises of Ayerve!

The family of Pedro Jordan de Urries long occupied the barony of Ayerve, but there was considerable friction with the inhabitants. This continued until, during the life of Hugo de Urries, the trouble became accentuated and the courts decided that the barony should revert to the Crown, much to the joy and enthusiasm of the inhabitants of the town. Hugo, however, considered himself seriously

* The following gives some idea of the growth of these little towns :
The population of Ayerve, according to Juan Juste García, in 1819 was 1239 inhabitants; Madoz gives, in 1834, 2170 inhabitants; Serrano, in 1879, gives 2610; Maurio y Escaso in the same year 2300, and the census of 1877, 2402.

offended by this sentence. He opened a criminal process against three of the judges who had made it, and on the 17th of July, 1768, obtained a vote in his favor. As an illustration of the kind of verdict which this proved,

it is interesting to note that one of the seventeen j u d g e s hereupon arose and declared that he had deposited in the urn a black vote owing to the fact that he did not clearly under-stand the case, and that he now wished to revoke his vote. A new vote was taken on the follow-ing day, resulting in a reversal of the first

PALACE OF THE MARQUIS OF AYERVE

decision. Don Hugo was thereupon deprived of his barony. But he so won upon the king, when sent to Madrid to give an account of his conduct, that he was returned to his country with the recompense of an annual rent of 2000 ducats.

From here the scenery grows bolder until we get to the old town of Murillo, where two great cones of rock rise high above the houses at the entrance to a gorge through which runs the river. These columns are really imposing; there is a hint of Yosemite in miniature.

We cross the Gallego on a bridge of stone and iron, and climb an ascent before reaching the village, which stands above the river where it breaks through the rocks, only stopping a moment below, on the edge of the town, long enough to drive a bargain for figs with a little girl who has a heaped basket. Twelve for one cent is the price. My companion says it is extortionate! Then on, under the gigantic masses of rock where, above the Gallego, there is a stunted growth of pines among the *débris* of the fallen cliff.

Our next stop is at an inn, before which a light suspension-bridge crosses the river. On a board is written a warning to passers. Nothing must go over weighing more than 1500 kilos. The number of persons must not be above twenty-five and they are to go gently to avoid *grandes oscilaciones.*

Everybody takes *aguardiente*, and we go on. The embankment of the, as yet unfinished, railroad to Canfranc is above us now. We pass under a ridge with a line of rocks like the Hudson Palisades, ending in a sweeping knoll with a square ruin on its top, and soon after descend and come in sight of an ancient bridge with a great pointed boulder above it. Here is the third change of animals; then on through the rock, by a tunnel, with hollow rush and clatter. We have only two horses,—the rest are mules, all closely and beautifully clipped. We reach Anzanigo at 5.15 and the light is getting so dim that a woman below by the river, washing clothes, looks a mere picturesque shadow.

As we turn up the valley a great mass of exquisite pink cloud lies before us, and on the cliffs as well, far ahead, the pink light has fallen. The man beside me, (I am now on the roof of the stage) wears a purple head-handkerchief with a red figure in it, a purple sash or *faja*, linen drawers projecting below cloth trousers at the knee, whose sides are slashed and tied with ribbon ; blue worsted stockings, a brown worsted shirt covered by a low-cut vest and two blue striped jackets. On his feet are sandals. It is growing rather cold, so I get down as soon as the light fails, to go back into my old quarters with the man from the mountains and the *cura*. The moonlight begins to be clearer, and the pink dies out and leaves the clouds ahead snow white.

Our last change (6.35) is at Bernues, and the horses are covered with foam. As we leave the place a bell tolls faintly in the distance and the dark closes in. Except for a momentary flash of lights on the arms of the last pair of silent *Guardias*, there is nothing more. At eight, we gallop into the half-moon-lit streets of Jaca, turn to the right, pass the cathedral and stop.

XII

JACA—PANTICOSA

AFTER patient waiting our bags are gathered up and
we start off in search of the hotel, through narrow,
dimly-lighted streets.   As we turn a corner we lose sight
of the little group by the stage, the *mayoral* holding a
lantern up above a dozen faces shaded by over-hanging
caps, and cursing vigorously over a piece of obdurate harness.   It is only a step to the *Fonda*, but late as it is, we
find the place in a state of confusion.   The proprietress is
in the midst of moving her worldly possessions prepara-
tory to a sale, and household belongings strew the ground.
I am at first altogether refused admittance, though at last
a room in the other building, where they are about to go
themselves, is promised me, and there, supper over, I sleep
soundly, after arranging with a driver to take me to Panticosa, starting the following day at twelve.

My earliest exploraion on this next morning is of the
low, solemn little Cathedral of Santa Orosia, with its gigantic columns and memories of Ramiro, its founder, of
the ninth century.

The air is cool as I start to walk around the town.   A
few birds are singing in the trees by the walls, a goat's
bell tinkles, and now and then a hog goes by, grunting.

The *Octroi* collector is having a vigorous argument

with some women about the value of their donkey's load of
wood as I pass the San Pedro gate. He evidently has grave
suspicions, for soon they begin slowly unloading the animal at command before his eyes, with gesticulations and
anger. There are three of these women of whom the
most energetic seems to be the oldest, a huge creature
whose skirts are a foot above the earth, and whose two
clumsy legs project from the upper vast like the columns
of the cathedral I have just left. I stand and watch until, stick by stick, the load is piled by the roadside—and
something is laid bare. It is a something wrapped in
paper bound close upon the animal's back. There is silence now, and the guard takes it with unchanging expression, opens it, considers and then turns into his little office
by the gate.

More to the east you come on the valley lying below
the town, and farther still the peak of Oroel is in sight.

I re-enter town by the restored gate of San Francisco,
and walk back to the *Fonda* along the *Calle Mayor*. A
baptism is going on in the house opposite and a crowd of
children have collected and are calling for coppers (which
it is the custom to distribute on such occasions). They
dance, and shriek, and yell, and scramble over the scantily
distributed coins, falling about in wild little heaps, their
butting, noisy heads rising here and there above the mass.
They are all ragged, all dirty, all healthy, with the firm
faces of little mountaineers, only, here and there, gleam a
pair of beady black eyes transplanted from the south *en el
tiempo de los moros*.

This morning, taking advice received in Huesca, I hunt
up a certain Padre Felix who had made a study of San
Juan de la Peña, chief of the things I had come to see.
He is very willing to aid me, even proposing that we go

out together to San Juan, if I would go on Sunday, for during the week he is busy with his pupils.

My room at the *Fonda* is filled with works of art. There are some pictures of fine, blue dolphins with red tongues and fiery eyes, which are incomparable for vividness of action, as they pursue certain creatures, which a false respect for perspective on the part of the artist has rendered by long, narrow, purple blots. Two portraits of Sagasta also decorate the desert wall above my bed, and a number of small vases stand in military row on two narrow shelves at the head of the bed.

We leave Jaca for Panticosa a little after noon, and it is cool even at that hour for we are nearly 3000 feet above tide. The drive to Biescas, where we are to spend the night, is pleasant though cold. We cross the Aurin above its junction with the Gallego, and then follow the course of the latter stream. A town lies just ahead, and a little farther, between that and Olivan, half-way up the side of the mountain, stands a solitary tower. The driver, Leopoldo, a young fellow of twenty, of pure Arabic type, calls it the *Moors' Tower*,—a not uncommon name in a land where *El Moro* is so deeply impressed upon the very landscape. He wears a red handkerchief, this Leopoldo, tied in a band about his head and cocked rakishly on one side. His face is clear-cut and refined ; very different from the general strong, heavy-featured peasant face hereabouts. He is lithe, clean-limbed, smiling, keen-eyed. " It is where they used to retreat when the Christians came," he continues, turning the delicate outline of a countenance which might have been witness from the walls themselves of a scouring band of mounted Christians sending up their war-cry of St. James against his half contemptuous and but half-spoken, " No God but God."

THE CATHEDRAL OF JACA

We turn along the left of the valley and have a view of piled-up mountains, the clouds resting on their tops. The opposite peak comes in sight—Biescas lying down between two foot-hills. As we draw nearer, the town divides itself into its two *parroquias*—San Pedro on the left of the river, and San Salvador on the right, and with the usual clatter we drive into a sort of *cul-de-sac* court, about which is the hotel. From the upper window leans the fat proprietor, bare-headed, indifferent.

After giving a hasty account of myself and a promise to return, I cross the bridge to the other town which is on rising ground, and was probably the original settlement. A sharp walk up the mountain-side brings the town at my feet. The blue, supper-time smoke is floating up from its chimneys. There are brush fires on the mountain above, and the two clouds of smoke float off together up the pass, from which direction comes, mingled with the tinkling of goat bells, the sustained, monotonous bray of a donkey. Down the valley it comes, that sound, in long waves and echoes, in sobs and complainings, choked, gurgling, cursing, dying, reviving, finally floating away with the fading light in one final burst of desperate animal profanity. The sun, just sinking below the mountain opposite, comes out of the clouds for a moment and sends a last blaze of light over the valley and up into the rocky *barranca's* dry bed behind me. The light marks the sides of the hills more clearly, for a moment fading the green of the valley below. The cry of a child, or the bark of a dog rise, quaveringly, at long intervals, through the hush, as through some denser element, while the sun sinks lower and throws up light on the clouds from underneath with splendid effect.

A little girl goes by driving two black and white hogs.

" God be with you," she replies to my *adios*, and disappears leaving me to continue my walk further up the mountain. As I return, the sun has sunk lower. The clouds take fire, like balls of loose cotton, and over the peaks there is a strange luridness like the flash of cannon, in the lead-colored masses.

On reaching the bridge it is late, and I hurry on paying no attention to a little girl who keeps calling after me —" *Caballero—buen caballero.*" I suppose her to be a beggar, but have not been in the hotel a moment before she appears at the door with a little red, excited face, and demands justice of the proprietor against me.

" What is the matter, *niña* ?   What have I done ?"

" What is it ! when I have run a mile after you to pay me—calling ' Caballero—Caballero '—and you get away because you are so big and walk so fast—and then you ask me, what is the matter ?" and her little face puckers up with wrath.

" Pay you ?   Pay what ?"

The proprietor comes to my assistance, explaining that strangers are expected to pay a tax of one cent for crossing the river by the bridge, and she before me is the toll-gatherer ; I pay my toll and retire, but as I look back I can see the little figure, slowly and with great dignity, marching back to her post by the bridge.

" Come up into the Casino," says the old man, " and I 'll light the lamp"; and up into the Casino we go, for here as everywhere there must be a local club—to which strangers are always welcome.   The room is of the ordinary type, with cushioned seats around the walls and tables down the centre.

A moment later, speaking of the grape harvest of the year he says :   " God knows when we will get such another." Turning up the lamp he comes and sits down by me and takes up the *Huesca Diario*. Opening he reads— "'*El Colera en Hamburgo*, 27,—Yesterday occurred in this capital according to the official reports 126 cases of Cholera and 47 deaths.'—*Jesus!*"

He turns over the paper and reads further—"'The Aragonese Giant—There has arrived in Barcelona the so-called Aragonese Giant, native of this province.'"

Just here someone calls, and he pushes the paper over to me, in size an octavo, resembling somewhat the *Barcelona Diluvio*.

"Here, read it yourself," and he totters away, sliding his feet, at the same time tremulously taking off and pocketing his spectacles.

The small size of these papers in the larger cities makes it easy to send out repeated editions during the course of the day, and news reaches the public very soon after its arrival at the central office.

That evening at dinner, the conversation turns on the Aragonese giant. It seems he has been a laborer in this district, and has been to Biescas once or twice, where his measure has been taken by a mark on the door-frame. A violent discussion of his points occupies an hour. Thereupon it is suggested (naturally by a tall, sturdy-looking fellow in high boots) that we all go out and make our mark under that of the giant. The little dark officer takes his turn last, and is least by five inches; whereupon, not to be left at that, he rushes at the pop-eyed girl who waits on the table, and drags her, screaming and struggling, amid peals of laughter, to take her height. She escapes, however, and he remains at the bottom of the list.

Discussion in the Casino turns on railways and their construction in Spain. By way of comparison I give some statistics as to English and American engineering feats which I chanced to recall.   Up to that moment I had been listened to with that mild and gentle toleration which the Spaniard is, by some effort, able to extend to such unfortunates as have not been born upon Peninsula soil.   Now, however, I could see a slight change, and before four statements had been made I understood clearly that I had been set down as a liar.   My remarks on the Brooklyn Bridge produced only one "yes?" from a hang-dog looking man whom I had thought slightly unsound of mind.

"Impossible!" said the strong, heavy-faced man finally, hitting his leggings a blow with a stick, from the end of which projected a point of iron two inches long.   The soldier seized his moustaches in each hand, put his elbows on the table, and stared.   "Why, such a bridge as that" said the strong man, poking the floor, "would have to be a hundred yards wide—at the very least."

"Ninety" said the soldier, emphatically.

I stated the number of railroad tracks, foot-passenger ways, and carriage roads on it.

"*Jesus!*"

"A hundred yards certain," said the strong man.

The argument as to the width of the bridge from that moment became furious, and it was half an hour before electricity had its turn.

And so we talked and talked until the room was fogged with smoke and all the glasses were empty.

At a little after dawn, with a second horse hitched tandem, and leaving our white mule of yesterday to rest, we drive out of Biescas as the bells are tolling for mass.

The morning is cold and clear, and I am glad to roll myself up in a rug and wait for the sun to come in sight. The clouds hang low down on the side of the mountains,

and at every few hundred feet we pass the water-swept
mouth of some small *arroyo*. Somewhat beyond the entrance of the hills, we come upon a picturesque castle
perched above the cleft in the rocks, through which runs
the river, and across which is flung a stone bridge. On
the other side, a line of loop-holes peer threateningly from
the cliff face, for this is one of the important passes to
France, and the government has fortified it accordingly,
Above in process of construction is another fort up to
which a road leads, and farther along the valley on the
dividing lines of the two countries, like an emblem of
peace, a church is built on an over-hanging crag. Farther
still a cascade breaks down through the rocks and pine
forests of the abrupt declivity.

At *Polituera* we pass under gigantic cliffs, rising on the
other side in a sort of magnificent semi-circle, with a great
column at one end ; the clouds hang above them.

Here, our horse having cast a shoe, we are delayed
a while, the driver paying the blacksmith one *centavo* for
his services. As we drive on, the clouds have a touch of
gold from the rising sun, and at one point to the left, high
above us, they thin a little about the abrupt sides of a cliff,
showing the bald rocks peering through and seemingly
suspended in mid-air.

Now and then a peasant passes, sometimes walking
and prodding a lazy mule or sleepy donkey, or mounted
in a silent, inexpressive, collapsed heap upon his back. A
purple *faja* or red head-handkerchief marks him far up the
road, and nearly everyone carries a green cotton umbrella,
in eternal preparation for rain.

At a turn to the right we come to a group of houses
with cleanly slated roofs, that look more French than
Spanish, standing amid a military group of poplars above

13

the rich green valley below.   Soon after, as we enter what
might be a little New England forest, we pass two horsemen in cloaks of bright velvet, who bow with the true dignity of highwaymen, but allow us to pass ; and then leaving
the valley of the Gallego on the left and crossing it on the
stone bridge of Escarilla, we turn up the other side and off
towards Panticosa, for the first time getting a view of the
cathedral-like peaks, under which we have been passing,
and the bright patches of snow in the clefts of the mountains to the left of the valley we are about to ascend.   A
little later we see the town of Panticosa, a pretty little
place with ninety or a hundred houses, crowded together
just above the church.

On the left of the road, where blackberries are growing in dense patches, falls a frigidly cold stream, which
disappears among steep fields of potatoes and cabbages.
Now the gorge narrows, and we pass under a splendid
cliff with a fine thread-like waterfall near it.   Then up
along the river *Caldares* which boils below with a surging
noise and far from whose edge a straggling army of fear-
stricken pines are trying to scale the steep sides to a place
of safety.   Soon the road begins to zig-zag, and, in spite
of the sun, it is so cold that we are glad to stop at the
road-master's house and go in to warm ourselves at the
fire.   Three children are seated in the middle of the floor
about a wooden bowl, eating a kind of scrap-pudding with
wooden spoons.   The cat tries now and then to get a bite,
but a determined little three-year-old has his eye on him,
and at last gets in an all but fatal blow on the thief's back
with his wooden spoon.

But it is too cold to let the sweating horses stand long,
so we start on again past a rocky cleft and a bridge where
three *carabineros* stand leaning on their guns.   We rise

suddenly up to the level now, and entering a rocky valley pass through it, turn a corner, and all at once come to the waters of a small lake. We have at last reached the baths, and a moment later the great bare hotels, with their rows of closed windows and deserted gardens and walks, appear. We are at the end of our journey, in the very heart of the Pyrenees.

This Spanish mountain-bath after the season seems utterly abandoned. The lonely solemnity of the little valley is brought home as it could never have been had those long, hideous hotels been full of clamoring invalids eager for news of the last comers. Their deserted weather-beaten look seems to suggest in a measure some sort of secret unexplained triumph over the insults of man in the place. One has to have seen the Pyrenees to realize their influence on the character and history of the Spanish people. This great spiked collar about the neck of Europe has truly been tight enough to choke off international communication. It is as though the bareness, the chilling, sombre, deserted, lifeless grandeur of these mighty Dons of stone had set the fashion of dignity and forbiddingness to a whole people whom they look down upon. How could the light grace of France be ever brought to struggle across this line of grimness? Or, if across, how muffled up and chilled must it be on arrival!

I wander about the deserted place for an hour. Torn letters are scattered in the stream below. A fragment lies on the bottom, the water flowing across the lines. It reads: " It is but a step across. José has gone and I have told Maria. When you pass—" He might have torn the letter finer—or burnt it!

Leopoldo, as I am pondering this possible romance, brings me a huge piece of brown bread, with a lump of hog's fat on it.   The first I can eat very comfortably.   The *carabineros*, stationed here for the protection of the frontier are communicative and tell me about the place how it looks in summer, and how the snow falls ten feet deep in the winter.   But now the valley is really magnificent, shut in as it is by huge mountains of bald rock on each hand.   At the end and from both sides fall streams of water, great dashing cataracts, tumults of white foam, the one to the right forming the source of supply for the baths. From the little cottage above one gets a view of the northern fall which is the largest.

" The way to France," says one of the *carabineros*, pointing to a narrow mule path winding up and disappearing in the cleft beside the fall.

One of the hotels—the *Fonda Española y Francésa* has, in large figures, the height above the sea—1637 metres —written upon its wall.

We leave at eleven, by the clock in the *Casa de Inhalacion*, and as we are driving down the long grade, Leopoldo suddenly turns to me letting the blanket in which he is rolled to the eyes fall below his mouth.

" Did they talk about the smugglers, those *Guardias ?*" he asks.

" Yes."

" What did they say ? "

" That smugglers never got through here."

Leopoldo chuckles, jeeringly.   " They get through fast enough," he says.

" How ? "

" Oh, the little ones get caught, but when a big load goes through—what would you have?   There is enough to pay every one ! "

We get back to Biescas for breakfast, and after the

mule has been changed for our old, white animal of the day before, we are about to drive off, when a voice calls above. I look up and there at the window of the Casino are my friends of the night before. " Do you know," says the soldier, leaning out, " we 've been talking over that bridge, and it *must* have been 80 metres wide." " It *must* be " says the strong man emphatically, and someone says " Yes ? " inquiringly inside, as we whip up and drive off.

" *Adios—adios,*" their voices float back : " *Adios—Feliz viaje ! Adios.*"

XIII

SAN JUAN DE LA PEÑA—THE CAVE OF THE VIRGIN

AT six on the following morning I am sitting, like Alfred, before the fire, only instead of the cakes he watched so badly, my charge is the milk and eggs which are to serve for my breakfast a little later. And with more appetite and less state cares I am doing pretty well. The woman has gone around the corner for bread. We are back in Jaca, and are about to start out for a trip to San Juan de la Peña. The day-light is not yet clear.

Finally the eggs are hard, and the milk hot, and the woman has returned with the loaf, which she has evidently dropped by the way, for it is covered with mud. By careful trimming, however, she removes every trace of dirt, without losing much of the bread. These shavings will doubtless be useful later—nothing is wasted. This woman's hair is of a mildew color. She has a slight limp, a harsh voice, a private mutter deep in the throat, and very large, thick finger-nails with half halos of dirt.

Shortly before seven, the old white mule to which I am gradually becoming attached, (in spite of a cynical expression on his face, whenever he sees me coming,) is before the wagon and we are soon under way out of town, with the rising sun shining on the battlements.

SAN JUAN DE LA PEÑA

We turn into the *carretera* of Navarre, and break into
a trot. *Oroel* towers before us with the sun gilding the
cliffs of his face. The mule even seems affected by
nature's grandeur. I am beginning to feel the romantic
influence of the morning myself and the stillness and
the curious light, when Leopoldo suddenly turns around
and calls :

" And the luncheon—where is it ? " My heart sinks. I
have made such trips before without luncheon ! I help
him turn out the rugs and pry under the seats. It is not
with us.

" Well, I 'll go back for it," he says, and leaves me
bundled up in my rug, and holding the reins under one
arm. The patter of his feet dies away in the distance. It
is very quiet and very cold. Black crows and *picarazos*
with their black and white markings and long tails fly about
the fields, and now and then flash in the light of the sun.
Behind me a blue haze risen from the kindling of innumer-
able breakfast fires, hangs over the walls of the gloomy,
silent town. By and by I hear the Huesca coach descending the hill with a jangle of bells and the cries of *mayoral*
and *zagal* floating back. I can just see the leather-hooded
top over the bank of the road, sliding along as though on
the surface of the ground. A little later, far down the
grade, the road makes a coil back on itself, and I watch
that point for the last glimpse. The heavy, lumbering old
affair rolls into view for a moment, swings leaning around
the curve, and turns out of sight for good, in a cloud of
dust, with a rattle as of distant artillery.

Two peasants pass talking earnestly, about the crops I
judge, for I hear one say " The potatoes "—but lose the
rest. His companion stops to give his donkey a blow as
he replies, not with the idea of urging him on at a faster

gait—long experience has taught him to hope for nothing but the steady, regular walk—but from a sort of contemplative habit he has acquired of striking hind-quarters at given intervals. These men have set, square-jawed faces, and their motions are slow, sometimes clumsy, but they give an impression of rough strength, and honest good nature, which one is far from getting in the southern provinces. Here shrewdness takes the place of subtlety and coarse jests that of the wonderful, instant replies of the quick, warm-blooded *Sevillano*.

Leopoldo now returns out of breath, panting from his exertions, and muffling himself up, to ward off the cold, he takes the reins, and we start on. Here and there the sheep, gathered in the night before, still stand crowded in their folds, looking very cold, and waiting patiently for the bars to be thrown down. We cross the small river Gas, as Leopoldo calls it, and keeping on down the valley of the Aragon, pass the usual solitary, ruined tower in a break of the hills on the left.

At 8.30 we stop at a little *venta* and unharness our mule. We have reached the limits of the carriage road, and must ride and walk the rest. My affection for the old white animal with the upper half of his body close shaven, grows deeper as we go on up the *Barranca de Santa Cruz*, Leopoldo walking ahead, muffled in his cloak, a fitful blue line of tobacco-smoke floating out now, and again, from his *cigarillo*. We soon come to an opening, a sort of enclosed valley, and going through, pass by a curious ridge of rocks, which comes sheer down from the side of the hills like the broken, upturned edge of a gigantic razor. Rising high into the air, and only a few feet in thickness, it runs down the slope, and suggests the remains of an ancient wall.

Far ahead the row of washed cliffs stand out, blocking the sky view up the valley, and as we turn a corner a group of peasants, driving *burros*, with plows strapped upside down on their backs, come in sight, and about twenty yards ahead of them, like a drum-major heading his band, with great, white-ringed, staring eyes set under gigantic ears, comes a small, grotesque donkey.

His look of astonishment is splendid. For a moment he gazes at us, all four feet planted apart, and then poking out his nose, but keeping both his eyes wide open, begins to send forth that series of noises not to be produced by other lungs.

We rise now into the district of box-wood, which here covers the hills, and pass a very small shrine behind a wooden lattice, with a glimpse of the Virgin in a dirt-smeared glass case inside.

It grows colder as we rise, until Santa Cruz comes in sight below us, and Oroel towers far off on the left. Higher, the peaks beyond the Aragon, toward France, come in sight. On the mountains beyond Oroel there is snow. Through a narrow gorge of composite rock, then zig-zag up the face of the cliff, the mule goes very slowly and carefully among the rolling stones, until the sun strikes us in the face, and we turn and enter a forest. This, after a short, cool ride, is passed, and we come out on a level, in the centre of which appears a long, low building.

We have reached the so-called New Convent, although itself old enough to be in ruins, and now all but deserted, its former inhabitants reduced to a single family. As we ride up to the main entrance a child and two puppy hounds fly in terror, the latter barking vigorously. A woman with a shy, nun-like face greets us at the door, and we pass into the entrance of the main hall, and the part occupied by the present inhabitants.

Some writing on the wall opposite the door catches my attention. "What is it?" I ask the woman. "Something to do with the congress that came," she says, in a timid and very gentle voice; "but my husband can tell you all about it." He appears, and explains that there has been a French and Spanish congress here some time

THE NEW MONASTERY

past, which I judge was about the new railroad. The man could not read.

As I am anxious to see the monastery as soon as possible, we do not wait to take breakfast; but, securing the service of a good-natured looking boy who has the keys, we start for the real object of the journey, the cave.

Entering the forest once more, somewhat to the left of where we had first come on the open ground, we begin a descent of perhaps fifteen minutes through a thick pine growth, swinging slowly to the left until, passing along the side of the gorge, the cliffs above and in front come

into sight.   Then, turning sharply, the monastery is before us.

There it stands, crouched under the over-hanging ledge
of the composite rock, looking out between the walls of the
narrow valley towards the plains below, solemn and silent,
the last resting-place of the ancient kings of Aragon.

The historical interest attached to this building can
scarcely be over-estimated, although the graves here are
not those of men whose memories the world has been at
great pains to keep fresh.   But when the lives of these
shall have all been more fully examined and the details
laid bare, perhaps this little heap of royal bones may gain
the attention it deserves.

The monastery of San Juan de la Peña is historically
the most important of all the ancient kingdom of Aragon.
There, according to the tradition, the Saints Voto and
Felix of Zaragoza laid the corner-stone of the Aragonese
Re-conquest, and there a handful of men, fragments of
what had been a part of the Spanish nation, gathered together about their new king-elect, Garci Ximenez.   From
such mountain clefts and caverns as this was the new nation to take its source, and such names as San Juan and
Covandonga ring with no uncertain sound in the memory
of the Peninsula.

St. Hubertus of Luettich met a wonderful stag in the
forest with a blazing golden cross between his antlers and
was a changed man from that day.   St. Voto of Zaragoza went hunting in the mountains about Jaca, and a
fleeing stag drew him to the edge of a great cliff beneath
which lay hid a deep cave.

The Saint dashed upon his quarry, forcing the latter
over the precipice and all but following himself, so head-
long was his speed.

With great presence of mind however he prayed fervently to St. John, and in the nick of time his horse was stopped miraculously upon the verge and he was enabled to dismount in safety. As he did so he perceived the cave beneath him.

The descent was steep and dangerous, dense undergrowth checked him, and the foothold was treacherous. At last, however, he cut or forced a way into the cave and found a fountain of clear water at which, says the chronicle, he thought none but the wild creatures of those hills had ever drunk.

But he soon found a small hermitage, and coming to the door, saw the body of an old man whose head rested upon a stone. On this stone was carved his story.

So moved was the pious Voto on reading this record that, after burying the sacred remains, he fell praying and pondering for a considerable time, after which he returned to Zaragoza and communicated to his brother Felix, a pious soul like himself, his wonderful discovery, telling him, moreover, that he had formed the resolution of spending the rest of his days on that holy spot.

Felix at once joined with his brother. They were rich and of noble lineage but they sold all, and dividing the proceeds among the poor Christians living under the Moorish rule, they betook themselves to their mountain cave, constructed two small cells, and there under the torments of cold and hunger and solitude and even the *temptation of devils* they passed the rest of their lives.

At their death those who buried them perceived most strange things, among others a wonderful light which came down from heaven itself. Their day in the Calendar is the 29th of May.

" Here," says a writer, " the race of invincibles arose ;

here was formed the Aragonese character, and here justice grew up under such names as Sancho, Iñigo, Ramiro, Pedro, the Jaimes and the Alfonsos."

The younger and greater in extent of the two monasteries was constructed as a result of a fire, the last of several, in 1675, and the monks, no longer in fear of an ever-ready enemy, were this time at liberty to seek a higher, dryer and more suitable situation. The accusation has even been made that the fires in the older building were not so much the result of chance as of the rheumatic joints of the fathers, who were so long forced to dwell shut in under their damp, over-hanging crag, surrounded by the wild, dense forest above which their view was ever outward toward the desolate snow-covered wall of the Pyrenees.

At the time of the monks, these dense masses of pines filling the abrupt and broken *barranco* below were everywhere intersected by pleasant walks and lanes, of which, however, no traces are now visible. The grandeur and deep stillness make a profound impression as we go slowly through the untouched wilderness, and the sudden appearance of the building has something awe-inspiring in it.

As we draw nearer the great overhanging wall of the cliff seems to advance upon us, looking like the lip of some gigantic mouth, stayed a moment before it closes forever upon the already half-engulfed building. Were the latter swept away we should find ourselves before a great fissure two hundred metres in length by fifty in depth and stretching open some fourteen metres.

Many indeed are the kings and grandees whom these low, dull walls have welcomed. Many a time has the echo of rattling arms, or the tinkling bells of the caparisoned mules, been awakened in the rows of narrow cells of the monks, or in the more imposing apartments of the Abbot himself. In the great library, where afterwards books were printed, and in the broad garden, royal feet have passed or rested, and many a war council has been held of which history has all but forgotten to make mention. Hospital, garden, library, monks or Abbot—little of all these remains, little indeed more than the very stone walls themselves and the heaped up bones in their damp cellars, or behind rust-eaten gratings.

A CHAPEL OF SAN JUAN.

The building, inside, is interesting, but in no way striking. The long, curved depression in the side of the rock into which it is built, is hardly deep enough to be called a cave. The greater portion of the structure is outside, the older being the deeper. The roof under the ledge stands open although this does not appear from without, for the line of sight brings the rock and roof seemingly together.

As we enter the monastery, on the right is the so-called Hall of Council, where the chief interest at once centres on the line of moulded and damp-destroyed tombs. From before the door here, rises the stairway, once of stone, now wood, and at the end of it, the hall containing the tombs of the ancient nobility of Aragon. These tombs are of the utmost interest. They are in two rows of Byzantine arches, one above the other, are twenty-six in number, and may date from before the year 1000.

The uniformity of the plan of these arched tombs
would seem to indicate that they were erected simultaneously, which may indeed have been the case, with the
same intent, at that early date, of forming a national sepulchre, as that which prompted the restoration of 1770.

EARLY TOMBS

Many of the tombs, however, have been opened, and
no doubt rifled of such valuables as they may have contained ; even the bodies in some instances have vanished.
But that this rifling should have taken place is in no way
to be wondered at, and the archæologist may be thankful
indeed, that after much puzzling and conjecture he is able
to read such names as those of the Etenzas, Ferrenches
de Luna, the Garceses and others so often repeated in
the chronicles of their times.

Here, too, lies the Count of Aranda, Minister of

14

Charles III., whose long-suffering bones were made to journey to the court, to form part of that conclave of remains of kings and celebrities, which it was once the eager plan to unite at the national capital. But when the plan came to naught—as plans sometimes do in Spain —and each province once more loudly claimed her own illustrious dead, then were the bones of the Count of Aranda gathered anew and honorably returned to their long-time resting-place, and a slab relating their journeying placed in plain view of the curious.

The monastery of San Juan possesses a tomb which has puzzled more than one historian. In an inscription we are told that Doña Ximena, daughter of King Sancho

ROYAL BURIAL CHAMBER

and wife of the Cid Campeador, is buried in this spot, and that her body was here brought in 1122. We are, however, taught to believe that her *other* body is still at Burgos.

We now reach a door of walnut carved with the arms of Aragon, and above which two angels with trumpets support a slab on which is inscribed :

In this worthy monument,
The noble liberators of their country,
And defenders of the true faith
In hither Spain
Are guarded with veneration.

This, then, at last, is the entrance to what we have come to see ; this, the sacristy of the ancient church. Here we are at the portal of the spot where five centuries of monarchs of Aragon and Navarre have been buried. Beyond that door, in all the severe simplicity of Gothic or Byzantine, we shall see the last resting-place of no less than thirty-two royal bodies ! Thirty-two noble names which, were space unlimited, we might print down the page.

And then we enter. Alas ! the dream has flown as we cross the threshold above which sit those trumpet-bearing angels. We are in a long, narrow, high room. On the left wall large reliefs give detailed portrayals of the early battles of the Re-conquest. Those nearest the altar represent the encounter of Garci Ximenez and Iñigo Arista ; the third, the king swearing to the charters and the laws in presence of clergy and nobility. These three are between the pilasters on the left, and are of stucco. They are difficult to see well, owing to the bad light.

The figures of the altar, however, are of finest Carrara marble, by the sculptor Salas. The bronze and polished surfaces gleam on every side, but dignity is wanting. There is no simplicity, no grandeur, no effect.

Before us, at the farther end, the church has taken up

her place of vantage, with altar and marble crucifix, the slanting light falling across it from above, to strike upon the long rows of bronze plates, twenty-seven in number, behind which in 1770, by order of Charles III., were im-

GOTHIC DOORWAY.

prisoned for all time —unless some other king reconsider it— the bones of the monarchs of the north. Unlodged i n d e e d, they were, or almost so, for this place, the ancient sacristy of the church, was all but a mouldering heap, with time and dampness, when the good-intentioned king turned his attention to its restoration.

On the floor, marking the spot where twelve tombs have been united in a single one, is written: *Hic jacet famulus Dei* . . . *Rex.*

The ancient church dedicated to St. John was finished and consecrated by Pedro I., whose father, killed before Huesca, had begun it. Finished and consecrated on the same day, Dec. 4, 1094, the dead king's body was deposited in it, and the Archbishop Amato, papal Legate of Urban II., performed the ceremony of consecration.

The edifice, crouching beneath its over-hanging rock,

is seventy paces long.   Behind its three Byzantine arches
the gaudy *retablos* strike the eye with barbaric glitter from
the dark.

Below there is yet another older church dating from
before 842.   Two naves of narrow arches are sustained
on short heavy columns.

There is a door in the building which must be examined with some care for it brings to us, suddenly, amid
this grave picture of Christian domination, a lighter, more
graceful impression.   Even here an influence out of
the far East has been felt and marked in stone, just as
it has in almost every
part of Spain.   It is
the door which unites
the church with the
cloister, and it has the
delicate curve of the
horseshoe arch. Above
it this sentiment is
given in Latin :

" By this portal to Heaven
    the faithful pass
  If, beside the Faith, they
    guard the laws."

The bodies of the
abbots of San Juan
rest in the Chapel of
San Victorian which is
Gothic and most inter-
esting.

DOOR OF THE FAITHFUL.

What remains of the cloisters is of the best of its kind.
They cover about 12 by 20 metres, and part of this has been

repaired in a coarse manner with brick. The arches themselves are excellent. Straight double columns with elaborately carved capitals enclose the little garden, and upon the whole falls a subdued, religious light. Of the faces of the cloister, that to the south has suffered much, but the western one, with its fantastic details and grand heavy manner in the capitals, is still excellent.

I sit on the edge of the altar and note the names on the brass plates, while the two puppies chase each other about the building, and the boy and my driver utter undertone comments on what I am doing.

After a careful examination we return to the new monastery and continue our voyage of discovery. The church looks dismal enough, and in the old halls of the monks the plaster is falling and the doors of their sleeping-rooms stand half open as though they had only just left. After breakfast and a walk about the open space on which the building stands, we start down again, saying good-bye to everybody, and are soon passing once more through the box, *enebro, herizones* and *hallaga*, which line the pathway.

We reach the house where our carriage has been left at a quarter to three, and here Leopoldo begins to make up for sparing use of the wine-skin. A few peasants gather about the door, and the drinking and merriment go on for half an hour. There is the usual, big, good-natured fellow who treats everybody and drinks almost a full skin himself.

Two hours later we are in Jaca once more, and at six my dinner is ready, and I am making preparations for the ascent of Oroel in the morning and seeing the Virgin of the Cave, on the other side, where tradition has it that the independence of Sobrarbe was proclaimed.

It is dark by this time. The old landlady, who has

CLOISTERS; SAN JUAN DE LA PEÑA

charge of the coaches, has only just finished her moving and is in the midst of a confused heap of boxes, bales, chairs, tables and pans.

"Sit down, sit down, *caballero*," she exclaims, as she draws out a chair for me in the centre, with my back to the hearth-stone (which fills a quarter of the room) and there, surrounded by her staff and camp followers, prepares to do battle for the price of new expeditions.

On Tuesday, the 4th of October, we were out of town by half-past six and under way to the Cave of the Virgin. We descended into the valley in the face of a chilling wind, and started for the spine of Oroel, stretching far back and away from the cliff ahead.

At an iron cross, mounted on a brick column, the road forked. We took the right, picking our way across a half-ruined, double-arched, stone bridge, beyond which began the ascent. Yet already in the clear, icy water, the washer-women, with red arms, were plunging their clothes, and along the bank above an old man with two mules was painfully ploughing on the sharp angle of the hillside.

WASHERWOMEN

A little farther on we met another stray donkey, larger and older than the one of yesterday and with less of the latter's expression of surprise. He had already, perhaps, tasted some of the sorrows of Spanish donkey existence, and was slowly assuming that dignified indifference which is his universal stamp.

" More rain," says a man by the wayside, and Leopoldo nods solemnly under his mufflings.   It is a dark, cold day, and the wind comes in puffs, sharp and piercing.   We cross the level to Maros and begin to climb again.   The massive form of Oroel, its outline like that of a great Egyptian face, stands out clear and cold above, staring down the valley of the Aragon towards Navarre, just as it stood when, from the monastery of Leyre, Sancho the Great, stopping for a moment in his rapid march to Ribagorza, and La Ainsa to meet the rebel Counts and defeat them, might have seen it towering in the distance.

Near a small town, with a bold, square church tower, we pass through a lane bordered by a field of black grapes.   Soon we reach the second rise, and approach the break in the mountain.   A great, gray, washed gorge lies below.   In front, high above us, stretches a solemn forest through which we slowly ascend.   Far ahead, on the utmost sky-edge of the cliff, the faint outlines of a wooden cross can be seen marked against the gray clouds, dizzying to look up to as the path grows steeper, turning back upon itself at every few yards.

We pass through the pines, and on.   Leopoldo stops, loosens a heavy stone and starts it rolling, bounding, crashing, down the dry bed of a torrent.   It disappears at last in the pine forest directly beneath us, followed by an angry hiss and swish of branches and a farewell thud and growl.   Then a goat-bell tinkles overhead, the sound intensified by the stillness.

After steady climbing, we reach the cross and pass out upon the top of Oroel.   The view below is magnificent. As we stand there looking down on the red, plowed fields, a dark shadow appears from beyond the mountain and a magnificent eagle sweeps past us not fifty yards away. He turns his head a little to look at us, and then sails majestically out over the tremendous abyss. It is worth a hundred climbs to see him take that long, silent plunge. Not a feather seems to stir, there is not a motion of the broad wings—steadily and with fearful velocity he sweeps on moving his head now and then as he watches the valley. As I stand and watch him out of sight I seem to hear the wind whistle over the outstretched wings and the hiss of the quivering feathers at their edges. And the words of the great poet come back : "She dwelleth and abideth on the rock, upon the crag of the rock, and the strong place. From thence she seeketh the prey, and her eyes behold afar off. Her young ones also suck up blood ; and where the slain are, there is she."

From the highest point the view is even grander. The country towards San Juan de la Peña is clearly marked, and the view down the Aragon wonderfully impressive. Jaca lies to the right, and behind it the pass of Canfranc, with only Castillo in sight near its entrance. It is through that pass that the railroad to Pau is to be built, to put an end to the individuality of the place and bring upon it the blight of the tourist.

We now begin the descent of the other side where the cave lies, by a sharp declivity, through box, brush and a second scanty pine forest, and soon come upon a square building, from the upper windows of which a man is leaning—the individual who has gone up ahead to open the place.

The cave is now seen for the first time—not unlike a huge, half-open, toothless mouth. At one end, a part has been walled up to form the church, inside which is an altar, covered with the usual tawdry ornaments. Only half visible in the sombre light, and fenced off by a grating, is a fountain of clear, cold water, falling into a basin encrusted with a deposit which hangs over the sides.

A careful and detailed examination of this birthplace of the ancient kingdom of Aragon is not an extensive or exhausting undertaking and may be well done in a few minutes. We devote an hour to it, however, and then, after disposing of a chicken, start back, the man who preceded us returning with us. A good type of these strong northern people he is ; people who here stood their ground well against the Moors, and a curious contrast he makes to Leopoldo. The latter with his light, delicate, refined body, clear-cut features, and soft womanish mouth with scarcely a trace of beard or moustache, has indeed little in common with the ruggedly built, heavy-paced man beside him, on whose clean shaven face the muscles and deep lines are alternately marked, and whose firm, square chin, large, powerful mouth, keen eyes set far apart and steady, unyielding carriage, mark him the mountain Spaniard of to-day as of yesterday. Here are the two types of Moor and Goth, as clearly defined as if we were still in the 10th century.

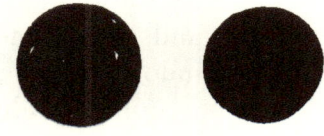

XIV

LEYRE—PAMPLONA

TWENTY minutes past four A. M. The white mule and another stand shiveringly huddled together, harnessed to the light wagon at the door of the hotel. It is perfectly dark and cold enough to make our rugs welcome. The girl with sleepy eyes stands holding the flickering lantern which casts long, waving shadows into the silent side-street beyond. At last, with a final " *Adios!* " replied to by a wave of the lantern, we clatter out along the *Calle Mayor* to the city gate, where the guard looms up indistinctly, his face partly illumined by the light of his cigar. The *Sereno* stands near him muttering something while he peers up at us as we pass. I have heard him earlier in the night, crying the hours and weather and once or twice the ominous *nublado* or *lloviendo* has made me dread a bad day, a fear to be realized.

A few stars shine dimly with a bleared, uncertain light, and on Oroel there is a heavy, white mist, soon touched and given a blue, ghastly color by a few faint traces of dawn. At 6.30 we cross the Aragon on a six-arched bridge, and approach Verdun in a fine rain.

" *Señores—Señores,*" calls a voice to the left, and a tall man with soft, curly hair and a skin as brown as a negro's comes out from a low shed, which stands alone in a broad, desolate field.

"*Cigarros, Señores*—Do me the great favor. We have been without them these two days." He takes off his hat with a smile. His companion stands in the doorway in the distance. Leopoldo hands him several cigarettes, and he bows gracefully and retires.

"A gypsy?"

"Yes."

"There are many here?"

"Plenty, plenty, more than we want."

"How do they make a living?"

"Make a living!—they steal."

"You imprison them?"

"*Ca!* No. What good would that do—they would eat and drink at the expense of the Government, which is all they want." It is raining now in torrents, and we splash along solemnly.

A SPANISH GYPSY

"Good for the sowing," says Leopoldo philosophically, pulling his blanket over his head. We stop at last at a carpenter's shop to feed the mules and escape the rain. Upstairs there is a fire, and, at the invitation of the old man at the doorway, we go up. By the small blaze sits a woman of perhaps twenty with a young baby on her lap.

"Five months old," answers the father to my question, lighting a cigarette. The woman is almost beautiful, with a sad, worn face.

There is something peculiarly alluring, too, in the accent of these peasants. The pronunciation of the final "a" has a curious, mournful sound, conveying in some way an idea of refinement and delicacy, out of keeping with the confusion of noises which rises through the chinks of the floor. Below, dogs growl and bark, and hogs grunt unceasingly amid the quacking and cackle of ducks and hens. As we go down the creaking stair a large goat eyes us inquisitively. We soon start on, leaving the men just sitting down to their dinner, of which they had urged us to partake. I shall not forget that simple interior with its festoons of beans and onions, the fire, with pots and kettle huddled about it, the brown walls, the open planking of the floor, through which the wind whistled, and the carpenter's shop knee-deep in shavings, the pots and pans each upon its nail, and, more than all, the mother and child. The last I see of her she has come to the lower door, and is standing, with the baby in her arms, watching us drive away up the rain-washed road. Then a turn hides her, and we sink down under our blankets once more.

Verdun stands on the crest of an abrupt knoll, the road going straight up to its foot, and then turning to the left. The church tower rises from the centre and on the left is a high, black butte covered with pines. We turn and, skirting the town on our right, come into more broken country, cross the Veral River on another broad, stone bridge of five arches, and at ten are driving along under an abrupt mountain range, capped with a sheer wall of rock. Dull, lead-colored clouds hang above it and upon it, and almost reach the face of the cliff. One might fancy a battle upon the top, the armies hidden beneath great, rolling masses of smoke. This is the *Sierra de Leyre* and we are drawing near the famous convent. · Oroel is still in sight behind us.

We pass another house of gypsies, a few hundred feet before crossing the Esco on a stone bridge of three arches, and then swing off and up to the level of the foot hills on the other side.

" *A noche te vi la card—a—a—a—*
Por la luz de mi cigarró—o—o—o—
No he visto cara mas bonitá—a – a—a—
Ni clavel mas encarnadó—o—o—o—"

sings Leopoldo, impelled perhaps by the sight of a pair of black eyes in the gypsy doorway. We pass Esco, perched among the foothills and half hidden, behind a low, bare knoll, the church dominating it and the houses stringing down from it, in a long, irregular group. It is a small, but rather picturesque little place. On the other side of the Aragon, a little farther down, ruined towers appear in a break in the hills, and behind, out of sight, lies Ruesta.

All along here, at intervals, one sees small heaps on the plowed land ; brush (box, *hallaga*, etc.), dried through the summer, and at this season piled in little mounds (*hormigueros*) upon the fields. After sprinkling these on top with earth, the brush is lighted, and the whole reduced to a mixture of earth and ashes, which is then scattered over the land as fertilizer.

At about eleven we sight Tiermas. It is somewhat higher than Verdun, and upon a more abrupt hill, standing on the right of the valley, with a square church tower, as usual, in the centre. Below and beyond, by the river, rises a slate-colored, water-washed cliff ; and behind, on the right, stand the bold, black walls of the *sierra*.

The green water is running quietly below the three

great stone arches of a bridge near which we come to a
halt, before the *Posada de la Guama*. Leaving Leopoldo
with the team and trap, I walk along the highway, around
the hill to the other side, and then climb up through the
town which stands on the top of a sharp knoll, and is a
well-preserved remnant of the days when safety was only
to be found in a fortified place.

The solemn sadness of desertion and decay fill the
lonely, brokenly-paved streets. Nothing is to be seen
but signs of neglect and poverty, and even the dozen ragged, forlorn-looking children who peer after me as I pass,
but do not follow, intensify the loneliness. The impression is perfectly indescribable. A completely deserted place
is often sad enough, but there will usually be something
to make the loss of the human element forgotten. A
bird may sing, or the wind blow suddenly in the face refreshingly. Here, however, the few signs of life to be
seen bring with them such a wonderfully overpowering,
and oppressively real sense of human desertion and im-
potence that one seems walking in some burial-ground
where a few of the open graves have in them persons not
quite dead, but dying, waiting patiently, with half-closed
eyes, for the end.

After breakfast at the *Posada*, I make inquiries about
Leyre, and find that we can get there well enough on
mules, and as soon as we like. A man of fifty, claiming to
be French, presents himself, and offers his services as guide.

" I know the country perfectly " he says, " surely I
ought. I have lived here now twenty-five years, and am
married here." He insists on talking French, with a remarkable accent, until I accept his services, and we start,
keeping the road for some distance, and then turning to
the right, and ascending through an oak forest, more or

15

less dense, and by the side of a dry bed of a mountain torrent. The monastery stands out, a square shell, above us.

"Wait a moment," says my guide, "I live by here; I want to go and get my gun. There are lots of rabbits on the way up." To this, however, I object.

"I know the country perfectly," he says again, "I ought to by this time, after living here twenty-five years, and marrying here." He is short, and livid of complexion, with large speckled ears and furtive, doubtful eyes. When looked at he deems it necessary to say something, which is usually about his peculiar ability in some direction.

We soon reach a fountain of clear, cold water, beside which lies a long slab, where, my guide volunteers, the monks took chocolate. Tradition long ago jokingly linked the drinking of chocolate with the lives of the good monks, perhaps in memory of the days of its then recent importation from America when the work * of Rauch was being secretly sought out and destroyed by the holy fathers, for its attack upon them and their use of it.

A bee-house with hive above hive, strongly resembling a modern receiving-vault, stands just beyond the wall. In one or two of the spaces bees are still flying in and out, lineal descendants, no doubt, of the first inhabitants, who began life in this establishment in the year of 1790 (the date is conspicuous upon the face of the little building), and who are, perhaps, the only living things left who could give us the traditions of this place as it was.

The monastery is now near, and we go up to it as fast as my mule (I discover him to be lame) can walk. We find the place seemingly deserted, its heavy walls rising

* *Disputatio medico-diaetetica de aere et Esculentis nec-non de potû* (Vienna 1624).

without sign of life about them. But recently-cut stone lying about shows the progress of the renovation going on, and after a search I discover a foreman who takes me over the ruin. The church is extremely interesting, although at this moment in a state of confusion. Many fine capitals, now scattered about at random, will find their proper resting place eventually when all is completed. The doorway is excellent.

Inside, workmen are cutting stone at the foot of the stairway leading into the crypt. Here I find what most interests me, for here is what was the old church, which may date back as far as the eighth century.

This, like San Juan de la Peña, is one of the oldest monuments of the Christians, and, like it, is to be made the resting-place of the bones of the rulers of its ancient kingdom, for we are in Navarre now, having crossed the boundary line between this place and Tiermas.

The Crypt presents a curious sight. The low lines of arches have not yet had all of the earthen floor, the accumulation of ages, removed from around the bases of their columns which will make the latter much longer and add lightness to their appearance. In one corner of this half-dark vault, I notice a gray pile, and, going towards it, in astonishment find it a mighty heap of bones: skulls, vertebræ, ribs, femurs—a general débris of bodies heaped in utter confusion.

" What are they ? " I asked the foreman.

" Bones of the monks," he answers, with an indifferent shrug, turning to give an order to one of the men.

" But where did they come from—whose are they ? "

" *Dios sabe !* We picked them up here and there as we came to them in the excavations, and as there were no marks or inscriptions they were all piled up here out of the

way until we can finish the work. See—here are shoes,"
he continues, picking up the sole of what may once have
been a sandal, and snapping it with his finger.

I thought of the temptation of Gough who preached
against light-fingered antiquaries and who yet at the disin-
terment of the bones of Edward the First, was seen, it was
told, by the hoax-maker Stevens, to pocket a finger bone.

The haunting legend of this vicinity is the famous
sleep of St. Biril, the local Rip Van Winkle.

"Oh, yes," says the foreman, "it is not far, I'll send
my boy with you."

So, mounted once more on my lame mule, we start out
to see the spot where St. Biril took his three-hundred-year
sleep. The place is all that imagination could demand,
and until the day comes when tourists arrive to bear off
mementoes, will remain one of the most weirdly interesting spots in all Spain. The gigantic cliffs have toppled
down, here and there, in tremendous fragments, and between them has arisen a wonderful mass of dense undergrowth in fantastic irregularity ; a tract of upturned
boulders and impassable brush, threaded by the path
which winds to the tomb of the old monk.

After a slow tramp of twenty minutes, we reach the
spring by which the Saint slept, where, by its side, is
shown the very tree on which his head rested for three
centuries.

The good St. Biril, in the middle of the eighth century, was, we are told, Abbot of Leyre and was a very old
man, and, if we may judge, somewhat given to speculation
after the manner of later school-men upon details of the
celestial life to come. One day, when he had somewhat exhausted mind and body in the fatiguing inward contempla-
tion of the cloister, he determined to walk abroad and

recover in the open air from the despondency which was creeping upon him. The dense and secluded undergrowth near the monastery was just suited to his mood, and there he went, and was soon moving deeper and deeper into the maze of trees and upturned rocks and brush. The Saint went slowly and laboriously onward, his attention little fixed upon his surroundings, until he came to a small fountain, where he sat down to rest.

Soon the soft flowing of the water produced a drowsy effect upon the old man, and he was just slipping into the realm of sleep when the notes of a bird in wonderful and delicious harmony came to him and the next instant the creature perched upon a branch above him. As the Saint listened to the marvellous song, the thought came to him : " Beautiful and soft is the song of this little bird, and I could listen to it without fatigue an hour perhaps, but, would it be possible to listen, without fatigue, forever— always—for all eternity—to the very choirs of the angels ?

" Eternity !" exclaimed the old man " what flower hast thou in thy dominions whose perfume forever pleases the sense of smell ; what beauty that forever refreshes the sight ; what song that forever charms the ear ?"

The bird continued singing, and little by little the Saint fell under the wonderful charm of the mysterious melody and, noticing no change as time slipped away, he did not know that the minutes grew to hours, the hours to days, the days to weeks, and months, and years, until at last three whole centuries had slipped away before the bird took wing, and the holy man awoke to shake himself free from the heap of débris that had accumulated about him. He arose to find himself closely shut in by the surrounding undergrowth, and it was with the utmost labor that he was able to force his way out.

But once out, his difficulties were only just begun. Surprises began to meet him at every step. The road, so familiar of old, had changed. The face of the country was different, and by the time he arrived in sight of the monastery, he began to think he had taken leave of his senses.

His first impulse was to seek the familiar door, but that too was missing. He could find no trace of it. He continued to examine the building, and noted that many windows had been closed, and others opened, which had not existed before. The monastery, too, was larger, and great trees stood where he remembered only small ones.

Finally he stopped before an iron gate and knocked. A monk, whose face he had never before seen, admitted him to a large room. Here he was soon surrounded by the entire community of the monastery filled with curiosity at the strange figure of the old man. The chief then spoke to him and inquired who he was.

After several questions the old man said simply : " I am Biril, the abbot, who a short time ago went out walking in the forest."

Little by little at the old man's tale, the monks, at first incredulous, began to believe that something remarkable had happened. He was questioned closely ; old manuscripts and records were overhauled, and it was learned that a certain Biril had actually been Abbot of Leyre three hundred years previously, and that he had mysteriously disappeared and, it had been thought, had fallen a prey to wild beasts.

When the good Saint realized what had befallen him he exclaimed, " Merciful God, if the tongue of a simple little bird moved by Thy holy love may give a man such ineffable delight during three centuries, what delights hast thou not in reserve for the chosen ones in the choirs of the angels which shall endure for all time !"

Thereupon accompanied by the whole community, he descended to the sombre crypt to pray, and, two days later, having received the last sacrament, the good St. Biril died.

We return to the monastery now and begin the descent. It is almost dark before we have gone far, and quite so before reaching the road. The guide repeatedly reassures me, as he stumbles along, with his unending refrain, that we shall have no trouble as he knows the country perfectly—having lived there twenty-five years, and having married there. When at last we arrive at the *posada* it is raining. After a hasty supper, I go to bed, and spend the night in battle with vermin.

At half past six of a rainy morning, we are once more on our way and pass along down the river, muddied by the rain. We again cross the dividing line into Navarre, and, half an hour later, come to Yesa, which lies on somewhat rising ground. We stop before the old church in the drizzle, which has chilled us and makes the interior even more dismal and uninviting

PEASANTS OF NAVARRE

than I had pictured it; and the quest—the remains of kings—is not enlivening. They have been placed here while the repairs go on at Leyre.

The remains are in a long, ancient, gilded, and emblazoned box, which stands temporarily to the left of the altar. The names are written on the top, but, as the box appears to have been opened, they may or may not be the real names of its present occupants.

The little building is somewhat interesting as an excellent example of a small, ill-kept, smelly, provincial church, with tawdry altar and more than usually bedecked Virgin, before which, during my entire stay, an old woman kneels, resisting the genuine temptation to look around at us.

As we are preparing to drive on, the *cura* who has heard of our arrival, appears, and I stop to thank him for his trouble. His gown is torn, and he looks poor enough, but there is a certain dignity of manner about him, not to be mistaken.

He is tall and emaciated. Yet you feel that you are in the presence of one of those men of magnificently small lives, to which Roman Catholicism points now as she has always done. He stands erect, and has a clear, grave look in his eyes, fearless as it is simple. His torn gown flaps about his ankles and shows the worn, heavy shoes beneath, Yet we know that he is patient and calm for he has all the light of the self-battle in his eyes. The light of the daring to do less than his heart tells him he is able.

At 8.25, looking back from a crest in the road, Oroel is still visible, although only the lower part, for the top is buried in a great rolled-up heap of cloud. At Yesa we have left the bank of the Aragon, which there turns away south, while our course continues, bringing us under Liedena in a quarter of an hour, after which we curve to the left and come down to the river Irati.

Here we find one of those peculiar, local, ferry-boats,

managed by ropes, and which, as is always the case with a Spanish ferry, is on the other side. With creak and groan and much talk of the crops and a discussion of the relative merits of all governments, we are at last across the few intervening feet of water, and, after bumping ashore, and a final hand-shaking, which as we look back at the boat we have left,

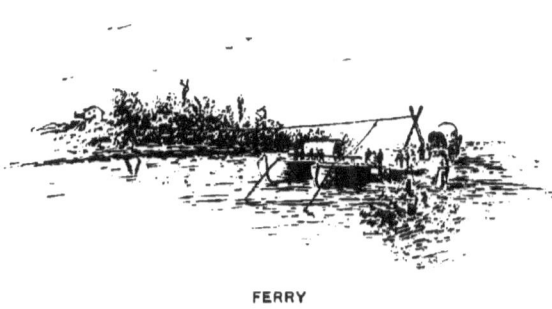

FERRY

we feel to be a partial congratulation at having cheated the watery element of its prey, we once more start on, leaving Lumbier on the right, but not going near the town.

At half past nine the rain has stopped, and twenty minutes later, with rush and clatter, the Sanguesa stage passes us and disappears with a sullen rumble behind, only giving time for a rapid glimpse of peering, curious faces, and the momentary sound of a buzz of voices and clatter of wheels and harness.

SANGUESA

Aldomate, a little town, lies below on the right of the road which here ascends, with Lumbier in sight from the broad, uneven-surfaced valley.

"*El Aragones fino despues de comer tiene frio*," says Leopoldo, pulling his blanket over him.

Passing Izca and several other small towns we reach

Idocin soon after eleven, where I take advantage of the "hour's rest" demanded by Leopoldo for the animals, to eat a hurried breakfast and explore the single, narrow street of the little place.

SPANISH SOLDIERS

The Posada is clean, and two sweet-faced women, one of whom I am somewhat surprised to find bent over an American sewing-machine, are the only occupants at the moment.

By Salinas de Monreal we go, where salt is mined (and the process looks dirty enough) and on to Monreal itself, under the mountain called "The Fig." There is a building above Salinas, which looks to me much like a monastery, but I can get no information about it. By Coello's map it might be Santa Barbara. Leaving Monreal, with its octagonal towered church, we pass the *Portazgo Provincial*, or toll-gate, and out upon a straight bit of road, the arched, Roman-looking aqueduct taking its stream into Pamplona on the left, with the railway passing beneath the middle arch.

At last, at half past two, we enter the broad, uneven plain of the capital of Navarre and Leopoldo puts a new lash on his whip. Soon the two towers of the cathedral appear, and it is not long before we cross the dry moat in which rope-makers are busily at work with their great wheels, and enter the city of Pamplona. A military procession is slowly winding along the streets, and for a while we are blocked watching the soldiers file by. Finally, however, we are before the door of the *Fonda de la Perla*, and at last at the end of our drive. Ten minutes later Leopoldo takes his leave, wishing me every manner of good fortune.

His departure has in it the sadness of a parting of old friends. We shake hands very earnestly twice, and I watch him from the window as he mounts to his seat, in the corner of the square below, and slowly turns the light carriage and drives off down a side street. And so Leopoldo and the white mule disappear forever.

PLAZA DE LA CONSTITUCION PAMPLONA

XV

ESTELLA

THERE is but one serious disappointment for me in Pamplona. This is the impossibility of gaining access to the famous Arabic carved ivory box at the cathedral, which is in reality my chief object in stopping in the city at all at this moment.

My first attempt to see this is astonishing. At the cathedral I find one of the priests, and ask him to help me.

" Box ? " he says in answer to my inquiry, " What box ? "

" What box ? " I explain.

" I suppose you are another Frenchman."

" No, I am not another Frenchman."

" The English are as——," he stops.

" Well ? "

" Suppose there were such a box ? "

" Suppose ! "

" Well, how did you know of it ? "

" It is well enough known."

" That is no answer. You are from a commission ? "

" No."

" You want to photograph the box ? "

" Not at all, I wish merely to see it."

"I don't see what good it would be to see it. You want to photograph the box."

"I have no camera."

"You want to photograph the box."

"But, my dear sir, the box has already been photographed, and I have a copy."

He looked at me for a moment, and then laid his finger on the side of his nose.

CAPITALS OF THE EARLY CATHEDRAL OF PAMPLONA—NOW DESTROYED

"You want to photograph the box," he said, "it cannot be seen," whereupon he turned his back upon me and marched away, his black robe floating behind him in stiff uncompromising folds.

As my other attempt turns out as badly I give it up. To this day, after a dozen visits to Pamplona, I have never seen the famous box.

A peculiar spirit seems to pervade this cathedral. My inquiries of a choir-boy as to access to a tower, are answered, after a furtive glance up and down the long aisles, to the effect that he will guide me.

"Are you from Pamplona?" I ask, as we climb the stairway.

" Yes, my father is Tomas · Izgarre. Do you know him ? "

" No."

" He makes shoes."

" Ah."

" On the street of the Martyrs of Estella. He is an old man now—more than fifty." And so this frank boy needs very little urging to tell me that he has three sisters, two married and one living at Sos.

" Ferdinand the Catholic was born at Sos," I say, pedantically.

" Was he ? " He is a delicate little fellow, in his flowing gown which he holds up at the side, and has large, brown, melancholy eyes. We ascend slowly, and I notice a certain anxious look on his face. We reach the top, however, without accident. The view of the city is excellent, and my small guide points out the buildings in answer to my questions.

Suddenly he is gone, and at the same moment comes the sound of a heavy step and deeply-drawn breaths. Turning, I am just in time to see a fat man dash wildly across the open space in a vain attempt to catch my boy, who dodges him with every appearance of terror.

" Oh, if I catch you I 'll teach you—I 'll teach you ! " (here a desperate lunge) and he almost lays hands on his adversary who, however, ducks instantly. A moment later his flying footsteps patter away down below us.

" What is the matter ? " I inquire, innocently.

" The matter ? " puffs the newly arrived — " the matter ? The Devil catch him ! (puff, puff) the little thief ! (puff)—I knew he would (puff) try to do it. I knew it ! "

" Do what ? "

" And it 's the third time I have caught him—the third time. My wife 's a poor woman, *señor*, and she can't afford it—no, *señor*,—the little devil ! " (puff)

" What has he done ? "

" Did he not offer to come up here with you ? "

" Yes."

" Ah, I knew it ! "

" But why not ? "

" My wife is a poor woman, *señor*—a poor woman— she cannot afford to lose what the *señores* may give—and this little, lying son of Satan is always sneaking about and getting the *pesetas* from the *señores* who come—she being a little deaf—and that she sleeps so much —Ah, *Dios !* "

It is two o'clock in the afternoon of a pleasant day when we drive out of town, with a fine horn-flourish from the *mayoral*, and, after galloping a mile, settle down into a trot, somewhat faster, I must confess, than is usual with these coaches. We are bound for Estella. A cross by the roadside soon after starting, marks the place of death of Ramon Alaregui (I think that is the name). Before reaching Zizur we pass two churches, one in ruins. These are the first interesting objects.

At half-past four we enter Puenta La Reina, with its little fort,—" named," says the historian, " from the con- struction of its great and beautiful bridge over the Arga by some unknown queen." One of the passengers, a tall, thin man, and myself, walk across the bridge and wait for the stage on the other side. It gives a good view of the town and the Arga.

Our driver has been out the night before with his

friends, there is not a doubt, for he is scarcely able to keep his eyes open.   He sways from side to side with half-closed lids, his cigar drooping, unlit, from the corner of his big, thick-lipped mouth.   But we get speed at least, though at some risk, for he lashes his horses unmercifully. At last, just at nightfall, the final horn is blown, with a shaking hand, and suddenly and unexpectedly we come to the town and the entrance of a narrow street.   It is dark now, and a long line of lights dimly marks our way. As we sway along between the narrow rows of houses, from whose second stories heads peer and waving lights are thrust, the snap-snap of the whip becomes incessant, a warning to the crowds of children.

Suddenly a ruddy glare bursts out.   We are passing a blacksmith's shop.   The owner appears at the door and thrusts into the street on high uplifted tongs a great mass of red-hot iron which flares and hisses and lights up all about with a lurid glare as he waves it above him, the muscles of his great, right arm marked out in red-touched knobs and black hollows, and his up-turned, sweat-covered face ablaze.   He laughs good-naturedly as the horses shy and the *mayoral* curses ; then the thump, thump of his hammer sounds again as we pass on up the street.   A few moments later we are in the *Posada San Julian.*

In the early morning, as I come down-stairs, I am confronted at the door by seven or eight tattered old women, who, at sight of me, exclaim, simultaneously :

"*Ave Marta Purissima !*"

Not knowing the cause of this sudden welcome from so many strange ladies, I no doubt look confused, but the outstretched hands are not to be mistaken, and I find that a copper in each settles the question most satisfactorily.

Each bears about her neck a brass star with what seem cabalistic letters upon it. I am not sure that I am not the centre of a group of witches. However, a side door of the hotel opens, and a boy comes out, and as I had done, distributes coppers with blessings, whereupon they betake themselves off.

"Who are they?" I ask the boy.

"Only poor people. They come every Saturday to beg."

"And that brass plate?" I pointed after one.

"Oh, that is given them by the *Ayuntamiento*. It is a permission, and to assure the people they are really poor."

"So you have no means of telling the beggars from the others here except by a brass plate?" I ask.

"None," says the boy, innocent of satire.

I watch the group that has been by the door. They are out under the arcade now, arguing over a division of the spoils. A fantastic group they are, old and wrinkled, and bent, but loud-voiced and clamorous. There is only one old man—by far the feeblest of them all. It is amusing to see how they push him aside and ignore him, and finally, when the division is made, dole out his share half contemptuously.

By and by it seems settled to their satisfaction, and they break up into little groups. I can overhear a few words :

"Mass is striking," says one.

"And Roberto—is he better?"

"Ah, no—last night he died." A series of exclamations follow, and I catch no more.

I depart, wondering who Roberto may be—some time-honored veteran of the staff, no doubt.

A short walk brings me to the little town of Ayegui, beyond which is the convent of Ihrache, where I find, to show me about, a talkative old door-keeper, who gives dates of historical happenings in a confused and mumbling way. On the return, a man going the same way, gives me the names of the peaks in sight, and tells me the story of the young count who fell over the cliff near the town, and also the pathetic tale of his nurse.

"You came last night, I hear," he says.

"You heard it?" I ask, "how?"

"Oh, they said at the Casino that an *Ingles* had come from Pamplona on the coach—and I did not think there could be two."

Hurrying along back to the hotel through the narrow streets, I turn a corner suddenly, and find myself face to face with two women, one perhaps fifty, and the other a girl of less than sixteen. For a moment, I confess, I stop short. The younger, is one of those wonderful Madonna child-women, rarer in Spain than in Italy. I turn home slowly and begin getting ready for the coach.

ESTELLA

Perhaps an hour has gone by, when the girl from below comes to say that two *señoras* would like to speak to me. I start to descend, but they meet me at the door.

I think my face is expressive when the same mother and daughter enter.

They seat themselves at my invitation and the elder proceeds to explain, at first with some hesitation, the cause of their visit. They had heard, they said, that a " North American from the United States " had arrived in town, and passing me, had at once come to the conclusion that it must be myself. Now, had I ever been in New Orleans? The question is sent at me without delay, and when I confess that I have, both smile and nod to each other.

" And is it possible that, having been in that city, I had ever been acquainted with Señor Juan Gomez y Leon ? "

I regret that I have not had that pleasure.

Then comes the story. The said Señor Juan Gomez y Leon, appears to have been the uncle of the lady now before me, who, with the daughter is the rightful heiress of the said Don Juan.

This gentleman, being of a roving and affectionate disposition in days gone, had after many like adventures fallen at last under the seductive influence of some fair lady of New Orleans, soon after which he had suddenly languished and passed away (without due reason, as my excited visitors seem to think), leaving this final recipient of his affection also the recipient of his worldly wealth.

Suddenly then there appeared before the eyes of his startled heirs, who deemed it merely necessary to write and demand that wealth, a will, leaving " *to my beloved wife Juana Romero* " his entire fortune, with the exception of certain old pieces of furniture, which, by the contemptuous tone in which the ladies mention them, can scarcely be of buhl or ormolu.

" And what we want to prove," says the younger, on whose exquisitely refined face the signs of impatience have been growing during the last few minutes, and can no longer be controlled, "What we want to prove is, that this woman was only our uncle's mistress, and can have no legal share in the property."

"Ah," I say, contemplating the young lady who has just given vent to this modest sentiment. "I see. You wish to prove that your uncle was not living with this person——

"Just so," interrupts the damsel. "That she was his mistress, besides, we have proof that she was a common character."

"And what was the amount of this income, if I may presume to ask?" I say, turning again to the mother.

The latter bends forward and lowers her voice, and the daughter's eyes assume an eager expression.

"When I saw my uncle last," she says, "he told me himself that his fortune brought him an income of over one hundred and twenty-five pesetas a year" ($25.00).

"Impossible!" I say, recovering my upright position. "But the will? Did you see it?"

"No, only a copy—and it was in English, which we could not read, and it was a long time before we could get it translated."

It has always been a cause of deep regret to me that the conversation, begun under these circumstances, has never been completed. My stage leaving so soon after this I was forced to bring the interesting interview to a close. Under stress of urging, however, I was drawn to promise that if I *should ever* be in New Orleans, and *should ever*, while there, chance to meet with the mistress of the said Señor Don Juan Gomez y Leon, I would surely inform them by letter.

Thereupon they took their leave, thanking me most heartily, and I assured the daughter that her eloquence alone had convinced me that her uncle was a most depraved character, which she received as a well-earned compliment.

When they had fairly gone, I made a rapid rush for my things, put two hard-boiled eggs and a piece of cheese, wrapped in brown paper, in my pocket, and flying downstairs, paid the bill and just barely caught the coach.

After leaving Estella, the road turns to the left branching from the one I took in the early morning to Ihrache.

Here we are joined by two priests, one a tall well-built, square-jawed man ; the other small and thin-faced, coughing continually, and whose great, priest hat increases a most peculiar expression of unceasing surprise. To add to this, his small, wide-open eyes are surmounted by up-raised, astonished eyebrows, and a half open mouth, and two deep wonder wrinkles in the middle of his forehead confirm the unavoidable impression that he is in some occult way beholding always, just beyond his nose, some strange and fantastic thing. When he is not looking straight before him with hands folded in his lap, or coughing, he is wonderingly engaged in taking a lozenge. And this is the Vicario General of the order of the Esculapians of Spain—a force indeed, for into the power of his order fall a great percentage of the children of the country ! He told me that the order had (I think) some fifty schools.

At Morento (11.30) I found time to talk with one of the stone-breakers—(*camineros*)—by the roadside. The amount of road allotted to these men varies with its physical difficulties. This one has five kilometres. They are paid by the amount of stone they break, and average two pesetas a day (40 cents).

There is much talk at Sesma of a wonderful surgeon

who lives here, but I cannot recall his name. The vines
are much injured by cold, and there is a great lack of
water. We turn to the left, on sighting Alcanadre, which
lies far off across the Ebro, and is seen through the break
in the hills. Approaching Lodosa, with the river below
us, a curious sight presents itself. On first seeing the
town lying under a hill, I am struck with the curious
patches of red on walls and roofs of the houses and in
some places whole parts of the town.

"Why do they paint the houses red here?" I asked
the *mayoral.* "They don't do it anywhere else in Navarre."

"Paint the houses red?" he replies somewhat gruffly,
for during the last half of the journey he has been sitting
on the edge of the dash-board, the stage being filled to
overflowing (in spite of government rules to the con-
trary).

"Paint the houses red?" he says again. Then it
seems to dawn on him, and, giving a snap to his whip,—

"*Ca !*" he exclaims, "those are peppers."

And peppers they are. We are soon near enough to
see the great red masses of fire, some eight inches long,
millions of them. It is a good-sized town, and one can
guess how many it must have taken, strung in great, pen-
dent lines a foot thick and ten feet long to give a red
color to nearly the whole place three miles away.

We drive between the blazing, scarlet walls, and stop
for breakfast. Here I see more of the Vicar General.
He turns out to be a bright little fellow, for all his
astonishment, with a somewhat surprising knowledge of
the outside world.

Breakfast over, there is singing, and playing on a
guitar by a man who rolls his eyes as he thrums, intend-

ing no doubt, to express feeling. The coach takes us over the bridge with a clatter to the station where the train comes after a long wait on the platform. I keep my new friends, the priests, taking the same coach with them to Zaragoza, in spite of the calls of the other members of the group, who say something unpleasantly jocose about "*Los Curas.*"

The amount the little Vicar General knows about America, especially the Southern States, astonishes me. He tells me how and where they are preparing men in Spain who are to go to America and urge on The Work.

He in turn seems surprised that I know several of his school teachers, one in Jaca, and another in San Pedro de Cardeña near Burgos.

" I am glad," he says, " to meet someone at last from your country who is willing to go into the little towns of Spain and see the people. Most foreigners think we are a nation of bullfighters."

It is moonlight, clear and cold, when we reached Zaragoza. The streets have an old-friend look about them, but it is too late to feel anything but cold.

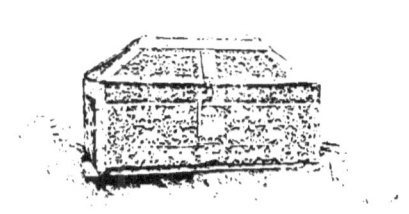

XVI

RONCESVALLES

THERE was a curious old woman, now dead, I believe, who, weighted down with a glass-topped tray filled with Virgins (of the *Pilar*), was always at Casetas, with her never-changing call; "*Imagenes del Virgen del Pilar—muy bonita,*" the last syllable prolonged and accented into a sort of pathetic wail, which still rings in my memory.

When, therefore, I passed Casetas this morning, and did not hear or see her, I felt quite as lonely and disheartened as if I had lost an old friend. I was going north from the *Sierra de Moncayo*, whence it was that an Arabic expedition once marched against the towns at the mouth of the Aragon, to whose aid Sancho the Great came down the river. Caparrosa, Milagro, and later, the bold outlines of the castle of Olite are in sight from the train window.

At Pamplona there is time only to take luncheon, and change from train to coach—the latter leaving for Burguente at 2 P.M. Out past Villaba, with its paper-mills, we drive, and on to Urroz. On the top of the coach with me, in his yellow and black uniform, there is a *Guardia Civil*, who is willing to beguile the way with his adventures.

" Do you mean is there much shooting and robbery ?" he says in answer to my question on that score.

" Yes."

" Well, not so much, of course, as in the South, but we have our share. There," he continued, " is a pistol," drawing out a revolver beautifully inlaid with gold, " which was given me last year for killing a couple of thieves."

I was at once interested and he continues.

OLITE

" I was over in the hills by Burguente on a trip of inspection, and stopped for the night at a friend's. It was about midnight and we had just turned in when I heard some one at the door below knocking and calling. I went down and found a man, out of breath with running, who told me that there were four fellows in his house, and that they were stripping it. He knew I was there and had come over for help. Well, I took my gun and got my shoes on in a minute and started with him. The house was just around the curve in the road, and we were there in three minutes.   As we came along I saw a light ahead, and then somebody ran by me.   I called to him to stop, but got no answer.   Then two came running by.   I did n't wait this time, but fired, and one went down.   The

RONCESVALLES

light, which had been stationary until that time, then began to move away, and I followed at a run.   The fellow, as soon as he suspected that I was coming, threw the lantern down with a crash.   I fired just as he did it, and when I got there he was dead.   We went back and hunted up the first man who was making a great noise, lying on his back and groaning.   We got him into the house and tried to fix him up, but he died before morning.

" And the other two got away ? "

" Yes, we never got the others."

" A few friends at Burguente gave me the pistol," he continued, unclasping the barrel and handing it to me.   It was self-acting, of the old style, richly inlaid with Toledo gold-work.

At Aois, which lies under a round, swelling mountain with a rocky knoll at the end, this hunter of men left us. After a change of horses we went on with a new *mayoral* to Burguente, where the rest of the night was spent. Part of this ride was shared with a little girl of four, put in by her mother, on the trembling edge of tears, and confided to our tender mercies.   Poor little thing, every now and then when a match was struck to light a cigarette, I looked down and saw her sitting bolt upright, her hands clasped desperately in her lap, and her little, round eyes almost popping out of her head.

Next morning at five, in a coach loaded with five wine skins, I started, the only passenger, for Roncesvalles. After a rapid drive between long rows of trees bordering the road, we stopped at last before the little church.

Inside they were celebrating mass, and the high altar was lighted up. It was still dark, although the morning was coming, and the mysterious light of the church was rendered more solemn by the deep melancholy voices of the priests and the double rows of bent, uncovered heads, across which the candles sent a dim, flickering yellow light. I walked on through the little town, passing under an arched way like a tunnel, and then up out of the streets, and, by a foot-path, along the side of the gorge till it joined the road again.

It seems almost a pity that Roncesvalles is so pervaded by the Charlemagne legend. Its individuality is quite as lost as that of Waterloo and other over-historied places, with the general difference, however, that there was here an individuality to lose. It would be really a beautiful little place to discover and enjoy by one's self. One goes along instinctively distributing and arranging the position of the famous Rear-Guard. Suitable places are found for Roland to stand, amid a ring of dead, and sound that last, tremendous blast which pierced across the maze of hills and valleys to the ears of the great Charles. After reading and seeing illustrations to the poem a disappointment may await the traveller at Roncesvalles. The scenery is infinitely less grand than one expects. The walls of the mountains by no means rise sheer out of the valley in monster precipices and gorges. The little rolling vale, though quite fitted for a surprise and defeat, is not what we picture for the heroic setting of the great poem and Roland, mounted on his faithful *destrier*, his Durandal in one hand and the great horn in the other, stands out less vividly.

There is in the church here a little bit of iron which recalls an event of perhaps far more importance than ever was the death of Roland.   A slight memorial indeed it is ; a bit of iron chain ; yet I think this little church can be more justly proud of its trophy than even the ancient Basilica in Rome, possessed of a like relic, and the additional prestige of a horned Moses.

This link of iron is said to be one of the fragments of that chain which, surrounding a portion of the Moorish chiefs' forces in the battle of Navas de Tolosa, was burst asunder by Sancho the Strong of Navarre.

After some time the coach comes by and picks me up and I am glad to get in behind one of the slightly warm wine skins which, not being quite full, folds a clinging embrace about my knees.

Then we go on slowly up the ascent passing the hermitage, a little ruin on the left—where Charlemagne is said to have emerged from the valley, and on top of the divide between Val Carlos and Roncesvalles we have a magnificent view.   In front lies the valley—Charlemagne's route back into France—and behind, the little hollow of Roncesvalles filled with trees, the whole end blocked by the heaped-up, blazing gold of a glorious sunrise.

Then we begin the descent along the road winding snake-like below us.   The sight of France, or perhaps it is the long down-grade, seems to infuse new life into our driver, for he whips up his horses and breaks into songs, set to Basque words.   The wine skins, against which my legs are pressed, are trembling like great bowls of jelly. Suddenly he pulls up.

A woman stops us in front of a small low house.   " Bring me a loaf when you come back," she says to the driver,

handing him some money. He takes it and nods.
"*Adios,*" she calls after us, and we drive on.

At Valcarlos, with its white houses in a beautiful, rich,
green valley, all looking bright, and fresh, and clean, and
quite unlike anything on the other side, we part with
the little stage and its driver, and wait for breakfast and
the other stage. A walk down through the town brings
me back with a healthy anxiety for food, and I watch the
baby getting dressed by the fire where my breakfast is
cooking. There are a great many little white pigs running about—all of the same family, and the old sow lies at
some distance with her small eyes intently fixed on their
actions.

At last the other stage arrives, and we get under way
once more, picking up, very soon after starting, an old
lady dressed in black who seems to be the mother of a
priest of about thirty who puts her into the stage and says
good-bye. From now on we stop every little while to speak
or to be spoken to by the passers. Our driver this time
is even more jolly and French than before, and sings martial songs and whistles operatic airs. He is a great favorite with every one, it seems, and has, for reward of his
good nature, a long list of messages, errands and purchases to be gone through with before his return. French,
Spanish, Basque—all tongues are alike to him—as indeed
they are to all these people. Naturally the accent is
Southern, but it is not bad, and at one point where we are
stopped by a pretty girl of eighteen to discuss the possibility of matching a piece of cloth, it seems quite satis-
factory.

At St. Jean Pied de Port we meet with a difficulty in
the fact that the stage is over-crowded. An army of pilgrims, it seems, are *en route* for Lourdes, and we are

threatened with a possibility of delay.   But another coach is put on at last and we get seats on the roof, whereupon up comes my old lady in black and seats herself beside me.

"Yes," she says in answer to my question, "I am going to Lourdes too.   You see I am old—very old, and I want to see if I cannot attain to Heaven—that is the best thing, you know—the best thing," and she reverently clasps a string of heavy beads lying in her lap.   At this moment there mounts with us another woman, quite as old as the first and quite as eager for the pilgrimage, and soon these two fall into an earnest conversation in Basque, for one is a Spanish and the other French Basque.   The words and the conversation are beyond me, but by the aid of the free interpretation of gestures, it is evident that their one theme deals with things not of this world.

"Whoever has been in the land of the Basques," says Victor Hugo, "wishes to return to it; it is a blessed land." These people are attractive to an American in their spirit of enterprise and energy.   Thiers calls them the "most gentle, the most active, the bravest and the most industrious of all those in the Peninsula."   It is quite true, if in some respects we except the Catalans, who have been to no small extent under the influence of France and the commercial intercourse of the Mediterranean.   Castelar once spoke of them as "the four most ancient provinces, the most historic, of character the most independent, of the oldest traditional liberty."

At last, the old coach creaking and groaning, we start on, out under the arch in the wall, and through the narrow street.   Our eyes are on a level with the second stories. There are old coats-of-arms carved in walls or over doors, and plates giving the date of erection of the buildings. Then we go out by a little river, up which the railroad is being built, and on along the road to Osses, which is crowded with people—old people mostly, where we finally take train for Bayonne.

As I enter Bayonne I recall distinctly a description of the customs of the ladies of this town by Madame Aulnoy, who passed through it in 1679. She says:

"These Women begin here to feel the scorching Heats of the Sun ; their Complexion is dark, their Eyes sparkling ; they are charming enough, their Wits are sharp : And I could give you a farther Account of their Capacities, could I have better understood what they said : not but that they could all speak *French*, yet with such a different Dialect as surpast my Understanding.

"Some who came to see me, brought little sucking Pigs under their Arms, as we do little Dogs : it's true they were very spruce, and several of 'em had Collars of Ribbons, of various Colours : However, this Custom looks very odd, and I cannot but think that several among themselves are disgusted at it : When they danced, they must let them down, and let these grunting Animals run about the Chamber, where they make a very pleasant Harmony. These Ladies danc'd at my Intreaty, the Baron of *Castlenean* having sent for Pipes and Tabors.

"The Gentlemen who attended the Ladies, took each of 'em her whom he had brought with him, and the Dance began in a Round, all holding Hands : they had afterwards long Canes brought them, and then each Spark taking hold of his Lady's handkerchief, which separated them from one another, moved very gracefully at the Sound of this Martial sort of Musick, which inspired them with such Heat, that they seemed not to be able to moderate it. This seemed to me to resemble the *Pyrric* Dance so much celebrated by the Ancients ; for these Gentlemen and Ladies made so many Turns, Frisks and Capers, their Canes being thrown into the Air, and dexterously caught again, that it is impossible to describe their Art and Agility : And I had a great deal of Pleasure in seeing 'em ; but methoughts it lasted too long, and I began to grow weary of this ill-ordered Ball : When the Baron de

Castleneau, who perceiv'd it, caused several Baskets of dried Fruit to be brought in. They are the *Jews* who pass for *Portuguese*, and dwell at *Bayonne*, who transport them from *Genoa*, and furnish all the Country with them. We wanted not for *Limonade*, and other refreshing Waters, of which these Ladies drank heartily ; and so the Entertainment ended."

INDEX.

Abadía, Juan, 154, 155, 156
Adamaro, bishop of Huesca, reconstructs the cathedral, 172
Africano, el, see Bellón
Ager, archives of, 168
Aguardiente, 146
Alabaster carving, *see* Huesca
Albardas or pack-saddles, 63
Alcala de Henares, 129
Alcanadre, 246
Aldomate, 233
Alfonso II., captures Teruel in 1171, 138
Alfonso III., church of Santiago reconstructed by him, 37
Alfonso of Castile, 140
Almanzor, 11
Alpargatas, 78
Amphoræ vinariæ, 66
Anzanigo, 182
Aois, 250
Arabic box in Pamplona, 236
Aragon, character of the Aragonese, 145; peculiarities of the architecture, 146; river, 224
Aragonese giant, 191
Arbor day, 124
Arbues, Pedro de, Master of Epila. His persecution of the Jews at Zaragoza, 152; plot to kill him, 153, 154; his death, 155
Arga river, 239
Arjona, Francisco, called *Curro Cuchares*, 118; his generosity, 120
Art, religious, in Zaragoza, 162
Astorga, 46, 49

Athanasius, companion of Saint James, 36
Athenasia, 60
Atienza, 133
Aulnoy, Madame, quoted, 87
Avignon, 151
Ayegui, town of, 246
Ayerve, Marquises of, 180
Ayuntamientos of Huesca, 167
Azagra, Don Fernandez de, 141

Ballabar, Ezmel, a Moor, associated in the building of the Torre Nueva of Zaragoza, 161
Banderillas, 103
Baptism in Jaca, 185
Barabas, the bull, 97
Barbastro, Jews there invited to aid in the murder of Pedro de Arbues, 153
Barcaiztegui, Martin, called *Martincho*, 106
Barranca de Santa Cruz, 202
Becerro, Jaspar, his *retablo* at Astorga, 46; his Christ inspired by the Virgin, 46
Beggars of Estella, 240
Bell of Aragon, 175
Bellón, Manuel, *El Africano*, his history, 105
Bells, constructed for the Torre Nueva of Zaragoza, 161
Bells of Santiago set up in the Mosque of Cordova inverted as lamps, 40
Benedict XIII., *see* Luna
Berenger, Count of Barcelona, 168

Berlina of a stage-coach, 59
Bernues, 183
Biescas, 186
Bilbilis roa l, 7
Biscuits, 70
Bitorino Parejo, 69 ; her insanity and treatment, 71
Blacksmith's torch of red-hot iron, 240
Boccacio, 137
Boticas Hondas, 155
Bowring's description of the religious condition in 1819, 3
Brick-work on the Torre Nueva of Zaragoza, 161
Brigantium, Roman road to, 36
Brooklyn Bridge, discussion as to its width, 192
Bullfighting in Italy in 1332, fatal results, 98 ; origin, 97 ; slow development in the thirteenth and fourteenth centuries, 98 ; its cruelty, 95 ; its effect, 97 ; it becomes a popular sport no longer confined to the nobility, 102 ; mutilation, 97
Bullfights, grandeur of, under Philip IV., 101
Bull-ring, the, 94

Caballero de Plaza, origin of, 99
Calatayud, 133 ; Jews there invited to aid in the murder of Pedro de Arbues, 153
Caldares, 194 ; river, 194
Candido, José, 106 ; his death, 107
Canfranc, the railroad to, 182
Caparrosa, 248
Carabineros ; a halt at their house, 194
Carlos III., his attempt to stop bullfighting, 107
Carlos of Navarre, his bullfights, 98
Carlos of Viana, 172
Carmona, Antonio, el gordito, 121
Casetas, 248
Casino in a Spanish town, 190
Caspe, 157
Cataño, Baltasar, 90

Caves of *Rey Cintoulo* and *A Furada d'os Cans*, 11
Cave of the Virgin, start for, 217 ; arrival, 219
Chain, broken at Navas de Tolosa, 141
Charles V. as a bullfighter, 101
Cid Campeador, 133 ; called the first bullfighter, 98
Cimborio of the Seo of Zaragoza given by Pope Luna, 149
Clavijo, battle of, doubtfulness of the event, 37
Coffee toasters, 77
Coffin of the Emperor Charles at Yuste, 72
Cofradias, 4
College of bullfighters, 115
Complutum, 130
Compostela, *Archivo* of, 34
Corn bread and wine for a horse, 44
Coruña, arrival there from Cuba, 14 ; city of, 10 ; province of, 15
Coso of Zaragoza, 147
Costillares, see Joaquin Rodriguez
Crosses, 66, 238
Cross of Yuste, 72 ; the Angels, Oviedo, 57
Cuarentenas, 58

Dacian ; his persecutions, 131
Damas Hinard ; his edition of the Cid Poem, 85
Delantero of a stage-coach, 23
Delgado, Jose—*Pepe Hillo*—Pupil of *Costillares*, 110 ; rival of Pedro Romero, 110 ; his life, 111 ; recklessness, 111 ; his dramatic death, 112, 113
Departments, Spain divided into, 164
Dominguez, his loss of an eye in the bull-ring, 97
Doña Ximenez, wife of the Cid, said to be buried in San Juan de la Peña, 210
Don Juan of Aragon and Navarre, 172
Door of Arabic construction in San Juan de la Peña, 213

Drake, fear of him in Spain, 42 ; Spanish conception of his character, 42

Dress of the *Zagal*, 24

Duero and Tamega rivers ; marble brought from their shores on the backs of captives for the construction of the church of Santiago, 37

Durango, Vidal, 154 ; drawn, quartered and burned, 156

Eagles in the mountains of Aragon, 167

Ebro, the river, 157

Ebro y Cinca, Huesca, capital of, 167

Education, 6

El Tato, lost a leg in the bull-ring, 97

Enchanted lady of the *Mount d'as croas*, 13

Esco river, 224 ; town of, 224

Esculapians, the Vicar-general of, 245

Espinillera, or *gregoriana* first used, 102

Estella ; start for, 239 ; arrival, 240 ; a question of inheritance, 243

Fences ; wanting in the Spanish landscape, 178

Ferrer, Jaime, of Lerida, 161

Fever, treatment for, 75

Fig, the, 234

Figs, 182

Fonda de la Perla, 235

Forment, Damian ; his Gothic altar in the Cathedral of Zaragoza, 159 ; his *retablo* at Monte Aragon, 177

Fountain, first in Zaragoza, named after Isabel II., 156 ; method of drawing water at, 156

Frotardo, Abbot, 175

Galicia, province of, 10 ; a misty country, 15 ; language ; 10 ; homesickness, 10

Gallegan, interior, a, 24

Gallego river, 164 ; 181

Game in the mountains of Aragon, 167

Garcès, Fortun, 138 ; Martin, 138

Garcia de Moros,. 153 ; burned, 156

Garcia I., 138

Garci Ximenez, 203 ; and Iñigo Arista, described on bas-relief of San Juan de la Peña, 211

Garganta de Gargüera, 64

Garrocha, *vara* or *pica*, its introduction, 103

Gaspar de Santa Cruz, 153

Gas, river, 202

Gate of the *Martires de Guadalajara*, 131

Giant, Aragonese, 191

Girolamo and Salvestra, story of, 137

Gold of Galicia, 17

Gombao, Gabriel, master builder of the *Torre Nueva* of Zaragoza, 161

Gormáz, 133

Goya, Francisco, his pictures of *Martincho*, 106

Gregoriana, see *Espinillera*

Gregory XI., 151

Gypsies, 222

Hartzenbusch, Don Juan Eugenio, 137 ; his life, 138

Hogs, familiar with their own homes, 74 ; in the streets of Plasencia, 61

Horse-shoeing, cheapness of, 103

Horse ; the white horse of Saint James, at Clavijo, 38

House of the Seven Chimneys, 87 ; thought to be haunted, 88

Huesca ; population, 168 ; alabaster carving by Damian Forment, 159 ; Cathedral of, 170 ; purification of cathedral of, 172

Huesca Diaris, newspaper, 191

Huesca, province of, 164

Idozin, 234

Ibrache, convent of, 242

Illueca, birthplace of Pedro de Luna, 151

Ince de Gali, a Jew associated in the building of the *Torre Nueva* of Zaragoza, 161

Iñigo Arista, see Garcia Ximenez

Isabella, the Catholic opposed to bull-fighting, 100

Izca, 233

Jaca, start for, 178 ; arrival, 184

Jalon, 133

Jaráiz, 67

Jarama river, 129

Jerte river, 59

Joaquin Rodriguez, known as *Costillares*, his life, 108 ; invents the *volapié*, 109

Joppa, the remains of Saint James taken from there to Spain, 35

Juan Gomez y Leon, Don, 244

Judaizantes, 153

Justo and Pastor, Saints, 131 ; their martyrdom, 132

Keys of Monte Aragon, 177

Kjoekkenmoeddings, 12

La Mota and Segovia, towers of, 159

Landscape, monotony in Spain, 1

Ledesma, Juan de, 90

Leopoldo, 186

Leyre, start for, 221 ; the monastery of, 226

Liberodunum, 36

Llaguno y Amirola, Don Eugenio de, 84

Local priests, 232

Lonja of Zaragoza, 157

Lorenzo, *see* Saint Valero

Lottery tickets, 79

Lourdes, 253

Lovers of Teruel, the, 137

Lugo, 10

Lumbier, 233

Luna, Pedro de, Antipope Benedict XIII., 150 ; his life, 151

Madrid, its environment desolate, 124

Magdalena, La, 162

Maldonado, Doña Ana, 89 ; Don Juan Arias, 89

Manchino, Ascanio, special rights controlling bullfighting in Valencia granted him by Philip III., 101

Maragatos, 50 ; customs, 50, 51 ; Muria, a Maragato town, 51

Matcilla and Segura, story of, 137 ; Blasco Garcés de, 138 ; Juan Diego, 139

Maros, 218

Martincho, see Barcaiztegui

Matador, the office developed by Romero, 104

Mayoral, 17

Medinceli, 133

Miedes, 133

Milagro, 248

Millán, Pascual, discovery of early bullfighting, 98

Mirabel, Marquis of, owner of Yuste, 72

Miracles, 4

Miraculous, appearance of Saint James to King Ramiro at Clavijo, 39 ; ship in which the body of Saint James was taken to Spain, 35

Mojoneras, 179

Mona or *Espinillera* (q. v.) introduced, 102

Moncayo, Sierra de, 248

Monferriz, Master, associated in the building of the Torre Nueva of Zaragoza, 161

Monreal, 234, Monreal de Ariza, 133

Monte Aragon, 174 ; expedition to, 177 ; ruined castle of, in Huesca, 168

Monte Rubio, Pedro de, successor of Pedro de Arbues as Inquisitor of Zaragoza, 156

Montes, Francisco, 115

Montesa, Jaime, 153

Montpellier, University of, 151

Moore's house in Astorga, 49

Moorish pirates, 41

Morente, 245

Mozo de cordel, 78

Muleta, the ; its introduction, 103

Muñoces, family feuds between them and the Marcillas, 139

Murder of Pedro de Arbues, 155

Muria, town of, *see* Maragatos, 51

Murillo, town of, 181

Museo of pictures of Huesca, 173

National decline, causes of, 5
Navas de Tolosa, 140 ; a fragment of chain broken there, 252
New Convent of San Juan de la Peña, 203
Newspaper, a weekly, of Huesca, 170

Olite, 248
Olivan, 186
Olotzaga, Juan de, architect of the Cathedral of Huesca, 172
Ordoño I., gifts to the Church of Santiago, 37
Orense, 10
Oroel, the mountain of, 201 ; the top of the mountain, 218
Oviedo, 52 ; the chest of, 52 ; its contents, 54 ; its history, 53

Pablo, San, 162
Padre Felix, 185
Palace of the Kings of Aragon, 175
Palomo, Pedro, 116
Pamplona, 235 ; a small guide, 237 ; capitals from the early cathedral, 237
Panticosa, 194 ; out of season, 195
Pasaron, 66
Paseo de Santa Engracia ; fountain there, 156
Pastor, Juan, (el barbaro) see Justo, 119
Pastry, women selling, in Zaragoza, 157
Peasants of Lerida, 164
Pedro II. of Aragon, 140
Pelota, 81
Peñiscola, last home of Pope Luna, 151
Pepe Hillo, see Delgado
Peppers, 246
Perez, Antonio, 89 ; his daring in facing a lioness, 97
Pickled fish, 71
Pidal, Don Alejandro, 81 ; José, 85
Pilar, the Cathedral of, in Zaragoza, 157
Pilgrimage to Santiago, 21
Pius V.'s ordinance against bullfighting, 100
Plasencia, 179 : trip from Madrid, 59 ; the station, 59 ; Fonda del Oeste, 60

Plaza Mayor of Plasencia, 61
Plaza of the Seo, 155
Poem of the Cid, 81 ; sent to Boston, 86
Polituera, 193
Pontevedra, 10
Portazgo Provincial, 234
Posada de la Guama, 225
Prehistoric remains of Galicia, 11
Proposed railroads, 22
Provinces, Spain cut up into, 167
Prudentius, 147
Puente La Reina, 239
Purification of the Cathedral of Huesca, 172
Pyrenees, smuggling there, 196

Quicena, town of, 177

Railroads, slowness of their construction in Spain, 7
Ramiro, King, 175
Rauch, 226
Rejoncilla, the, 103
Relics of Saint James, 44
Robert of Geneva, 151
Rojas y Sandoval, Don Cristoval ; his fear at attempting to open the box of Oviedo, 52
Romero, Francisco, 104, 105
Romero Pedro, 115
Roncesvalles, 251
Ruesta, 224
Ruiz, Fernandez, 141

Sagasta, portraits of, 186
Saint Biril, legend of, 228
Saint Felix of Zaragoza, 205, 206
Saint Ferdinand, uses captives as beasts of burden, 40
Saint George, Church of the Huesca, 168
Saint Hubertus of Luettich and the stag, 205
Saint James, his journey to Spain, 158 ; his preaching in the Asturias, 158 ; the Virgin appears to him, 158 ; column of marble on which the Virgin appeared to him, 158

Saint Sernin, Church of, 30
Saints Valero, Vicente, and Lorenzo, busts of ; presented to the Seo of Zaragoza by Pope Luna, 149
Saint Voto of Zaragoza, 205, 206
Salary of bullfighters, 110
Salinas de Monreal, 234
Salto del testuz, invented by Candido, 106
Salto de Roldan, 169
Sanchez, Don Tomas Antonio, 84 ; Sanchez Gabriel, treasurer of Ferdinand, 152 ; Sanchez Gerónimo, 153 ; Juan, 153
Sancho the Great, 248
Sandoval, Prudencio de, 84
Sanguesa, 233
San Juan de la Peña, 198 ; discovery of, 205 ; Royal burial chamber, 210 ; the cloisters, 213 ; Abbots of, 213
San Pedro, Church of, in Teruel, 143 ; gate of Jaca, 185
Santangel, Louis Sanchez, 153 ; condemned to be decapitated and his body burned, 156
Santa Orosia, 184
Santiago de Compostela, visitors to, 41 ·
Santiago, Church of, restored by Alfonso III., 37
Sariñena, Juan de, associated in the building of the Torre Nueva of Zaragoza, 161
Seal of the Templars, in Huesca, 168
Seals first employed in Aragon by Pedro II., 168
Segura, Doña Isabel de, 139 ; her death, 142 ; Don Pedro de, 139 ; Church of San Pedro, 142
Seo of Zaragoza, 148 ; lacking in architectural beauty, 149 ; Pedro de Arbues killed there, 152
Sereno, or night watchman, 28
Sertorius, 171
Sesma, 245
Sewing-machine in Spain, 2 ; 234
Sierra de Guara, 168 ; Leyre, 223
Silo, the wife of, 68
Singing at Monte Aragon, 174

Smuggling, an attempt at, 185
Spanish, bravery, 133 ; cities, divergence in character of, 145 ; ferries, 233 ; knives, 128 ; pride, 2 ; railways, 191 ; soldiers, 234
Speech by a *mayoral*, 19
Sperandeu, Juan, 154 ; drawn, quartered, and burned, 156
Stage-coach, 8–21
Start for Pamplona, 231
Starting from Madrid, 123
St. Jean Pied de Port, 253
Street names, individuality of, in Spanish cities, 148
Substitutes for wood, 24
Suspension-bridge, 182
Swearing, 9

Tambre River, 24
Támega River, 37
Tejeda, 64
Templars, end of, 168 ; in Huesca, 168
Teruel, captured by Alfonso II., 138
Theodemir, Bishop of Tria, 33
Theodorus, companion of Saint James, 36
Thieves, the story of a *guardia civil*, 248
Tiermas, 224
Tin of Galicia, 17
Tizon, Doña Constanza Perez, 138
Toll-gatherer, 190
Tomb of Santiago, discovery of, 34
Tombs in San Juan de la Peña, 209
Tower of Hercules of Coruña, 15 ; *Torre Nueva* of Zaragoza, 159 ; Calatayud, leaning, 160
Towers in Spanish landscapes, 159
Trading spirit, absence of, 5
Trees, rarity of, 167
Trenque of Zaragoza, 154
Tumbo A of the manuscript of Compostela, 34

Urries, Hugo de, 180 ; deprived of his barony, 181

Urroz, 248
Uzeda, Duke of, 130

Valcarlos, 152
Valero, *see* Saint Valero
Veral River, 223
Verdun, 223
Vicente, *see* Saint Valero
Villaba, 248
Villanueva, 168
Volapié, invented by Costilláres, 109

Wyclif, 151

Ximenez, Cardinal Francisco, 130

Yesa, temporary resting place of bodies
    from Leyre, 231
Yuste, first view, 67

Zagal, 20
Zaragoza, 145
Zaragoza, best views of, 162 ; first im-
    pressions, 148 ; influences exerted upon
    it, 145
Zizur, 230
Zuera, 164

www.ingramcontent.com/pod-product-compliance
Lightning Source LLC
Chambersburg PA
CBHW030618030726
47497CB00006B/1551